A Type Of Beauty

"A beguiling tale and an imaginative mélange of historical characters with a sharp insight into women's lives – and the limitations of their circumstances – in the period. There is a meticulous attention to detail – India is exquisitely conjured up – and a narrative of great sympathy evoking the artistic and literary worlds developing in the 1870s and '80s. Kate's story is most compelling and this is an altogether fine literary accomplishment by Patricia O'Reilly – with a fabulous movie potential."

Mary Kenny

A TYPE
OF BEAUTY

the story of Kathleen Newton
(1854-1882)

by

Patricia O'Reilly

Cape Press

Distributed by Gardners Books, 1 Whittle Drive, Eastbourne,
East Sussex, BN23 6QH
Tel +44 (0) 1323 521555 | Fax +44 (0) 1323 521666

This is a work of fiction based on actual events, with imagined dialogue
written after extensive research. The main historical figures in this book
are real, some of the minor characters are fictitious.

Cover illustration: *October*, 1878 (oil on canvas) by
Tissot, James Jacques Joseph (1836-1902).
Private Collection/ © Agnew's, London, UK/ The Bridgeman Art Library

British Library Cataloguing in Publication Data
A catalogue record for this book is available from the British Library.

ISBN 978-0-9563632-0-6

Typeset by Amolibros, Milverton, Somerset
www.amolibros.com
This book production has been managed by Amolibros
Printed and bound by T J International Ltd, Padstow, Cornwall, UK

Dedication

This one is for Xavier.

About the Author

Priory Studios, Dublin

Patricia O'Reilly, a native of Dublin, is a writer and lecturer. Her work includes novels – *Time & Destiny, Felicity's Wedding, Once upon a Summer*; non-fiction books – *Dying with Love, Earning your Living from Home, Working Mothers*; print journalism; radio documentaries, plays and talks, as well as short stories. She runs writing workshops throughout Ireland and as part of UCD's Adult Education Programme; and is author of *Writing for Success* and *Writing for the Market.* Website: www.patriciaoreilly.net

Praise for Patricia O'Reilly's Time & Destiny, *the story of Eileen Gray:*

'A good read that goes very well with a glass of wine and a bubble bath' – *Sunday Independent*

'A wonderful book to curl up with and dream of being in Paris' – *Evening Herald*

'A rich, rewarding read' – *Books Ireland*

Acknowledgements

Thanks to the staff of:

National Library of Ireland, Dublin
National Gallery of Ireland, Dublin
Glasgow University, Glasgow,
National Army Museum Staff, London
National Archives, London
V&A Museum, London

and

The Burlington Magazine, London
The St John's Wood Society, London
Rick Fink, photographer
Debbie Awad, London
Asfari family, London
Xavier, Susanne and Peter O'Reilly; Pam
O'Connell; Pascale McGarry; Richard
McCormick, Helen & Richard Ryan

Prologue

It was one of those golden June evenings when sunshine bathed the astonishing greenness of the parks, dappled shadows on the tree-lined streets and glimmered and glowed off tall buildings. It was a perfect evening for a party, and the Leicester Galleries in the heart of London was hosting an exclusive affair.

The guest list was made up of the usual mixture of beautiful people: glittering socialites, the occasional right honourable and wide-eyed debutantes, as well as a scattering of art dealers and dignitaries from the Royal Academy. More contacts than anyone's friends. A string quartet plucked out the rhythms of 'Love is the Sweetest Thing', and a sweet-faced soprano with finger-waved hair and bright red nails echoed that sentiment. Waitresses in black frocks, frilled aprons and starched white headbands wove through the crowd, skilfully balancing silver trays of champagne and crystal platters of canapés.

A tall, slim man moved hesitantly across the marble floor of the foyer. He looked carefully around, not quite believing he was in, that he had gained admission to the launch of what newspapers, magazines and even the wireless were all calling the most important art exhibition of the decade.

He straightened his shoulders and ran his fingers over his rather sparse moustache. Turning sideways, he eased forward into the gallery space. He was oblivious to the elegance of the venue and to the buzz and hum of the crowd, hearing but not registering a snatch of conversation from a bony woman in pansy-purple, as she admired 'the courage of Huxley's *Brave New World*', or the burst of laughter from another at the idea of Marlene Dietrich arriving in Paris dressed in a man's suit. 'And darling, can you imagine, in brown too!'

He presumed Violet was present, the respectable Mrs Walter Burns. Unlike him, she would have received a formal invitation in the post. He had no wish to see her; even thinking of his sister had him doubting himself. All of a sudden, coming uninvited to the exhibition was no longer the clever idea it had seemed when he had sat on the edge of his unmade bed, in his greasy room, and plotted his grand entrance. His nostrils quivered as he gulped for air. He should have known he couldn't cope in this public place. *Inhale, exhale. Slowly.* Like the doctors in the hospitals said. But his breathing couldn't control his panic as his body began to quiver, as though made up of echoing and re-echoing harp strings. *Inhale. Exhale.*

He was on the point of turning back when the crush of people parted and there she was. Rows and rows of her, immortalised in paintings, etchings and line drawings mounted on the stark white walls.

Her impact on him was like taking a bullet in the chest. Despite her leaving him, he had never left her. How wrong he was to think he was prepared for this exhibition, for seeing her again. For quite some time he had not been prepared for anything out of his ordinary, which was as basic as getting out of bed in the morning and muddling through the day.

He took a few steps backwards. How beautiful she was, how she shone out from her portraits, and what memories she and they evoked.

His solemn face softened as he went up to the wall, closing in on his favourite painting of her. She was wearing the russet gown, playing the piano and singing, and looking down at the boy standing beside her, the child's intensity forever captured in paint. He could not have been more than five, wearing a pale green suit, his blond hair of then touching the back of his collar, as his greying hair did now. He knew she was performing especially for him. All these years and she still held power over him. Happily he drifted out of himself, away from the crowded gallery, back in time to the music room, with its clutter of books and ornaments and sunlight dappling through the long window leading to the garden.

In *Mavourneen* her expression of dreaminess was painted full on, although he could not remember her having a fringe of hair on her forehead. He wrinkled his nose in dislike. He nodded in approval of her black coat with its face-framing fur collar, and the hat with its turned-back brim. Running the pads of his fingers up the trousers of his uniform, he felt not the coarse serviceableness of military material, but the delicate ridges of her velvet titillating the tips of his nails.

His breathing steadied as he nodded at the pictures he was familiar with, greeting them as beloved and trusted friends. He was regaining control, although he knew his hands were still trembling. He clasped them firmly behind his back.

He had no recollection of that portrait of her sitting in the armchair in the small drawing room, an open book resting on her lap—she was a prodigious reader—but that was the way she was: smiling a welcome as though waiting for him to walk through the door for a chat. She loved chatting and telling stories; she said it was the Irish in her.

In *Octobre* she was waving a book and posed in playful flight against the golden foliage of the shrubbery. She had laughed and laughed at the idea of a footman polishing the leaves and of everyone drinking champagne, which a French critic had written after visiting their home in St John's Wood.

His body was loosening and he was beginning to relax, to lose himself in the world of the past, where he longed to be, when he came upon *La Frileuse* (*The Shivering Woman*), aptly titled, as she felt the cold more than most and shivered her way through the English winters. He took a step backwards from the black ink portrait, wondering why as a child he had so disliked it. As an adult he knew, but then as an adult he had come to know too many things, more than he could cope with. The simplicity of the picture captured her as she was then, closed away from all but the chosen few who were permitted to enter the Camelot-like seclusion of the inner sanctum, her lover had created for his *ravissante Irlandaise*.

His attention was diverted by a burst of female chatter. It was the Dietrich woman, all backless gown and jangling jet earrings, and waving an ebony cigarette holder. She was surrounded by a group of women whose feline eyes were turned in his direction. Surely they knew it was the pictures

4

and not him that they should be looking at? He turned away from them.

He could imagine her at an occasion like this. She would be the most beautiful woman present: her chestnut hair piled high, diamonds and pearls gleaming at her ears and throat, wearing one of her jewel-coloured gowns. Like an exotic bird, she would draw the other guests towards her, enchanting them with laughter and repartee as she sipped champagne and smoked the gold-tipped cigarettes specially imported from Paris.

When he saw the porter approaching, he went into his protective mode of bent head. Madness was his recurring nightmare, the fear of relapse into that mental blackness, the fear that took him one blameless day to the banks of the Thames and set him adrift on the river. He had been pulled back from the waters of oblivion on many an occasion and he knew the lead-up all too intimately: loss of energy and appetite, and whole days spent lying in bed when the fire in his brain and the weight of his eye sockets prevented constructive movement.

When he lifted his head, the porter was signalling him, and the faces of the surrounding crowd were bright with salacious interest. He had been identified. His closed, middle-aged face crumpled; his hands resumed their frantic clasping and unclasping, dividing, linking in an odd dance of fear, a choreography of panic, as he saw Violet coming towards him.

His mental images were liquefying. He could no longer separate his impressions of the past from what he was seeing in the pictures. Unease, like a drawstring, pulled his throat tight, filling every plane of his face, draining away the blood from his skin, widening his eyes. He turned and with awkwardly angled shoulders passed through the crowd, which briskly parted ranks, eager to hurry him on his way, to have him gone.

When he reached the door, the quartet was playing another popular tune, still extolling the virtues of love, although there was no sign of the singer. He faced his audience, paused momentarily, raised his arm and gave a military salute as befitted a lieutenant of the Royal Field Artillery. 'She was my mother, you know.' His eyes were steady and his voice was calm. He shuffled out into the square where he was swallowed up by the twilight.

Part One

Chapter One

Kate was wakened by the tumbling sounds of bells from the nearby oratory. During the night she and Louisa had become spooned into each other and their lumpy bed was moistly warm and treacly comfortable. As the last echoes of the bells died away, she heard the quick tap of boots along the bare boards of the corridor. Six o'clock. Miss Carmody gave her usual sharp rap on the door, and Kate pushed her face into the pillow and groaned.

As was her habit, Louisa woke slowly, rubbing her eyes and making little grunts of protest as she ran tickling fingers along the knobs of Kate's spine. It was her way of telling Kate it was time to rise.

Retaliating with a good-natured poke of her elbow, Kate eased her way along the hard sheets and stepped onto the floor, her toes curling in protest at the icy boards. The early spring of 1870 was particularly cold. Padding on bare feet in the inky darkness, she made her way between the other beds to the washstand by the window. Already the dawn-blanched streets of Kensington were thick with the steady clunk of boots on stone, the wordless tramp of workers—men, women and children, pale and glue-eyed with sleep, heads down, shrouded in the smoky mist.

After splintering the skim of ice with her thumb, she poured a few inches of water into the basin and dashed it up on her face. Dribbles ran and glistened on her cheeks and chin. She would like to drink a little but if she did and went to Holy Communion she would burn forever in the fires of hell, and if she did not receive she would have Miss Carmody to answer to. What a parcel of ifs.

After drying her face and hands, she wriggled out of her nightgown and shivered in her chemise as she began dressing—stepping into her drawers, putting on her corset, followed by the petticoat and the coarse grey frock, fastening the tiny buttons with fumbling fingers and tying the sash at the back with the efficiency that comes from practice.

The uniform was an uncomfortable and unflattering garment, hated by the pupils at Miss Carmody's School for Young Ladies. Not that they had say or choice in the matter. Kate sat in the chair to pull on the thick black woollen stockings, which she secured with garters, and from underneath she hauled out her boots, flattening the tongues that were constantly awry, and eased in her feet.

She rolled Louisa's underlinens and stockings in her uniform and threw the lot across the room, where they landed with a thud on the hump of her body. While Louisa, who blithely ignored the school's rule of early-morning washing, sat up and dressed, Kate buttoned her boots and took out their capes and bonnets from the cupboard. Next morning it would be her turn to lie in.

As they were leaving the room, they looked at each other, grinned and nodded—Kate's chestnut curls bobbing, Louisa's cap of dark hair lying sleekly against her head. In mischievous synchronisation they raised their hands and went clap, clap, clap. Sharp staccato sounds. As soon as the other pupils began to wake—they had been sleeping on, impervious to bells, footsteps, knuckle-raps and the sounds of toilettes, grumbling and disorientated—Kate and Louisa ran giggling along the darkened corridor, down the stairs to Miss Carmody, who was waiting at the door, enveloped in a maroon cape with her lantern casting a rosy glow.

Daily mass was part of Kate and Louisa's educational requirements, as laid down by their respective fathers. Miss Carmody had the greatest of respect for the fee-payers of the world, for it was they who made possible her ambition of running a finishing school for young ladies. Despite not being of the Roman Catholic persuasion herself, she ensured the wishes of both parents and guardians were her command, no matter how apparently trivial or eccentric. After all, he who paid the piper was entitled to call the tune.

With her plump body swaying from side to side, holding the light aloft and oblivious to the thick, smoky breath of London's fog, Miss Carmody led the way. Kate and Louisa, holding hands, walked behind, their enforced silence broken by an occasional cough as the damp air caught their throats.

If such a thing were possible, it was even colder inside than outside the tiny oratory, and the puffs of breath from the small, mostly elderly congregation floated up the nave like so many timid clouds.

Looking at the altar in purple mourning for Lent, Kate's heart squeezed in misery. The crucified Christ with droplets of blood running down his alabaster skin gazed back; his crown of thorns dug into her head; she tasted his vinegar; felt his spear in her side, and his nails throbbed in her hands and feet. She dreaded the joyless stringencies of the six weeks of Lent: each day an eternity marred by the sacrifices she felt she ought to make; the niggling penances and various indulgences that troubled her conscience. It was all so tedious.

'Religion is quite miserable, isn't it?' whispered Louisa.

Kate was glad not to be the only one thinking blasphemous thoughts. Miss Carmody said imagination had no place in religion but Kate knew differently. The colourful gods and goddesses of her childhood in India were imaginative, full of adventure and excitement, and the richness of their stories still beat in her like a pulse.

She looked at Father Mathew on the altar, his lean body resplendent in the black-braided purple vestments of the season. Her fantasies about him were so delicious that they must be a sin because, surely, she should not daydream about a 'man of the cloth' as Mama described priests. Closing her eyes against temptation, Kate's conscience battled with thoughts, words and deeds.

The thoughts, words and deeds of Miss Carmody's young ladies were single-mindedly concentrated on the trappings of love: coming out, having a wardrobe of fashionable gowns and slippers, doing the season, acquiring suitors and making a good marriage—good being a euphemism for wealthy and socially acceptable. Kate was not dismissive of their aspirations but, for her, love was more about the connection between souls. Before settling into a life of domesticity she hoped to have an opportunity to exercise choice and freedom. She wasn't sure precisely what she would do with this choice and freedom but she did know she would just die if Papa married her off as he had her sister Polly.

With rosary beads entwining her hands and head dutifully bowed, she took the long walk up the short aisle to kneel at the communion rail. Through the fence of her fingers, she watched Father Mathew approach, watched his capable fingers enfold the chalice. As he stood in front of her, host held between index finger and thumb, she breathed deeply. Words could not do justice to his fragrance. It bore no relation to the sour sweat of the labourers who worked around the school, to the men of India's smell of patchouli and garlic, and her father's tobacco. She hugged to herself thoughts of fresh linen, incense, wine—and perhaps a touch of lavender.

A jab of an elbow in her ribs from Louisa jerked her back to the present. Blushing scarlet to the roots of her hair and then growing pale, she opened her mouth and stuck out her tongue to receive the papery host. Hot dew was left on her forehead.

Ensuring her young ladies were occupied with French conversation and knowing she was unlikely to be disturbed, Miss Carmody settled down to the school's accounts. Nothing gave her more pleasure than a set of balanced books, but despite her economies throughout the winter, cutting down on heat, curtailing the amount of laundry and reducing food bills to the minimum, the school was seriously overdrawn with the bank.

Yet, given time and an injection of capital to allow for the taking on of more pupils, she believed the school could prosper. Opening up a bedroom on the return would accommodate another four young ladies. With pen held precisely between index and middle finger, the chilly spring sun fell on her copperplate writing as she made rapid notes. But would the board agree to approach the bank for the necessary funding?

As she worked, she looked out at the tiny garden, her kind, plain face breaking into a smile at the riot of yellow daffodils, purple grape hyacinths and tulips beginning to bud red and orange. She loved Elmwood with a passion.

Her initial reaction to the rattle of the knocker on the front door was a reflex of annoyance, but that quickly changed. Like many an only child and a lonely adult, she was curious, a trait she considered unladylike and went to considerable lengths to hide. But she found it difficult to resist any excuse to enjoy company. Presuming the caller to be for her—her young ladies were permitted only carefully vetted visitors on Sunday afternoons—she tackled her ledger with a new enthusiasm as she waited for Dolly's knock.

'If you please, ma'am, it's the major. Major Kelly.' Dolly, the young Irish maid, wore her customary cowed expression.

This was a pleasant surprise.

'What does he want?'

'Please, ma'am, to see you.'

Knowing he had not, she asked, 'Has he an appointment?'

'I don't know, ma'am. Shall I find out?'

Miss Carmody gave an exaggerated sigh and a pat at her hair, which was sensibly styled with a ruler-straight middle parting and neatly plaited coils over each ear. She was glad she was wearing her best black skirt and the grey pinstriped blouse. 'You'd better show him in.'

While Dolly bobbed a curtsy, Miss Carmody smiled, and it was not only because Dolly had mastered the simple movement. Major Kelly, as well as being an imposing figure of a man, was both a widower and a war hero, as she labelled any man who fought for queen and country.

As she rose in greeting, the major strode across the small parlour, arms outstretched, eyes sparkling, waxed moustache a-bristle with pleasure.

'My dear Miss Carmody, how delightful to find you at home. I hope I'm not disturbing you by calling unexpectedly.' He took in her cluttered desk and open ledgers. 'Oh, you are busy.' The comment sounded as titillating as a proposition and she found herself blushing. 'But if I may, I wish to ask your opinion on an important matter.'

She smiled and nodded, hope surging in her breast. But then, whenever a man—almost any man—displayed the slightest amount of interest, her hope had a habit of surging and she still dreamt of a husband and children.

'I could think of no better person to consult than your good self.' Charles Frederick Ashburnham Kelly could not help a gallant flirtation with both pretty and not-so-pretty, and young and not-so-young women, particularly when he had a request to make. He found the title of Major and with it the automatic assumption that he was a fighting man to be of considerable social benefit.

With a gracious movement of her hand, Miss Carmody gestured him to the sofa. She took the winged chair opposite, allowing the pale sunny light from the window at her back to flatter her complexion.

'And how is married life suiting Mary Pauline?' From what she had heard, it was a good match and that reflected well on her establishment.

'She's well, I believe.' The major drew out a pouch of

tobacco and a pipe from an inside pocket of his jacket and cast a questioning look in her direction. Despite disliking smoking in all its forms and particularly detesting the way pipe smoke lingered, she inclined her head. Hands folded in her lap, she relaxed back against the soft cretonne of her chair and enjoyed studying him while he filled his pipe, tamped, lit and finally puffed with satisfaction. In the company of men, her businesslike exterior was inclined to evaporate and frequently she ended up feeling somewhat out of control.

When Dolly entered pushing a trolley of tea things, Miss Carmody dismissed her and set about pouring, sugaring and milking, buttering scones and setting up a small side table, noting with approval the crisply starched cloth and napkins. The time and effort she was putting into training Dolly was paying off.

'These are good,' the major complimented, with his mouth full.

'Yes, they're an old recipe. We make up a batch every couple of days,' Miss Carmody fibbed without compunction. Irish soda bread in a variety of guises was Dolly's special skill.

'Hmm. I'd have thought you'd enough to do.'

'I enjoy all aspects of homemaking.'

'I can see that.' He felt expansive and looked appreciatively at the polished furniture, healthy plants, fresh antimacassars and gleaming brasswork. She seemed to know how to create and maintain a home, and she was modest with it. He had a penchant for self-effacing women.

Reluctantly he turned to the purpose of his visit. 'I wish to discuss Kathleen's future with you.' He had a soft spot for his younger daughter but he was the first to admit that she was too headstrong and too full of opinions, as well as believing she had the right to decide on her role in life. She was so unlike Mary Pauline, who behaved as a daughter should by doing exactly what she was told without argument.

Miss Carmody's hopes of the major's intentions being directed towards her evaporated, and she reverted to capability. 'How can I be of help?'

Better get this over with quickly. The major knew precisely what he needed to find out. 'How is Kathleen progressing?'

'Well. She's a quick learner with a lively mind.' Miss Carmody's answer was diplomatic. She was extraordinarily fond of Kathleen Kelly and, while she looked on her feistiness and wish for independence with awe, she considered her too interested in unladylike attitudes.

'Is she ready for marriage, do you think?'

Marriage was the making of most women and, invariably, it put an end to nonsensical goings-on, but she could not be sure it would have that effect on Kathleen. She countered with, 'Well, she's very young—not even seventeen.'

'But mature enough for marriage, do you think?'

That was a difficult question to answer without further information. 'I believe it would depend on her intended. Have you someone in mind?'

'Yes, and he is a deal older. Sensible. A civil servant.'

Try as she might, Miss Carmody could not imagine such a match. She considered Kathleen to be a flamboyant throwback to some distant ancestor. In her experience this was frequently the case with an emigrant colonial background as well as which Kathleen had an Irish recklessness about her. 'May I enquire what area of the service?'

'Mr Isaac Newton is a surgeon.'

That sounded more promising. There was a heroic frontier type of glamour about surgeons. She would like to have been a nurse, but even had he known of her ambition, dear Papa would not have heard of it. And rightly so, she thought from her vantage point of two decades on.

'He's currently serving in India.'

Ah. The land of the exotic. She read the newspapers avidly and, now that the Suez Canal was open, some day she hoped to visit India. 'Would the wedding be there?'

'That's the plan.'

'Will you travel with her?'

'No. Regrettably, my business interests keep me here.'

'Military I presume.'

'Indeed.'

So for the present the major was making his home in London. Miss Carmody squirreled away that nugget of information. She could not imagine anyone allowing a daughter of Kathleen's age and disposition to journey halfway across the world without being chaperoned. Still, it was not her decision, and when dealing with parents she had cultivated an air of discretion. 'Shall I have Kathleen called out of class?'

That was the last thing he wanted. The more he saw of his daughters, the less he understood them, although he knew enough not to want to be on the receiving end of Kathleen's reaction to her impending marriage. 'Thank you, no, I wished to sound you out first. Perhaps at a suitable occasion you might mention the matter to her.'

'I hardly think…'

'In the circumstances, I consider you the perfect person. After all she doesn't have a mother to guide her.'

After a second cup of tea and another scone, he bade goodbye, leaving Miss Carmody all of a dither and quite unable to return to her ledgers. As the morning was ruined for concentration on matters of finance, she might as well get this talk with Kathleen over and done with before luncheon.

Kate hated the way the cold dampness of the English weather left her constantly feeling chilled, and whenever possible she spent time in the warmth of Elmwood's big kitchen. She was touched and saddened by the melancholy way Dolly went about her chores.

'You shouldn't be here, miss. She doesn't allow it.' Dolly's pale face was haunted by shadows and she cast a worried look towards the door that led up to the hallway. She had been raised in poverty on the back streets of Dublin and she was used to living anxiously, expecting nothing and registering neither pleasure nor displeasure.

Kate sat at the top of the scrubbed table, snarls of wool scattered across its pale surface, glowering at a grubby tapestry depicting improbably shaped tulips. She heartily disliked needlework and when next Papa called she would beg him for lessons in drawing and painting. 'Are you happy, Dolly?' She jabbed the needle into the canvas.

For a moment Dolly looked startled, then her natural acceptance of her life asserted itself. 'I don't know, miss.' She opened the oven of the range, removed a batch of potato scones and propped them sideways to cool along the edges of the tray. Her hands were red and chapped.

Kate's belly was constantly puckered in hungry protest at the school's Lenten rations. She regularly dreamt of food: the reds, yellows and greens of exotic fruits, richly spiced dishes and flavoursome curries prepared by their Indian cook, as well as the more homely English boiled sides of pink ham; meat pies with golden pastry and coils of fat sausages. Dolly's scones were irresistible. 'May I have one?'

'You can't, miss. You know we're fasting and she likely has them counted.'

'Nonsense, she wouldn't. She couldn't anyway.' Kate jumped up, lifted a scone from the tray, broke it in two and handed half to Dolly. 'Mmm. These are quite delicious. I could eat the whole lot.' She spoke with her mouth full.

Dolly looked terrified.

'Only joking. Go on. Eat it before she comes down those stairs and catches you.'

As though Kate's words had the power to conjure, just as Dolly took a tentative bite, Miss Carmody's voice floated downwards. 'Kathleen Kelly. Are you down there?'

Kate put her fingers to her lips but, seeing Dolly's expression, changed her mind. 'Coming, Miss Carmody.' Carrying her tapestry and wool, she ran up the stairs waving a hank of deep blue. 'I'd mislaid this, but Dolly found it. Thank you, Dolly,' she called back to the kitchen.

'You cannot believe what's happened.' Kate caught up with Louisa on the way out of the dining room after a meagre meal of potato pie and boiled bacon followed by tapioca pudding.

Louisa was indifferent to what had happened to Kate or anyone else. Somewhat self-absorbed at the best of times, that afternoon she was in a thoroughly bad mood. Her mother had refused to pay for the muslin for the 'Marie Antoinette' gown she had seen pictured in *The Illustrated London News*. She knew she would just die if she couldn't have an exact copy to wear during the royal regatta at Henley-on-Thames, which was only a few months away.

'Swear you won't tell anyone,' Kate persisted. Her news was so exploding out of her that she disregarded Louisa's sulks.

Louisa's attention was caught by Kate's intensity. 'What is it? No, of course I won't.'

'Swear you won't.'

'I promise. Cross my heart and hope to die.' Louisa performed the ritual with automatic piety. 'What's happened?'

As Kate told her, Louisa's eyes widened with envy and her cheeks pinked in excitement. She crossed her heart again, duly hoped to die and hurried off to absorb the implications of Kate's news. Typically Louisa, she was unable to resist being purveyor of such an exciting event, especially in the middle of Lent when nothing happened. The word of Kate Kelly's betrothal spread throughout the school like wildfire and a midnight celebration was quickly arranged.

'*Amo, amas, amat.*' The girls lay on their beds, pantalooned legs scissoring in and out and backwards and forwards in time to their chanting. They were heady at the romance of a wedding in their midst. Kate would be the first to be married, and the excitement of a surgeon husband, added to the exhilaration of living in India, had them swooning and passing round the smelling salts. Someone produced a flask of gin; another had a half-eaten box of crystallised fruit, but most coveted of all was the pigskin box containing a few cigarettes.

Kate was the only one lacking in jubilation. 'I don't want to get married,' she persisted, insisting on having a whole cigarette and an extra mouthful of gin. After all it was her celebration. '*Amamus, amatis, amant.*'

Chapter Two

With hunched shoulders and arms clasped across her chest, Kate sat tucked into her corner of the saloon carriage, raging at her father, alternating between despair at having decisions forced on her and fury at women's inequality to men. Her belly was so knotted in cramps that she was scarcely aware of the clackety-clack of the express train as it journeyed down the centre of France to the port of Marseilles. Would she ever again know happiness? Probably not, she decided, holding herself even tighter. What was there to be happy about, being married off to a man you knew nothing of, cared less about and hadn't even seen a likeness of?

At least Polly had met her intended on a few occasions prior to her wedding, but from her closed face and shuttered attitude, Kate had no idea of whether or not she was happy. When she had asked, more out of curiosity than solicitousness, Polly had broken into an unaccustomed peal of joyless laughter. 'Pray, what could you do about my happiness?' Her eyes were wide with sadness and Kate was filled with powerlessness. The only silver in the black clouds of her life was that she was returning to India. If only she could live there forever without having to get married.

Miss Carmody, her shoulders straight and ankles neatly crossed, sat opposite Kate. Major Kelly's pleading eyes had flattered her into agreeing to travel to India and to act as Kathleen's chaperone, but as early as the railway journey from London to Folkestone, every turn of the wheels reinforced her regret. She fretted that the ex-governess she had appointed in her place was not up to the demands of running Elmwood. She worried at the escalating war between France and Prussia, about which she voraciously sought out snatches of gossip and rumour. She had sat mesmerised in the waiting room of the station as a tall man with a nervous sniffle speaking loud, slovenly English held forth on the possibility of the southern German states being drawn into the war. They were two unescorted, vulnerable women. The possibilities of kidnapping, abduction, robbery and worse were terrifying.

When a broad-shouldered man wearing the uniform of a captain pulled aside the sliding doors and entered their carriage, she smiled tentatively, not so much at him as at the sense of security afforded by an army officer. Her charge did not raise her eyes from her hands, which were tightly clasped on her lap. Despite her years of experience in dealing with young ladies, she was unsure of how to handle Kathleen Kelly and her attitudes, as she had labelled Kate's outbursts. Enforcing a code of behaviour in school was one thing, enforcing it while travelling the world with a reluctant young woman was another.

'I apologise for disturbing you but allow me to introduce myself: Captain C H Palliser of the Bengal Cavalry at your service.' He clicked his heels and bowed slightly. He had Saxon good looks and his voice was clipped British. 'When I saw you two ladies so obviously travelling alone, I came to offer my assistance.'

Miss Carmody, flustering with relief, ran a hand across her forehead. 'Oh, thank you. Thank you. That's very kind. But it's not necessary. Our arrangements are well in hand.' She needed to feel she retained control.

'May I enquire your destination?' The captain looked towards Kate who was still in contemplation of her hands.

'We're going as far as Agra in India.' Miss Carmody was unsure of how to proceed. Indeed, she did not know whether or not she should proceed. Presumably she should introduce Kathleen and herself but should she? While she was mistress and in control in her domain, she had little knowledge of social protocol outside her own experience, and she was at a loss to know how to take the conversation further. With his courteous behaviour, there was no doubt in her mind that the captain was a gentleman.

When Kathleen got up and left the carriage with a muttered 'Excuse me'—brushing past him as though he did not exist—Miss Carmody felt easier, less inhibited.

'The young lady is your sister?' he asked, looking down the corridor in the direction Kate had gone.

'No. That's Miss Kelly. She's in my charge. I am Miss Carmody.'

When the captain nodded in a gracious way, she knew she had been right not to offer him her hand.

She sat up a little straighter. 'Miss Kelly is on her way to be married.' She hoped she sounded like a capable woman of the world.

'And I must catch up with my paperwork. I hope you'll permit me to be of service during the journey.'

She pursed her lips and nodded in an equally gracious

manner. When the captain left she settled back, well pleased with her handling of the situation.

Cornelius Harold Palliser—Harry to his friends—had no intention of returning to his carriage. His mission was to find the young girl whose beauty and poise had captivated him from his first sight of her at the railway station in Calais. He did not have to go far: a few yards along the corridor she was standing by the window, gazing out at the passing landscape, her hands resting on the narrow ledge, her body swaying rhythmically with the train. Her hair, caught in a stray beam of sunlight, rippled warm chestnut, and her waist was little more than the span of his hands.

When he touched her shoulder she jumped, and turned towards him. He was surprised to see what he interpreted as unhappiness on such a lovely face. For her part she saw an expression in his eyes that she had never seen before, and while she was unable to interpret what it meant, it raised a newfound awareness that whetted her interest and somewhat blunted her feeling of despair.

Captain Palliser read her flicker of reaction as that first look of budding interest, the virginal awakening, which in his considerable experience never lied. God, she was so beautiful and luminously young; he would wager the whole of the family estates in Wiltshire that she was untouched. He bent close and whispered, 'If you'll permit, I'd very much like to get to know you.'

Cloistered as Kate had been, she knew enough to recognise that his behaviour was preposterous. She pursed her lips and raised her eyebrows in surprise, more at the idea of him thinking she had freedom to grant such permission than anything else. She didn't reply, not because she didn't want to but because she didn't know what to say. Louisa would take the captain's overture as an adventure and she'd have opinions on his height, physique, manners, the blue of his eyes and, doubtless, the way he had of smiling.

She turned away from him. The loneliness of isolation and fear of the unknown still cut into her but she walked a little taller, held her head a little higher and smiled a little smile as she continued along the corridor. Bloody hell. She was having her very own adventure.

The captain was as good as his whisper. The following morning, as the train drew into the station, he turned up at their compartment with a manservant and two porters. 'Come, allow me to organise a carriage.'

Relieved that she no longer had to worry about the complication of getting from railway station to docks, Miss Carmody, bossily ensuring her charge was in tow, followed him.

En route to the docks, the coachman drew up at a small cluster of stalls. 'This is the best place to stock up on those little luxuries so important to you ladies.' The captain was gracious and charming.

'We don't need anything. Thank you kindly. We're well provided for,' assured Miss Carmody. Their budget was as tight as could be: there was no allocation of money for incidentals and certainly not for luxuries.

Captain Palliser instructed the coachman to wait, ensured his passengers were comfortable, and with his manservant approached the stalls.

'He's going from one place to another and back again,' reported Miss Carmody, peering from the window. 'He must be buying a lot.'

Kate shrugged.

When the captain returned, his manservant was laden down with parcels.

After a light lunch, they arrived at the docks with time to spare. The captain disappeared on an errand. Kate took in her stride the noise and the hurrying, bustling and confusion of the burly dockworkers, anxious travellers and nonchalant sailors. But Miss Carmody was terrified, crouching down, refusing to emerge from the carriage until encouraged out by the captain on his return.

In the early afternoon they boarded the Peninsular & Oriental steamer, which would take them to Alexandria. Two stewards led the way to their cabin, flung open the door and stood back to allow them to enter. Miss Carmody gave a cry of dismay. 'Oh, it is so small and dirty.'

'It'll be all right. When Polly and I came back, our accommodation was much worse,' assured Kate with an airiness she did not feel. She was beginning to wonder who was minding who.

Captain Palliser handed Miss Carmody her small portmanteau. 'You're lucky. I was able to upgrade you.'

She was flustered. 'Oh, it's too kind of you to take such trouble. Thank you.'

He bent low over her hand. 'It was no trouble. If I may, I'll call later to ensure you've settled in.'

She was visibly brighter as she set about unpacking, humming under her breath as she punctiliously allocated space for their belongings, although she grew quiet as the afternoon advanced. She pleaded a headache when Kate suggested a turn on deck and refused to leave the cabin.

Evening light was fading into a violet sunset that stained the docks red as Kate stood by the rails watching a flock of gulls wheeling around the steamer. As the shallow light thinned, the day faltered and the boatmen released the warps securing the ship to the quayside. For a moment the steamer seemed reluctant to move; then it sighed quietly before sliding under its own power, out into the harbour. As it put out to sea with a fair and gentle breeze, Captain Palliser made his way to the women's cabin.

When Miss Carmody opened the door to his knock, her face lit up. He handed her some of the parcels he had purchased earlier and stepped inside. 'A few luxuries for you and Miss Kelly. I hope they meet with your approval.'

There were generous quantities of gossamer-fine cotton, scented soaps, toilet waters and perfumed lotions.

'I, ahem... .' She was in a quandary. The etiquette of running Elmwood had not prepared her for this. 'Thank you.'

'Are you English?'

'Yes.' She hoped his question was asked out of interest in her.

'And Miss Kelly? With that name she has to be Irish?'

'Yes. I believe her grandfather was from Ireland. A doctor from the county of Wexford, I understand, but her father is a major serving with the British Army in India. She was reared there and now she's going back to be married.'

He bowed smoothly and exited gratefully from the stuffy cabin.

The crossing was unseasonably rough and unpredictably warm. The ship was hardly out of the harbour when Miss Carmody was stricken by seasickness. She was reduced to lying shivering on the lower bunk, constantly thirsty but vomiting a brackish bile after the smallest of sips of water. As the majority of the passengers were confined to their cabins, equally affected, onboard protocol broke down.

With her chaperone indisposed, Kate was free to roam the ship. She was the only female to pace the decks and stand by the rails breathing deeply of ozone, and she became expert at dodging the rolling casks. The captain became equally expert at engineering meeting up with her, in the course of which he used his time and charm well: watching her grow more comfortable with him; hearing her laughter—for one so slender she had a hearty laugh, from the base of her belly; feeling his way with cautious flirting; making a game out of secrecy; graduating to the occasional humorous billet-doux to which, to his chagrin, she retaliated with equal humour but without a modicum of sentiment. Kathleen Kelly was the exception to his rule of avoiding virgins. She occupied his dreams and many of his waking thoughts, and he was growing impatient at his self-imposed restraint.

On a murky morning, Kate stood at the rails mesmerised by the metronome of the waves, their surging swell, grand arrival and long diminishing hiss and shuffle of the swash, heaving like the ghosts of buried giants. She felt for the physical discomfort of the passengers below deck. With the hatches tightly closed to prevent flooding when the seas chopped high, they were packed in the most uncomfortable of circumstances, together with a variety of dogs and other animals, and the ship's stores that had not been destroyed. The food being served to the passengers was reduced to little more than hard biscuits, dubious beef and watery ale.

Captain Palliser stood watching her and when he rested

his hand on her shoulder, she turned easily to him. 'The sea is wonderful, isn't it?'

'Yes,' he conceded. He would concede a ridiculous amount and subjugate his natural inclinations to ludicrous levels to possess her. 'The power of nature never ceases to amaze.' He slipped his cupped hand under her elbow. 'Perhaps, you'll allow me to show you my copy of Gosse's *History of Sea Anemones and Corals*? The illustrations are quite splendid.'

'Is it your favourite book?' she asked eagerly.

As he was not a reader, he did not have a favourite book, but that did not prevent him stating, 'Yes. Definitely.'

'Shall I tell you my favourite?'

He was not in the least interested in her choice of reading but he was running out of time. They would dock in Alexandria within a few days and he suspected Miss Carmody would be back on full chaperone duty. 'Please do.'

'It's *Lalla Rookh*, signed by Mr Thomas Moore. I could fetch it, if you like?' Her bright enthusiasm was quite enchanting. The book had come in the post a week after she had written in desperation to Aunt Muriel, her only remaining Irish relative. The letter accompanying the volume of poetry was in a frail, spidery hand and offered regrets that she could not intervene in Kathleen's betrothal but assured, 'Remember, there's always a home for you here in Rathmore.'

Captain Palliser congratulated himself that in an effortless few minutes he had moved up their relationship by several notches. 'Perhaps later? I've some business to attend to now but why don't you join me in my cabin around four o'clock and we can compare books?'

She nodded, her attention back at the swell of the waves, accepting the invitation in a fun spirit, as though entering into nothing more serious than a game of charades. 'My friend Louisa would love this, she'd have such amusement with us,' she told him.

Aided by the laudanum, which she kept on hand for those occasions when pessimism threatened to overcome her carefully cultivated optimism, by the time Kate returned to the cabin Miss Carmody had drifted into an uneasy sleep. As the voyage progressed, to Miss Carmody's horror and impotence, Kate had re-considered her wardrobe—vowing never again to wear anything resembling that restrictive Elmwood uniform. With the warmer weather, and in a burst of freedom, she dispensed with her corset and reduced her clothes to a muslin shift and a loose cotton dressing gown. That afternoon, seeing no reason to deviate, she got ready to visit the captain by re-pinning the loosened strands of her hair.

Putting the book in her pocket, she eased closed the door behind her. Going down the dark passage, her hands skimmed the surface of the walls to prevent herself from falling. The sea was swelling again. They were in for another rough night.

The door to Captain Palliser's cabin was open; his accommodation was considerably more luxurious than theirs. He was sitting in a brocaded armchair, complete with fringing and braiding; and his head was bent over a map. As she stepped inside, like fine dust a feeling of unease swirled in the air, and her breath caught in her throat. While she was flattered by his attention, the fact that she was not even a little in love with him gave her a feeling of power and security that enabled her to adopt a carefree attitude towards him. Kate considered she was well informed on the subject of love—after all, it was a topic of constant discussion at Elmwood—and she knew she would never feel for the captain as she had for Father Mathew.

Captain Palliser put aside the map and motioned her to take his seat while he made himself a place on the narrow bench built into the wall. His white shirt was rich with frills and flounces. Like the floor, the cushion of the chair was seeping and the damp of the upholstery was cool beneath Kate's dressing gown.

She gave a skimpy laugh, which did not quite hide her feeling of nervousness, and clutched at her book like a life raft. 'Shall I read some?'

He nodded. Running his hand over his pale stubble— his manservant was too ill to shave him—he watched the tilt of her head and eloquent hand gestures as she lit an additional lamp. His fellow-officers enviously referred to him as a Lothario and he joked that if he had a sovereign for every woman he had pleasured he would be a rich man. He was thirty-six and remained a bachelor by choice, favouring the less complicated scenario of short-term relationships with married women whom he wooed with tender words, romantic gifts and lingering caresses. He was a maestro of timing, playing the strings of seduction like a violin. With her chaperone indisposed, he had been sure winning Kathleen Kelly would be effortless, but her innocence was scuppering his plan. She appeared oblivious to the rules of flirtation and paid scant attention to the rites of courtship, although for a girl she was fun, lively to be with and the best of company. She would be perfect if only she did not insist on voicing such radical opinions.

As she read, her voice was mellifluous and her diction

as clear as the bells of his village church. Like Kate, the royal heroine of the verses was journeying to a marriage arranged by her father, although unlike her it was in comfort, and with a dowry including caskets of jewels. The princess had fallen in love with another traveller, a poet who was seducing her most romantically with tender words and amorous looks.

After a few pages, Kate paused and looked up.

Captain Palliser's expression was unfathomable. But his mind was racing. Was she flirting? Was she extending the most subtle and sophisticated invitation he had ever received? Surely she could not fail to see the connection between the young lovers and themselves? The time could not be riper. If he was ever to make a move, it should be now. He came and sat on the arm of her chair.

'Enough of that.' He took the book and leaning across her he placed it face downwards on his desk.

Her heart beat wildly and she was acutely aware of his nearness. In as calm a voice as she could manage, she asked, 'Have you got that book on sea anemones?' On a number of occasions, she persuaded herself that she was imagining his too familiar behaviour and habit of crowding her. Miss Carmody was always going on about the dangers of over-active imaginations, but his thigh pressing against the softness of her arm was real. She swallowed hard.

He leant further against her, slipped his arm around her shoulders, drew her towards him, and his breath was hot and heavy with whisky as he kissed her full on the lips. For a moment she went with the strangeness of this unknown rather delicious sensation before standing up, re-claiming her book and stepping out of the cabin.

With hands clasped behind her head, Kate lay on the

salt-water-encrusted sheets. Her first kiss. From detailed discussions at Elmwood she knew that a 'lip kiss' was compromising, whereas a 'cheek kiss' was not. She should not have gone alone to the captain's cabin but he was the only flicker of fun and lightness in the scary darkness of her life. And now…? She ran her index finger along her lips and felt very grown up, very confused and very sad.

The latest storm squall had left a good three inches of water in the cabin and everything was damper than usual. As she watched a rat trying to climb into her portmanteau, she envied his freedom, although considerably more unnerving than the constant scrabbling of rats and the clicking of hordes of cockroaches was the all-pervading stench of rot. What was actually rotting nobody seemed to know, but the rumour that it was a human body had spread throughout the ship like wildfire.

She was too upset to sleep that night. While listening to Miss Carmody's snores, she remembered Louisa's gossip about King George IV and his bureau drawers bursting with 7,000 envelopes, each holding a lock of hair from a woman with whom he had 'intimate relations'. Kate interpreted the ensuing giggling from the beds as knowing giggles. She must be the only one who didn't understand the meaning of 'intimate relations'. Lying in the damp darkness a year later, she wished she had not been too proud to ask.

Next morning she felt better after striding the length and breadth of the boat. She loved the sea in all its guises and moods, the way it streamed endlessly past—a silky glide forward, a trembling pause, followed by a swoon into the next wave. She believed she was protected, finding the grumbling of the bulkheads both soothing and hypnotic.

When Captain Palliser joined her he was freshly shaved. 'I apologise for my behaviour last evening. It was unforgivable.' His hands on the railings were strong and brown. She wished he had stayed away. 'Please say you forgive me.'

She did not laugh or make a joke as he had hoped. 'I do,' she muttered, feeling gauche and ungracious.

'Promise you'll read to me again.'

Politeness dictated that she agreed, although her instincts advised otherwise: 'I most certainly shan't.' She walked away.

He gripped the railings and scowled at the sea, cursing his misconstruction of the previous evening, and yet for the briefest moment, he was certain, she had responded to his kiss.

That afternoon after making sure Kathleen was on deck, he went visiting. Miss Carmody looked ghastly, grey-faced and with a boil on the side of her neck, although she had made an effort at grooming: her hair was coiled but the thick woollen skirt, over-heavy boots and limp blouse made a mockery of style.

'How are you?' He bent towards her. He was a master at projecting sympathy.

'I am all right.' She spoke bravely but it was obvious she was far from all right.

'I heard you were unwell.'

Her carefully managed aplomb almost deserted her. He was such an attractive man and caring too. She read kindness in his eyes.

He held out a wrapped package. 'I thought you might like something to read.'

'You're too kind.' She was quite overwhelmed.

'Now that you are up, perhaps you and Miss Kelly might do me the honour of taking tea this afternoon?'

Tea. Being an English military man, she presumed it would be proper tea and she thought she could just about manage that. She hoped he would organise the journey from the docks to the railway station for the train to Cairo. But he was offering more.

'I've taken the liberty of booking you and Miss Kelly into Shepheard's Hotel.'

Chapter Three

Kate had forgotten the power of Agra, the impact and sounds of the place. The railway station stewed in a mass of people of all ages, shapes, sizes and colour: elderly *paanwallas*[1] calling the delights of their aromatic morsels; watermelon men piercing the humidity with their noisy cries; a three-generation family of acrobats shouting through their sweaty exertions; spiced opulence combined with dirty poverty. The heat was oppressive, laden with a sharp dust that permeated everywhere. And music, always music merging into the gulps and hisses of steam from the train. She had come home.

She was dressed in sprigged muslin the colour of forget-me-nots and her straw bonnet had blue streamers, limply floating in the heat. Clothes clung to her sweat and her heart thumped under the command of a distantly remembered climate. Underneath her gown she wore corset, pantaloons and stockings, and the same remembered perspiration dribbled between her breasts and under her buttocks. Until now she had not realised the stifling clench of England's sensory deprivation—the dampness, coldness, drabness and greyness of its people. She stood entranced, breathing in the sounds, sights and scents, allowing India to nestle around her.

A small, plump, pink-faced woman dressed in purple wheezed forward. 'Miss Kelly? Miss Kelly?' She drew herself to full height. 'Allow me to introduce myself. I'm Mrs Montgomery. The wife of General Percival Montgomery.' A dimpling smile spread across her face. 'You're most welcome to Agra.' She began by pumping Kate's hand up and down but changed mid-pump to an all-enveloping hug. Turning her attention to Miss Carmody, she inspected her thoroughly before twisting round to the three expressionless, turbaned servants who stood behind her. 'The luggage. Look to the luggage.' She clapped her hands. 'Quick. Quick.'

As they moved to obey her command, she caught sight of Captain Palliser. Her eyes lit up and as quickly as her bulk would allow she moved to his side. 'You're most welcome,' she assured, looking up at him. Whoever he was, he was an unexpected bonus.

Her arm linking Kate's, nodding and chatting, Mrs Montgomery led the way to a battered barouche standing outside the station. 'We're so delighted to have you, my dear. We must set the date for your wedding ceremony as soon as possible, although we have to allow enough time to get your trousseau organised. You'll meet your fiancé, my cousin Mr Isaac Newton, tomorrow—he's a good man. We've arranged a small tea party.' Kate wondered how she could have forgotten the slap and sting and liquid brightness of Agra sunlight.

As the carriage, followed by a wagon carrying servants, bearers and luggage, pulled out onto the dusty street, the air was even hotter than Kate remembered. As they moved away from the station, the trading offices and the jumble of white, ochre and pink buildings, and headed towards the outskirts of town, it became tinged with a balmy breeze.

Captain Palliser cast surreptitious glances at Kathleen; he abhorred unfinished business. She was beyond his comprehension, which made her even more desirable. As long as Mrs Montgomery accepted him as one of their group he planned to remain. He was supposedly travelling to Delhi on family business before rejoining his regiment further north, but a telegram should buy him time. Shepheard's Hotel had neither earned him Kathleen's gratitude, nor provided an opportunity for seduction. He had ended up consoling himself during the voyage from Cairo to Aden with a well-endowed Italian lady travelling to join her husband. For the remainder of the journey, he had devoted himself to the Misses Kelly and Carmody, which was no sacrifice as there was a dearth of appealing women, but his total devotion had made no discernible difference in Kathleen's polite but cool attitude towards him.

Some forty minutes later, after passing a series of handsome residences set in their own grounds, the carriage rolled up the driveway of a rambling, one-storey house, sprawled against the backdrop of a gloomy banyan grove.

Having been brought up in the less affluent quarters assigned to the families of the staff of the East India Company, Kate was somewhat taken aback by the size and opulence of the place. Mrs Montgomery led the way followed by a phalanx of servants who seemed to appear from nowhere and multiply en route. She was an enthusiastic guide and a lively commentator, and she derived enormous pleasure at redressing Miss Carmody's lack of knowledge of life in India.

The bungalow was constructed as an interlinking series of large, darkened spaces and wide corridors cooled by blinds. 'Tatties,' their hostess informed, running her fingers along one of the blinds, 'made from the roots of cuscus grass that we grow in the grounds. It has a nice fragrance when the servants keep it watered.' The floors were covered in date-leaf matting, scattered with zebra and tiger skin rugs and groups of low-slung chairs clustered round ebony tables. 'The matting keeps down the ants and by placing the furniture away from the walls we avoid nesting snakes,' she assured airily with a courageous wave of her arm. She was terrified of India's insect and reptile population but went to considerable pains to present herself as a non-complaining, British flag-bearing colonial wife.

A deep veranda, trailing clematis, hibiscus and bougainvillea, encircled the bungalow. Like schools of shimmering fish, rows of slippers belonging to the servants lined the railings. Tailors sat cross-legged at one end of the veranda, needles varying in size from large to small, with different colours, lengths and thickness of thread jabbed into their turbans; children, their childhood stolen, tatted intricate patterns of lace; doe-eyed youths and young girls ferried covered dishes of food from the kitchens; others waved fans; more watered plants, blinds, dust and lawns.

'Such industry,' complimented Miss Carmody, 'everyone working so diligently.'

Hands grasping the railings, their hostess surveyed her kingdom, a look of satisfaction on her plump features. 'Ah, but if you observe closely, you'll notice that a job which fills the time of one well-trained Englishman requires the attention of six natives.'

Kate's bedroom contained a double wardrobe, hammock

and a bed with gauze curtains, a fat bolster and thin cotton comforter. Tarun, her personal houseboy, was produced with a flourish by Mrs Montgomery. He stepped forward, bowing his dark head and putting together his palms in the traditional greeting. Another boy, small and skinny, propped in a corner, wore only a *dhoti*.[2] With the string of a *punkah*[3] fan attached to his big toe, he paid her no attention as he began a slow-motion movement, resulting in the fan flapping and fluttering like an enormous moth over the bed. An archway led from the bedroom to another small, square room, which housed a private water closet.

With travelling firmly behind her, Miss Carmody breathed a sign of relief. She refused even to think that at some future date she had to repeat the journey back to London.

Next morning Kate was woken all too soon by Mrs Montgomery, followed by a grinning Chinaman and two skinny boys carrying bales of materials. 'Butterfly will make clothes for you,' she announced, positioning herself in the hammock and clapping her hands, which brought yet another scrawny boy with a large fan, which he proceeded to waft over her. Even with all the fanning, Kate could feel the stillness of the Hindustan as Butterfly unrolled, draped, tweaked and lovingly stroked his materials.

'That,' Mrs Montgomery pointed to a swatch of saffron yellow laid across the back of a chair, 'will complement the memsahib's hair.'

Kate shuddered at the thought of being dressed so vividly. 'Thank you. But I would prefer blue. It's my favourite colour.' She pointed to a length of pastel material as delicate as English bluebells hanging over the end of the bed.

'But, my dear, that's so very dull.'

'Blue very beautiful but this more nice.' Butterfly ran some yards of soft jade silk through his fingers, his eyes hooded as he watched for reaction. Kate smiled in agreement, and as Mrs Montgomery leaned over to feel the material, with a swish of his pigtail he pressed home his preference. 'This complement missee's beauty.'

Their hostess agreed as Kate was to discover she invariably did when directly confronted. While Butterfly took her measurements, their hostess issued directions about style and trimmings. Next she clicked her fingers at one of the boys, 'Pass over missee's corset.' She examined the corset in detail, clicked magisterially for Butterfly's attention, and when he glided to her side she ordered him to replace the original busks with silver ones. 'More comfortable and less likely to rust in this humidity,' she assured, with the blasé confidence of personal experience, as she swept from the room.

Butterfly smiled widely, displaying a mouthful of small teeth, stained carmine with betel juice, as he unfolded a bale of silk the colour of India's hot blue sky. 'Gorgeous sari for gorgeous missee.'

As Kate joined the tea party, the chattering faltered momentarily, then resumed. Undoubtedly, she was the most beautiful female present and that alone called for instant dissection, but together with the circumstances of her marriage there was enough gossip to keep the mongers supplied for days. Anglo-Indian society was notorious for its curiosity and jollity and the atmosphere was boisterously good-humoured. There must have been at least a hundred people present in the ballroom, a large space floored with date-leaf matting, with clusters of potted palms filling the corners, and sheaves of waxy orchids pinned to the walls.

The European men wore pale trousers, dark tailcoats and decorative cravats; their women had vibrantly coloured satin gowns with enormous puff sleeves and wide skirts. The Indians were in national dress: the men with traditional brocade tunics over trousers, and jewelled turbans; the women resplendent in buttercup yellow, sky blue, dazzling turquoise and peony pink saris shot with gold and silver embroidery. Precious stones flashed on their fingers and bracelets chimed on their arms.

In comparison Kate wore no jewellery, her hair was dressed casually and her gown was simple, untrimmed and softly bustled. The silk was sensual against her skin, the cambric petticoats cool; her white cotton stockings light and the restructured corset almost comfortable. If only there was not a bridegroom in the offing. Timed to perfection, like a ship in full sail, the general's wife, dressed in poppy red, appeared from the back of the room. She was accompanied by a slender young man of medium height with curling brown hair. As Kate and Isaac Newton came face to face, there was another patch of curious silence from those present: they were witnessing the couple's first meeting.

As Mr Newton bent over her hand, Kate saw Captain Palliser watching. He was in dress uniform, his gaze intense and his expression inscrutable. Although somewhat reassured by the ordinariness of her bridegroom, Kate's mouth felt dry, her chest palpitated and she had the strangest sensation that the real her wasn't present.

The introduction line was a tedious formality, which since the Sepoy Uprising[4] was adhered to punctiliously.

Mrs Montgomery presented the couple to administrators from the East India Company, government officials and army personnel, and, most importantly, several princes and their various entourages. As was expected the young couple circulated, made social small talk, drank tea and nibbled on fingers of seed cake.

The plum-coloured darkness came early, the moon was low-slung and the sky full of stars as Mr Newton led Kate outside. They had so much to talk about, she had so many questions and yet she was impeded by a sense of shyness. Still, there was no threat in the silence between them, it was almost companionable. As he moved from the shade to a rectangle of moonlight and took her hand, the light from the glimmering candles in the glass lanterns hanging on the railings of the veranda caught at their faces.

'Thank you,' he whispered.

'For what?' Kate found herself whispering back.

'For agreeing to marry me. You're more beautiful than your likeness.'

So that was the reason her father had the miniature painted. She might have known. 'I didn't have any choice in the matter.'

'I am sorry. I didn't know. I hope I'm a little to your liking?'

Kate may have been unsophisticated to the point of naiveté but she sensed integrity. He was so different to Captain Palliser and indeed her father. Perhaps, after all, Papa had not been totally cavalier in his choice of husband. She permitted herself an uncharacteristic flicker of satisfaction that owed all to the ethos of Miss Carmody's School for Young Ladies and nothing to her true self—if she had to wed, being married to a surgeon attached to the Indian civil service would give her status within both the British and native communities. From childhood she knew of the importance of status within the colonies. She loved the beat of India; she could and she would make a life here. Louisa had promised to visit, as had her brother Freddie who was stationed up north in Amritsar. She knew from his letters he was enjoying the hospitality of its powerful Sikhs.

'I think you may be a little to my liking. But time will tell,' she joked, gently disentangling her fingers from his.

'I promise I shall do all in my power to make you happy.' She read tenderness in the way he touched her cheek. 'I'm sorry we can't spend more time together but I must return to the hospital tomorrow. While I'm gone I do not wish you to socialise.'

As she was about to ask why, he placed a firm index finger against her lips.

He was gone before dawn but he left a letter in which he promised to write frequently, begging Kate to do the same and explaining he had an undertaking from Mrs Montgomery to come up country to visit within the next three weeks. 'At the least as you had not seen me before our betrothal, you should view your new home before the wedding,' he wrote.

Mrs Montgomery's running of the household was a chaotic mirroring of her good-hearted loneliness. The general was posted to the garrison town of Meerut up north where the revolution of 1857 had begun, and their four children were being educated in England. She had become resigned to filling her days receiving and paying calls, catching up on the latest intrigues within the community, having Butterfly implement the over-elaborate designs and trimmings derived from fashion magazines from London and Paris, failing to grasp the rudiments of chess, though succeeding admirably with écarté. With the arrival of Miss Kelly and her entourage—tiny though it was—she was greatly invigorated.

The previous year Major Kelly had been a frequent visitor. There was plenty of unfavourable gossip about him and his position in the East India Company but, flattered and delighted with his companionship, she paid scant attention. One evening, during which he considerably depleted Percy's stock of Gordon's Export, he confided his anxiety about his headstrong daughter. Relaxed from several glasses of Sandeman port, she not only advised marriage as the most practical solution to curbing waywardness, but was able to recommend a suitable husband.

Her cousin Isaac Newton had been brought up in a strict Church of England family of farmers in Hampshire. To his parents' chagrin, he had turned his back on farming for medicine—surgery, no less—and to quote his mother, 'in India of all places'. Mrs Montgomery was delighted to have kin nearby. But since his arrival he had eschewed her many attempts at matchmaking, confiding to her and anyone who would listen how horrified he was at the moral laxity of his fellow countrymen and women.

For Mrs Montgomery the arranging of the betrothal had been as simple and as uncomplicated as presenting the major to the surgeon. While the latter took a dim view of the former's enthusiastic imbibing of alcohol, the opportunity to marry a Catholic straight from the convent, as Kate was presented, was too good an opportunity to pass up. Even in India, Isaac was aware that Catholics

47

adhered to their codes of moral behaviour. With little more than a minor demur, he agreed to pay travel costs for Miss Kelly and a chaperone. The major would supply a likeness and fund the cost of the wedding, which Mrs Montgomery promised to organise in her home. When Isaac returned to his hospital, she and the major were enthusiastic in their toasting of the young couple.

Kate had spent her formative years in both Lahore and Agra in the care of Poonam, and it was through her ayah's eyes that she been seduced and fascinated by India and all things Indian. Mama believed people reacted differently in different places and that there was no escaping yourself in India, where happiness was the result of personal confrontation and acceptance of one's true self. Within this spirit, Kate felt a previously unknown freedom and a certainty that she was evolving into her true self: it was there in the new languidness of her attitude and the sucking way she gulped in lungs full of air. She decided to incorporate some Hindustani customs into her wedding service.

She'd never forgotten Shakti's wedding. Shakti, the bride, was Poonam's cousin. She was tall, slender and doe-eyed with a ready smile. Kate could still feel the love that had encompassed the occasion, and the beat of happiness that had coursed through her young body from the soles of her feet to the tips of her fingers. And, as Mama would say, the family was as poor as church mice.

Shakti's village, clinging precariously to the side of the mountain, was decked out in triumphal floral arches, the air alive with dancing butterflies and falling petals, and filled with the low penetrating sound of conch shells and the light-hearted music of the *shehnai*.[5] The bride arrived in a palanquin, decorated with woven blossoms of pink and red and purple, carried by four barefooted bearers. Through the rippling gauzy blinds, Kate could see her dark, veiled head and golden necklaces studded with precious stones. From Poonam, she knew that earlier Shakti would have been bathed in perfumed oils, her skin rubbed with turmeric paste and her insteps painted with henna, before being dressed in a sari of the finest red silk with embroidered brocade and ivory bangles decorating her arms.

Rhythmic drums and a procession of dancing girls making swooping gestures and jingling anklets heralded the bridegroom's entrance along the pathway. Madan was perched high on a waving howdah, the elephant swaying from side to side, stepping steadily, waving his trunk, seemingly as entranced as family and guests by the occasion

The ceremony was long, lingering and delicate: a combination of poetry, song, music and prayer. It included the exchange of leafy garlands, first Madan tenderly bedecking his bride, Shakti repeating the gesture. Kate, eyes filling with emotion, watched as the groom decorated his bride's forehead with the traditional red *bindi*, believed to bring prosperity and grant a new wife a place as the guardian of the family's welfare. This was followed by Shakti offering Madan a mouthful of rice from her fingers.

Kate doubted her bridegroom would permit either the *bindi* or rice but surely they could include some music and garlands in their ceremony?

'I'd like to visit the church,' she announced one afternoon during tiffin, which was served in a small anteroom. She had settled well into her new surroundings, particularly since Captain Palliser had taken off with several servants and bearers on an exploratory expedition down the River Jumna. She hoped he would be gone for many weeks.

'Whatever for, my dear?'

'I want to discuss the ceremony with the priest.' She decided against mentioning the Hindu element.

'Mr Newton is devout in his religious practice and I've arranged with his agreement for the minister to perform the service here.' Mrs Montgomery's autocratic voice was authoritative.

Kate was dismayed but she spoke firmly. 'And I'm a devout Catholic. Papa must have explained that to you. When Polly and I were in London, he insisted we attended daily mass.' She looked across the table for confirmation. Miss Carmody's mouth was full and she nodded; to her amazement she was developing quite a taste for goat curry.

'My dear, you'll find individual religions are not so important in India. We seek to be good Christians and indeed for centuries have tried without success to convert the Muslims and Hindus and all the other religions.' Mrs Montgomery's tone was placatory and she waved her arm as though embracing the world.

'I disagree. Individual religions are important in India, as is the culture. Remember I was reared here.' Daily, Kate's senses were assailed anew by the sights, sounds, scents and tastes of northern India, and she couldn't believe how much she'd forgotten. Until Cook presented it in her honour, she had not remembered as a child how much she had enjoyed the soft white bekti fish. When she married, she planned to learn the Hindustani language and to become familiar with its culture and music. She was also going to take up painting: the landscapes of contrasting lusciousness and desert, cirrus and cumulus skyscapes, as well as the people would provide rich sources of inspiration.

'I shall have to discuss the matter with Isaac,' Mrs Montgomery stalled. She hoped the education her two daughters were receiving in England would make them more amenable than Miss Kelly.

Religion was important to Kate, who saw it as a mighty river with millions of droplets glistening in the sun, all flowing towards God. She had no need to hear the priest's Latin or to observe Hindu rituals, their messages were carved in her bones, but she could not, she would not contemplate a Church of England marriage ceremony.

'There's no need for discussion. If I don't have a Catholic service, in the eyes of my Church I'm not married. Isaac wouldn't want that.'

'We'll see.' Mrs Montgomery returned to her food, but she'd lost her appetite and fretted she could lose her carefully cultivated relationship with the Reverend James Moncton, who conducted services in the old style favoured by generations of Montgomerys.

While the two women were taking siestas, Kate went to her room and unrolled the silk-wrapped parcel that Butterfly had delivered to her houseboy. She put on the petticoat and *choli* blouse, wrapped the sari around her waist, draping one end over her shoulder, slipped on flat sandals and took time to admire her cool elegance in the looking glass.

On the way to visit Father Jacobi, the local Catholic priest, Tarun ran alongside the fiacre, shouting '*Chalo!*' Kate suspected more to impress his countrymen than to protect her. The nearer they drew to the Taj Mahal, the more crowded the dirt tracks became, swelling with young and old. She loved the romantic story of the Taj built more than two centuries ago by the Emperor Shah Jahan in memory of his favourite wife. She remembered her father's anger about the time of the Sepoy Rising, at its defacement by soldiers who chiselled out precious stones and lapis lazuli from its walls.

While poverty was everywhere—in the fragile lean-to shacks and in the mounds of debris piled against the walls—she found the city hauntingly contradictory and exciting. She was fascinated by the haphazard slouch of neglected dwellings crumbling into lavish stalls of vegetables and silks; enthralled by the vibrancy of the colours and the dizzyingly delicious fragrances, she was also heartbroken by the liquid accepting eyes of the women and children.

Her father had forbidden the giving of alms to the beggars who set up home outside the gates of the compound and surrounded the family with outstretched hands and pleading voices whenever they left. From the time she was old enough to recognise the effects of want, Kate had ignored him, as did her mother, who saw nobody went hungry. Like so much else about India, she had forgotten its all-encompassing poverty, how it floated in the air she breathed and was baked into the ground under her feet.

'Stop,' she called to the driver. As she stepped out of the small coach, the air caught in her nostrils and fine grey dust settled on her sandals and stuck to the hem of her sari. Within seconds she was suffocatingly surrounded by women and children, but she was not frightened; there was nothing scary in their quest for alms, although she was scared at her houseboy's reaction. Wielding the whip, which he had snatched from the driver, Tarun beat off the small children who were clinging to her like the tiny cat-like monkeys that colonised the ruins. The whip swished down on their skinny shoulders and buttocks.

'Stop, stop it!' she cried, horrified, thinking how distressed the mothers must be, but they seemed impervious to their children's pain as they helped them to hang on to Kate, yet nobody made an attempt to pull at the purse of coins hanging from her waist.

'Shush,' she entreated, reaching for the money. The women and children drew back, watching with huge eyes and open mouths as she spilled out coins onto the palms of her hands. Wishing she had a few words of their language, she addressed Tarun. 'Tell them this is all the money I have but they're welcome to it. Can you distribute it fairly?'

The Montgomery servants knew the beautiful English lady was special but now Tarun had proof first-hand. Not that he approved of her behaviour. As her servant he would have more status if, like the other English, she held her head high and ignored the natives and their way of life. With hair that dazzled like the sun, pale skin and soft voice, she was like the goddess Lakshmi, embodiment of light, beauty, good fortune and wealth. His importance was mighty as he clapped his hands; she had given him the authority. He spoke a few staccato sentences, took the coins from his mistress, placed them on the ground, brushed the children to one side and called the women one by one.

Footnotes

1 *Paanwallas*: sellers of bethel leaf chew.
2 *Dhoti*: traditional garment of menswear in India.
3 *Punkah*: portable fan made from the leaf of the Palmyra.
4 After the Sepoy Uprising of 1857, the British government ruled India with two administrative systems, the British Provinces, comprising about sixty per cent of the country and totally under British control, and the remainder comprising the Indian 'princely' states, which recognised British rule in return for local autonomy: and it was the latter situation that accounted for the minor royalty.
5 *Shehnai*: double-reed musical instrument of good luck, widely used in marriage ceremonies.

Chapter Four

Kate settled into a low hammock chair on the veranda to read Isaac's latest letter. As she absorbed the contents, she blew softly through her lips: he was dismayed at the 'frivolity' of her suggestion to incorporate Hindu traditions into their wedding ceremony. His reaction did not overly surprise her. It had taken her insistence for him to dispense with the 'Miss Kelly'. She had wanted him to address her as Kate—it was the name she felt best suited her personality, but she couldn't budge him further than 'Kathleen' and he had agreed only after she confided that in her heart she thought of him as Isaac. Through their correspondence she learned that while he was an honourable and decent man, he did not have a sense of humour, adventure or fun, but she consoled herself with supposing you could not have everything in a husband.

Isaac had already written to Mrs Montgomery that as there was an outbreak of bloody flux at the hospital, under no circumstances was Miss Kelly to travel. Kate had been looking forward to going up country to see her future home, and as a break from the monotony of her current life.

She would have to look for tactful alternatives and diplomatic modifications to her original plans for the wedding ceremony, to which Father Jacobi had been agreeably receptive, even including a few ideas of his own. She was beginning to suspect that married life would involve the constant implementation of delicate compromise. Having seen her mother bow to a myriad of such concessions with her father, while she was disappointed, she was somewhat prepared.

In the shaded warmth of the veranda, she drifted back into dreams of childhood. A bearer worked a feather fan, with the air full of balmy scents and evening whispers from the foliage at the edge of the compound. In her memory she was little more than a baby, a plump little thing, just beginning to walk, dressed in white with dimpled elbows and knees, grunting with pleasure at the effort of clambering up and down from the muslin of her mother's lap. Keeping time with Mama's rocking, Kate moved her shoulders voluptuously; she loved the touch of lingering hands on her head. She did?

She jerked out of her reverie and turned round. 'What are you doing?' she asked Captain Palliser, who was supposed to be miles away, camping on the banks of the Jumna.

'I apologise if I scared you.' He looked more jubilant than remorseful. He had left the Montgomery household in an effort to clear his mind of Kathleen. As the trip was not fulfilling its purpose, he had decided to return. He was delighted to be back and even more delighted at what he took to be Kathleen's response to his caresses.

As he sank into the chair beside her, his bulk strained the tough canvas.

She should have got up then and left the veranda.

'I thought you'd be interested to hear of my adventures…'

She would love to hear where he'd gone, the sights he'd seen and what he'd done but she tossed her head in a gesture of indifference.

He knew her well enough to know differently. Kathleen Kelly was made for adventure and new experiences and would have thrived on his journey. He pressed home his advantage. 'So I hear all is not going well for the good doctor?'

'He's a surgeon.'

Captain Palliser waved an airy hand. 'Why is he concerning himself with the flux? It's everywhere in this God-forsaken country.' He lowered his voice and leaned closer to her: 'I thought a lot about you while I was away. We must talk. Please.'

'We've nothing to talk about.' Her voice was firm and without a trace of the coquette; she was one of those rare women who knew how to excite a man without wanting to or without having to resort to flirtation.

He had never before felt this way about any woman and, despite his reputation, he had no idea of how to proceed. In the dark of the nights, sleeping under the stars he had considered offering marriage, elopement, anything to possess Kathleen Kelly, but sitting with her next to him on the veranda his planned words of seduction deserted him. He arose from the chair, slipped to his knees, put his arms around her thighs and nestled his face on her lap.

For a brief moment in an instinctively sensual gesture, she allowed her chin to rest on the softness of his blond hair, but when she realised what she was doing she lifted her head and struggled to remove his face from her skirts. To her dismay he clasped her thighs tighter, then lifted his head and kissed her soundly on the lips.

In breathtaking sequence, Kate experienced enjoyment—yes, outrageous as it was she enjoyed the sensation of his closeness, his arms around her and his lips on hers. But the feeling was brief and was swiftly followed by disbelief at what was happening, which escalated into horror at discovering Mrs Montgomery, very much the general's wife, standing before them, gulping strangulated gasps of outraged air. The finale was the stomach-churning realisation that she was publicly and horrifically compromised. God knows the captain's behaviour on board was shocking but at least she had been able to keep it to herself.

In what she afterwards remembered as terrifyingly slow motion, Captain Palliser rose to his feet; Mrs Montgomery clutched at her bosom, her yelps filling the air; Kate escaped to her bedroom and sank into the hammock. Without the *punkah* boy's fanning, the air in the room was thick and stifling.

With hands folded prissily across her chest and an angry red staining her cheeks, Miss Carmody looked down on her charge. 'Have you taken leave of your senses?' She had been kissed briefly and only once on the side of her face by the son of a cobbler who wrote verse and claimed to be in love with her. She preferred not to remember how her father had erased any notions she might have had of romance by ridicule.

Kate lay supine, the strings of the hammock motionless beneath her. 'Mrs Montgomery came upon us as Captain Palliser was behaving most inappropriately. That's all that happened.' She wished it was as simple as that.

'Such behaviour is unforgivable,' Miss Carmody scolded.

'It wasn't my fault.'

'It was. You shouldn't have allowed the situation to develop.'

'I didn't.'

'My dear, sitting alone on the veranda is inviting trouble.' Miss Carmody walked out of the room, her head high with righteousness.

If the situation were not so awful, Kate would be amused at Miss Carmody's copying of Mrs Montgomery's 'my dear'. In different circumstances she could imagine giggling with Louisa over the incident. But with betrothal came duty and she knew the weight of it would lie heavily on her until she clarified the situation to Isaac.

She swung her legs over the hammock and picked up her writing case from the small bureau. Sighing at the thought of what she was about to do, she settled down to write an explanation of what had occurred. Words and phrases flew around in her head like bad-tempered moths, but when they landed on the page they were too explicit. She was compromised and she had compromised the man she was going to marry. He needed to understand what had happened but she did not know how to tell him. Should she talk to Mrs Montgomery, ask her to write the letter? Or would her attitude be the same as Miss Carmody's? She quivered with indecision and snapped closed her case.

Captain Palliser was unsure of his hostess's reaction to his breech of etiquette, and, fearing being asked to leave, he became an inconspicuous figure around the bungalow and grounds. But after a few days of careful observation, he planned his next move. Waiting until Mrs Montgomery emerged from her siesta he followed her to the dining room.

The room, airless and dark from being sealed by heavy wooden blinds, was more shrine than function, and, as the general's grandfather had stipulated, it looked as though it had been transported from a stately home in England. Indeed, with the exception of the installation of water closets, General Montgomery's home remained a memorial to past generations of his crown-serving ancestors. The dining table, chairs and sideboards were rope-edged mahogany—their legs stood in shallow bowls of water to protect them from wood-eating beetles; the panelled walls hung with portraits of sternly dutiful Montgomerys who, due to the climate, had grown rather mouldy. The heirloom china, Waterford crystal and fine silver service, which tarnished within twenty-four hours of polishing, were all displayed in glass-fronted cabinets. But after sunset the room was transformed into a place of sparkles when the candles were lit in the crystal chandelier hanging low over the table and in the candelabra between each portrait.

Captain Palliser came upon Mrs Montgomery sitting in the shadows at the top of the table with a half-full decanter of port and an almost empty glass. 'I feel I owe you an explanation,' he began, knowing his timing could not be better. 'I should have done so before but I didn't think matters with Miss Kelly would come to this.'

From boyhood he had been skilled in plausible justification and he had developed the ability to manoeuvre situations to his advantage. His father, a decorated general serving with the 2nd Punjab Cavalry of the Indian Army, was mostly absent from the family estates and had died in action during the Sepoy Rising. After giving birth, his mother handed him over to a wet nurse and spent the next three decades breeding toy terriers, which she trained as lapdogs rather than have them demonstrate their prowess in the popular rat pits. He graduated to a nursemaid to whom he became hysterically attached, then a governess whom he could not bear to leave out of his sight, and finally to a tutor with whom his relationship was one of mutual antipathy, and whose sexual conquests included his mother, various visiting cousins and even some of the upstairs maids.

Mrs Montgomery was at the mellow stage of being capable of endorsing the most bizarre of viewpoints. The captain lowered his voice to a suitably solemn tone. 'The poor child. I've the greatest of compassion for her. She can't help her hysteria and is inclined towards exaggeration.' Mrs Montgomery's nod was encouraging. 'I suppose it's understandable as she is so young—as a woman you'd have considerably more experience than I in such matters.' He shook his head perplexedly. 'And, regretfully, she's travelling with an inexperienced chaperone.'

Beaming pinkly, Mrs Montgomery relaxed into his explanation. She believed her fondness for port to be her secret pleasure but it was, in fact, common knowledge throughout the colony. 'Yes, you were right to help. People like us must assist where appropriate. It's unfortunate her father's business detained him in London.'

'Perhaps I should have realised earlier but I fear Miss Kelly has become attached to me.' Passionate as he was about Kathleen, he had neither conscience nor compunction when it came to wriggling out of a situation that could be potentially damaging to him, his career and reputation.

'Perhaps, as she is to be married, it would be better if this matter isn't referred to again. Leave it to me. I'll talk to her.'

'Thank you.' He accepted her expansiveness as his due. 'I'm grateful for your understanding. I expected no less.'

'Would you like…?' She gestured towards the decanter.

He declined. The last complication he needed then was an even more maudlin hostess.

Father Jacobi was a quiet man, deeply religious and intensely spiritual. Knowing he would be unable to stop the match between Roman Catholic Miss Kelly and Church of England Mr Newton did not prevent him grieving at yet another mixed marriage. He had been long enough in India and dealt with sufficient colonials to know that betrothals were entered into for a variety of professional, monetary and social reasons; religion was seldom considered. So it was unexpected to come across devotion such as Miss Kelly's, someone who was strong enough in her faith to sway her husband eventually to Catholicism (hopefully). He comforted himself that any daughters of the union would be raised in the faith of their mother.

Kate made her confession on the eve of her wedding, going through the motions of worrying about her relationship with God, wondering did she suffer from pride and questioning the sin of covetousness. Father Jacobi had heard it all before and he soothed her concerns as being natural. Before setting penance, he asked, 'Is there anything else troubling you?' Frequently at this stage he found brides-to-be nervous about the marriage act of consummation. As he had no personal experience, his advice never varied. It was to cleave to and obey their husbands in all matters and at all times.

Judging that a priest would be no more knowledgeable

than her in such matters, Kate had not planned on confiding those concerns, but there was something gnawing at her conscience. She had intended keeping it secret, but now that she had been asked, under the seal of the confessional, silence was not an option. She and Louisa were in agreement that the constant threat of the flames of hell for various misdemeanours was one of the major problems of being a Catholic.

'Yes, well…' she broke off unnerved, unsure of where to begin.

She wished for Father Mathew's soothing presence and assurance that no sin for which contrition was truly sought was outside the realm of God's forgiveness. It seemed an eternity since he had been her occasion of sin. She had made her confession before leaving London, received absolution and known the peace of forgiveness.

General Montgomery had come south for a few days over Christmas. His wife fussed the servants to chaos regarding the various entertainments that he regarded as a necessary part of his career. Because of Isaac's wish that she did not socialise, Kate spent much of the holiday alone reading, re-thumbing her copy of *Lalla Rookh* and empathising with the characters in *Great Expectations* and *A Christmas Carol*, living their lives, feeling their joys and sorrows, but invariably her thoughts would turn to Captain Palliser who had finally journeyed to Delhi to deal with that family business.

She had never warmed to him but she couldn't help but feel flattered by his attention. In the quiet of her room, she tried to explain her predicament to God. To make Him understand she went down on her knees to describe her relationship with the captain, embellishing rather than understating out of fear that He might think she was skimping on facts. With God's permission, which without manifestation to the contrary she took as being granted, she had decided against formally confessing. What was in the past was better left there.

Father Jacobi's question about the troubling 'anything else' left her with no choice but to alter her decision about keeping her secret.

'Take your time, my child.'

She started with the captain entering their railway carriage on the journey to Marseilles and finished with his kiss on the veranda. Her sessions with God were fresh in her mind and her story as recounted to Father Jacobi became one of sexual misconduct. The priest was too experienced in the foibles of human nature to show his surprise, though he never ceased to be amazed by the corruption of his penitents. How mistaken he had been about Miss Kelly.

'My advice to you is to be honest with your husband at all times. And as you've Irish blood in your veins, for your penance say the fifteen mysteries of the rosary twice.'

The marriage took place on Tuesday, 3rd January 1871. The ceremony was carried out by Father Jacobi, with the Reverend Moncton in attendance. In the end the sole manifestation of Hinduism was the large, informal floral decorations created by Tarun. Every corner of the public rooms bloomed with a combination of rosy pink lotus blossoms, delicate fronds of jasmine and trumpet-shaped hibiscus, as well as swirling swags of greenery from the silk plant.

Everyone agreed that Miss Kathleen Kelly was the most

beautiful bride within living memory. Butterfly surpassed himself with her golden silk wedding gown, which was worn slightly off the shoulders; it had a narrow skirt, small bustle and wrist-length sleeves, and was devoid of the flounces and furbelows so popular in London and Paris.

For the remainder of her life Kate maintained that her memory of her wedding ceremony was little more than a blurred series of impressions.

However, she clearly remembered her panic at walking the length of the ballroom, the way her breath was stifled in her throat—and the firmness of Mrs Montgomery's palm cupping her elbow, and the rustle of her saffron taffeta, as well as the shadow figure of Miss Carmody following in a gown of dove grey. As she reached the makeshift altar, she was amazed to see that Isaac looked smaller and more nervous than she remembered. She hadn't forgotten what she considered to be the ridiculousness of the Catholic edicts of 'love', 'honour' and 'obey': surely love and honour were earned and as for obey, she preferred not to think of having to live with the implications. 'I am the words and you are the melody'—the traditional Hindu wedding mantra ran seductively around in her head.

Her belief that she would be loved, cared for and protected by Isaac softened the enormity and lifelong implications of the service, and, pushing away her previous wishes for choice and freedom, she held onto those beliefs like a talisman, vowing she would love him in return, be a good wife and make a fine life for them.

The dining room had been opened for the sixty invited guests. At Isaac's request the meal included a selection of fruity curries and bowls of spicy stews prepared from *dhal*, and at their hostess's suggestion the Indian fare was augmented with smoked salmon pickled in brine and transported in small barrels by Fortnum and Mason in London, which Mrs Montgomery insisted be invoiced to Major Kelly. For dessert there was *kheer*, a form of rice pudding to which Kate was particularly partial, and *kulfi*, a nutty ice cream. The women drank tea and the men had whisky or India pale ale.

The meal could not be extended forever, and as the time drew close to be a wife—and not quite knowing what that involved—Kate's belly was a mess of cramping pains. She hated the idea of her transformation from virgin to wife taking place in the Montgomery residence—with, she suspected, everyone knowing, waiting and gossiping. Louisa said that in parts of the world, as proof that consummation had taken place, bloodstained sheets were thrown from the bedroom window. Kate presumed her husband would not go that far, but she did not even know why sheets would be bloodied. When she broached the idea of going up country to their home after the meal, Isaac had answered that he considered it 'inappropriate'.

Kate watched her bridegroom. He appeared soberly out of place among this rumbustious, red-cheeked crowd: the delicate tracery of his eyelashes, soft curl of his hair, the disciplined black of his coat, precisely knotted cravat and those short stubby fingers that would soon lay claim to her body. Why were women reared to believe that marriage was their only destiny? She bit her lip in determination: bloody hell, she would make it work.

When she could no longer stand the crowd or bear the anticipation, she whispered to Isaac, 'May we leave?'

Momentarily, what she took as a flicker of annoyance crossed his face, and then he nodded.

They left the gathering without fanfare but not without being noticed. The men, envious of the groom's prize, joshed and elbowed among themselves; the women were brushed with sadness for the pregnancies and hardships that would be the bride's life. A lamb to the slaughter, they said.

In the intervening hours, Tarun had decorated the marriage bedroom with scattered blossoms, drifts of petals and shallow bowls of fragrant spices and incense. Standing beside Isaac in the heat of late afternoon, Kate felt numb. She wished that instead of the two glasses accompanying the covered jug of lemonade on the bedside table, there were two chairs so that she and Isaac could sit down and just talk. As always, one of the skinny young boys was in attendance, his toe busily operating the fan. He was as invisible as she felt.

Isaac's behaviour did nothing for her feeling of security or to enhance her confidence. He looked so unsure, licking at his lips, blinking nervously, and this was the man to whom she had promised to cleave for the remainder of her life. She closed her eyes but opened them immediately as she sensed him approaching. He was undoing the first three buttons of his coat. Her legs felt weak, she needed to sit down but there was only the bed on which her bridal nightgown was laid out in lacy glory, pinched in at the waist and with satin ribbons streaming across the thin coverlet.

Eventually she sat on the edge of the bed, its hard surface digging into her buttocks. 'Isaac, there's something I need to tell you.'

He shrugged out of his coat, folded it neatly, and not

finding a chair laid it on the hammock. 'Later, my love.' Taking both her hands in his, he raised her to her feet and as he drew her towards him, his pale blue eyes mirrored Captain Palliser's expression. Her heart began to pound, her colour rose as he tightened his arms around her and, unbelievably, it was all right. It felt surprisingly good in a way she had not dared to hope. She felt the thump of Isaac's heart against her breast, wondered if he could feel hers and thought that some day she would ask him. He kissed her, his lips tentatively brushing hers, and it was so different to the captain's kiss that she wondered was it a proper kiss at all. She wriggled away. 'Isaac, please, there's something I have to tell you. Must tell you.'

'Not now. Can't it wait?' His voice had thickened.

'No. It can't.' She had wanted to start her new life with a clean slate but now that the time had arrived she found she was in no hurry to begin that new life.

'Well in that case.' With his arm proprietarily around her waist, he walked her out onto the veranda. The sky was turning a soft plum pink and the air pulsed with twilight life.

'What's so important?' he teased.

'When I was making my confession yesterday, Father Jacobi told me to be honest with you.'

'And rightly so.'

'It's nothing really.' She was sorry she'd mentioned anything about having to tell him something, and she was experiencing difficulty conjuring up the words. 'Well, it's about Captain Palliser.'

'What about him?'

She took courage from his disinterested tone. As far as she was aware, he had scarcely registered the captain.

'He made advances towards me.' Now that it was said, she breathed a sigh of relief. It was out, it was over and she could get on with her life.

'What sort of advances?'

She hadn't expected questions. 'I…well… .' She couldn't go on.

Isaac's arm stiffened. 'Did he touch you?'

'Yes.' This was dreadful.

'Did he kiss you?'

'Well…yes.'

'More than once?' Kate nodded and Isaac removed his arm; then he did what Kate least expected. He walked away from her. As she followed him inside, he was putting on his coat. His face was sheet white and his eyes blazing. 'You know what I must do?'

Kate shook her head, puzzled at how telling the truth as advised by her confessor could cause such a reaction in a man she knew to be a true and caring Christian.

'I'll arrange your passage back to England and inform your father. I'll also instigate immediate divorce proceedings.'

'Isaac, you what?'

'You heard me.' He had his coat fully buttoned.

'You can't. We're married.'

'We're not. We have not, nor will we complete the marriage act. You should've thought of the implications before you compromised yourself and me.'

'But I didn't…'

Her words fell on deaf ears as Isaac walked through her room, outside to the corridor, as still the young boy worked the *punkah* fan.

Again Kate found herself sitting on the edge of the bed.

This time she was staring into space, unaware of its hardness. She knew she should feel something but she couldn't—just a numbness, and that wasn't a feeling. After a while Miss Carmody came in, sat beside her and just held her hand; some time later she raised her to her feet and began to undress her. Kate stood mute, like a child rising up and lowering her arms as the whispering lace of her nightgown replaced the rustling silk of her bridal gown. Miss Carmody held back the coverlet and the two women—she still in her dove grey—climbed into bed and still they did not speak.

Kate must have dozed because some time later she half-woke, and in that sleepy moment teetering between sleep and wakefulness she was distantly aware of angry voices in the corridor. She hoped she had dreamt what had happened and looked forward to waking up to a new dawn. When next she opened her eyes it was morning. The boy with the fan was missing and the room was heavy and dank.

Miss Carmody came in from the veranda; she was dressed in her travelling clothes and her expression was inscrutable. 'We're to leave today for Bombay to wait for the next ship back to England. Mr Newton has left a little funding and we'll be all right. We'll have to be.'

Kate said nothing. She climbed out of bed and looked around.

Kathleen Kelly—or was it Newton? She was seventeen and about to be divorced from a marriage that in the eyes of her Church was null and void, while in the eyes of Victorian society she was a ruined woman.

Chapter Five

Kate braced her feet on the floor and moved her shoulders against the rough wood of the bench. Their first-class train journey to Agra, which Miss Carmody had regarded as primitive, was luxury compared to this, although the amount of force required to board this train had been no less or no more than the amount of politeness necessary to ensure that their cramped journey was as pleasant as possible.

That was her beloved India. A place of dizzying extremes: disastrous floods and consuming earthquakes, deadly cobras and springing leopards, monkeys climbing trees and green parrots flying against the bowl of blue sky. Trapping fireflies in jars and munching on raw sugar cane. Travelling by steam trains and riding in rickshaws, maharajas and mahouts, magic tricks. It was a continent where goddesses were worshipped and women were powerfully matriarchal, yet it remained a male-dominated society.

'Bloody hell,' she muttered under her breath. It was Freddie's favourite swearword and when Mama caught him at it she had his mouth washed out with soap; it was Kate's favourite too and she'd never been caught. This was a bloody-hell situation. Perhaps if Freddie had come to the wedding she would not be in such a pickle.

Through the echoing tunnel in her head she was aware of the chattering crowd: deep, accepting adult accents, shrill-voiced children and the tiny peeking bird cries of babies. The thick air, hot and dusty on her face and clogging her nostrils, was full of a thousand excessively pungent smells. She struggled to keep open her heavy eyelids, because closed they created a kaleidoscope of pictures she wanted to forget. She was squashed against a large woman breathing out ragged gasps of spicy breath, who was pressed against her so tightly she could feel the pulsation of her thighs through the flimsy material of her sari. Every available inch of train space was occupied. The men in the corridor took turns to sit or squat on a section of floor, every man feeling the press of at least two other bodies against his own.

Miss Carmody, her eyes tightly closed to the harsh reality of their railway journey, had the added trauma of a basket of squawking hens spilling onto her lap. She was aware of the implications of her return to England—failure from start to finish, and she dreaded coming face to face with the major. With each clank of wheels on the metal of the track, she shuddered at her situation, a shuddering amplified by the resonating image of Mrs Montgomery's anger-fuelled words and Mr Newton's white-faced rage. She had never come across such naked fury and she was glad Kathleen had been spared the scene.

As a child she remembered embroidering a sampler with the words 'This too shall pass', one perfect stitch after another. Unable to recall and not caring what happened to the finished square of cream linen, with its flawless blue cross stitching, she hoped the little adage was based on fact and wondered when the current situation would pass.

The sense of *joie de vivre* that she had experienced during her stay in India had disappeared. In different circumstances she believed she could have lived there and had a good life. She liked Agra's relaxed social rules, the constant entertainment and the likelihood of marriage, even for older women. Now her reputation was almost as tattered as Kathleen's. How could her school for young ladies survive the scandal? Desperation clawed at her as the full force of reality struck.

Mr Newton had been parsimonious in the extreme in providing money to get them back to London, and when she had plucked up the courage to query the smallness of the amount, Mrs Montgomery, lips pursed in annoyance, had tartly pointed out that in view of the circumstances her cousin was extremely generous as he was under no obligation to fund any part of their return journey.

When the train drew into Bombay's railway station, with its cathedral interior and birds fluttering beneath a metal heaven of vaulted ceiling, the two women disembarked without the aid of porters or bearers. They managed the high step down from train to platform and manoeuvred their portmanteaux without a helping hand from either the crowding natives or the few Europeans who threw them curious glances. Even in the more enlightened 1870s it was not usual for white women, particularly those who were obviously from the upper classes, to travel alone. The station was filled with people, luggage, bundles of goods, and an assortment of live and recently deceased animals.

Miss Carmody felt she had been through so much that no matter what happened she was beyond surprise, but the sight of Captain Palliser striding along the platform quite took her breath away. She felt a delicious surge of relief and was filled with the belief that his presence would make all well.

For once the captain was not his confident self; his demeanour was sombre as he reached out to rest one hand on each of the women's shoulders. 'I am so sorry you are in such a situation.' The expression of sympathy was out before he realised it and if pressed he would be hard put to state specifically for what he was sorry. Truth to be known, part of him was glad to have them indebted to him as their predicament allowed him the opportunity to play the role of a knight in shining armour. He had used both his influence and money to get to Bombay in the shortest possible time.

'You were gone before I was even up,' he said. He glanced at Kate hoping for some sort of an explanation but she was looking at a point over his left shoulder and would not meet his eyes. He had no idea of what had happened between the time he had enviously watched her leave the wedding party with her husband, and his discovery when he arose the following morning that she had left Agra without her husband.

The whiff of scandal was potent but Mrs Montgomery had been unaccustomedly reticent and had to be pressed even to admit that Mrs Newton, accompanied by Miss Carmody, would be embarking for England at Bombay. Mr Newton had disappeared too—no surprise there. Privately the captain had labelled the surgeon a milk-and-water man. Despite bribing the servants, he got no information, notwithstanding their reputation for being see-all, know-all and hear-alls; when it suited they could be incredibly tight-lipped.

'Where are you staying?' He addressed his question to Kate.

'We don't have a reservation,' Miss Carmody answered.

If the captain was amazed at the thought of two white women wandering around the city on their own, and in all likelihood without introductions, he did not show it. 'That's no problem.' He put his fingers to his lips in a shrill whistle and two white-robed servants appeared. He swung the portmanteaux as though they were featherweight. 'Is this all the luggage?'

'Yes,' Miss Carmody answered. 'Mrs Montgomery is forwarding the remainder.'

He spoke in brisk Hindi and, as the servants scurried off, he followed with the two women. Outside the station a barouche and two elegant white horses waited. They drove along the wide streets with rust red herringbone rooftops, skilfully negotiating the barefoot boys on bullock carts, soldiers carrying weapons and bejewelled Indians.

Watson's Hotel was sited in a quiet part of the city, although with several horse-drawn trams in evidence, and with a promise of much future building, the area had the air of a place about to be discovered. The hotel, modelled on the Crystal Palace commissioned for London's Great Exhibition of 1851, was for whites only, and with the rooms built round a central atrium it was considered even more impressive than Shepheard's Hotel. Not that either Kate or Miss Carmody were particularly aware of the opulence of their surroundings.

The captain's unselfishness did not last long. Kathleen was now even more intriguing and desirable and, best of all, she was available. But immediately he had arranged the accommodation, with a quick, gracious 'thank you', she retired to her room.

He came upon Miss Carmody wandering disconsolately round the lobby and invited her for tea. Her navy blue gown was travel-stained, her boots were scuffed and she was worn out. She hoped he was returning to London so that they might have the benefit of his company. She dreaded the thought of an unaccompanied journey. They sat among the trappings of colonial décor—golden embroidered tapestries, marble floors and beaten brass accoutrements—sipping sedately, the silence between them broken by an occasional comment ebbing and flowing harmoniously. He had a relaxed personality and he was companionable, knowing when to speak, when to remain silent and when to ask interested questions.

Having concluded that Miss Carmody was as she appeared, an unworldly innocent, he leaned forward, and in an apparent burst of confidence explained how prior to seeing Miss Kelly on the platform at Calais he had been bound for Delhi on a matter of private business. 'I cannot explain what came over me but I fell in love with her at first sight and when you told me she was betrothed it in no way changed my feelings.'

He was on the right track; Miss Carmody's eyes grew moist with romantic sympathy and her question was full of awe. 'Did you wish to wed her?'

'Yes. I wanted her for my bride from that very first moment. And I still do. I don't care what has happened between her and Mr Newton. I want to help and protect her. Well, both of you.' In quiet moments he had imagined being married to Kathleen, envisaging her gracing the manor house, presiding over the breakfast table in the sunlit morning room that looked out to the pond. But as well as himself, his mother was always present, surrounded by her yapping terriers. Now that the situation had changed, winning Kathleen without having to make a commitment would be his ideal solution. 'But she's already wed.' He raised his voice in incredulity. 'Weren't you and I at the ceremony?' He leaned closer and lowered his voice confidentially, 'And why, might I ask, are the three of us here?'

Miss Carmody liked his 'you and I' and 'us'. 'Perhaps she will not remain married for long.' Having said too much, she clamped her lips closed.

It never occurred to Palliser that he could be the reason for Kate's summary return to England, but then he had never come across a man with Isaac Newton's moral code of behaviour. If asked, he would ridicule the idea that such men existed. 'You and I are people of the world,' he confided. He had no feelings for Miss Carmody other than as the means to his end. 'Whatever happened back in Agra, it appears Miss Kelly's—or should I say Mrs Newton's—reputation is compromised, but if she comes under my protection she will be shielded from the crueller elements of society. It would be in your interest if you could make her aware of her position.'

Hands primly crossed in her lap, she nodded solemnly. 'What does being under your protection mean?'

He had not expected such astuteness and he considered his next words carefully. 'I will take care of her travelling expenses, food and clothes, and I will also care for you, as her companion, until we reach London.' Having Miss Carmody's respectability on his side would be an added advantage. He hoped she would not look for clarification on what precisely he meant by 'care'.

'I believe Mr Newton is issuing a decree nisi.' Miss Carmody did not know whether that would change the captain's proposal but she suspected it would soon be common knowledge.

That the captain had not even considered. Divorce proceedings after a few hours of marriage. But why? What had happened? Nothing sexual, he was sure; more moral, he reckoned. So Newton was not as ineffectual as he appeared, but the wheels of law were slow to grind and the implementation of a divorce would buy him time. 'Obviously the legalities have to be clarified but by now her father will be aware of the situation.'

As if Miss Carmody's spirits weren't low enough, they dropped even further. 'How does Major Kelly know?'

'Mrs Montgomery sent him a telegram. Perhaps you might explain the position to your charge. In case you are unaware of the seriousness of your situation allow me to spell it out.' He used his capable fingers to count. His nails were surprisingly pink. 'One. You have nobody to turn to but me. Two. You have virtually no money; you could be stranded indefinitely in Bombay and reduced to inferior lodgings. Three. If you succeed in booking a passage back to England, you would have to travel steerage class.'

Miss Carmody nodded weakly.

The captain was as capable as Mrs Montgomery of making use of the telegraph and, if his gamble paid off, it would give him additional leverage.

Kate was lying motionless on the bed, still in her travelling clothes and boots. She had not responded to Miss Carmody's knock on the door and she did not acknowledge her presence by as much as a flicker of movement. Miss Carmody dragged over a stool and sat by her side; this was going to be difficult. She took a limp hand in hers. It felt chilled. The room was white and airy, and cooled by the latest belt-driven air pump. 'Kathleen, you have to listen to me. We have to think of your future.'

When there was still no acknowledgement, she bent over her and shook her shoulders.

'Stop. Stop that.'

'Not until you listen.'

Kate wriggled free, sat up and hugged her arms around her knees. 'I have been thinking, wondering at our best course of action.' It was only now that the shock of Isaac's behaviour had registered. She was unsure of what to do but she felt it was up to her to come up with some sort of a solution. While she was not impressed by 'society', as such, she had been reared in India and was familiar enough with the way London society operated to realise that she must be seen to conform, if only somewhat.

Miss Carmody could have coped with tears or tantrums. While she was nonplussed by Kathleen's sturdy courage, she considered the captain's offer to be their only hope. She believed him to be a man of principle with honourable intentions. But how best could she word his proposal to Kathleen? 'Have you come to any conclusions?'

Kate pursed her lips and shook her head. She had come up with a solution of sorts but it was too outrageous to mention to someone as innocent in the ways of the world as Miss Carmody.

'Captain Palliser is deeply in love with you. He has been since he first saw you.' Jane Carmody saw herself as instrumental in the outcome of a most romantic situation, better than any of Jane Austen's novels. 'He wants to wed you.'

Kate carefully absorbed that bit of information. The fact that the captain had spoken of marriage to Miss Carmody put a different perspective on the situation but, she wondered, could she make him believe she cared for him long enough to get them back to England? The idea of taking advantage of him repelled her, but if she succeeded, somehow, she would make it up to him. 'In case it escaped his attention, although on the point of being divorced, I'm married.'

Miss Carmody could have done without the sarcasm. 'Of course,' she soothed, 'but in the meantime he is willing to offer us his protection.' The details would have to be sorted out initially between them and eventually with the major, and she didn't want involvement because as far as she was concerned her objective was to get them safely back to England. 'Your captain cares deeply for you, which is more than can be said for anyone else in your world or mine, either.' She gave an unexpected little smile. 'You're lucky. We're lucky to have such a protector.'

Kate wanted to laugh at the ludicrousness of the situation: Miss Carmody in all earnestness offering on behalf of the captain the solution she had come up with. Her head was spinning. She was ill-equipped to start negotiating. 'I'll talk to him in the morning.'

Miss Carmody looked in admiration at the feisty girl with the wild Irish ways.

Instead of the bustling tearoom, Captain Palliser guided Kate towards a quiet corner of the atrium that led to the ballroom, which was used for the grand balls integral to the Anglo-Indian social season. The area was empty except for an impassive servant who hovered in the vicinity of a beaten-brass table and two uncomfortable chairs.

Kate was pale but composed. She was still wearing the travel-stained muslin, and had made no attempt at grooming or prettification, but she was well-rehearsed in what she wanted to say. The captain was entranced by her unkempt appearance and air of abandonment, all heightened by her smudged eyes, streelish hair and rumpled gown.

She felt alone, yet strong in her decision. 'You asked to see me?'

'Yes. First let me offer my condolences on your situation.'

She broke eye contact to nod gracefully. The skin of her face felt tight and the harsh maroon material of the seat ate into her thighs.

He reached across the table and rested his hand on hers. He would not make the mistake of rushing in. 'Secondly, let me once more say that I care for you deeply.'

Another nod. Her hand lay lax under his.

'Thirdly, I have here,' he tapped at his pocket, 'a telegram from your father entrusting you to my charge on the journey back to London.'

She snatched her hand out from under his. Her skin tightened further. Her father couldn't. He wouldn't. But he could and he had. Her well-rehearsed words were pointless. Her father's actions weren't new. Hadn't he passed on Polly to her husband; her to Isaac and for a second time to Captain Palliser? Together with the hurt and sadness was that feeling of uselessness that comes from having no control over your life. She looked down to her lap but saw nothing, not the blue of her gown, nor the slenderness of her tightly clasped hands, their knuckles showing white.

She stood up without speaking. Palliser rose too, faced

her and reached out to draw her to him. He was speaking, saying something about booking the return voyage, but she was receding, her mind unfurling, rolling back on its own and then she was running away from him, through the lobby and out from the hotel.

The street was broad with elegant palm trees and a scattering of bustling Europeans. The sun burned through the sleeves of her gown. A cluster of flies scribbled around her face. Out of nowhere she remembered Aunt Muriel's promise, 'There's always a home for you here in Rathmore.' From their correspondence she felt familiar with the square stone house set against the rumpled hills; the elastic skeins of barnacle geese coming in each autumn from Greenland; poplars and willows giving way to emerald fields with their crop of dawn mushrooms; spring hedgerows alive with birdsong; and winter woods, quiet and dark as a cathedral. She craved the security of belonging.

She passed back through the lobby of the hotel, unaware of Miss Carmody and Captain Palliser in agitated discussion. Approaching a porter, her mind was clear, as she outlined her requirements. It was good to feel in control.

The following afternoon when Captain Palliser came upon her leafing through *Lalla Rookh*, Kate looked up with a confident smile. His mouth was set in a tight angry line. In his hand he held a telegram. 'This is from Wexford in Ireland. Your aunt is dead.' Once again Kate had the bitter experience of having control snatched from her, and she knew there was no more buying of time.

Chapter Six

Kate waited in the foyer of the hotel, half-shielded by the fluttering foliage of a large butterfly palm. As the captain come down the stairs, she stepped forward to meet him. 'May we talk?' she asked unsmilingly. She was wearing the green gown that Butterfly had made for her betrothal. In the midst of the panic of leaving Agra, Miss Carmody, in a moment of astuteness, had tucked it into a corner of her portmanteau.

As he led the way to a quiet corner of the tearoom, Captain Palliser hoped the drip-drip of Miss Carmody's persuasive worry had worn down Kathleen. The situation had him worn out. After being ceremoniously served fragrant Darjeeling tea in fluted porcelain cups, he asked, 'Well, are you about to relent and read to me?'

It was the last question she expected but she picked up on his humour and answered smartly, 'It depends on what that involves.'

'Touché.' He liked a woman with spirit but not too much. He rested his elbows on the table. 'What do you want to talk about?'

'Protection. I want to know what your protection entails.'

As well as being the most beautiful woman he had ever

come across, she was the most complicated and she was no more than a slip of a girl. He chose his words carefully. 'To mind, provide and care for you.'

'Is that all?'

'And love you,' his voice was barely audible.

'If I agree to your protection will you organise and pay for Miss Carmody's and my journey back to London?'

'Yes.'

'It is wrong for me to lie with you as my husband.' Her voice was as unflinching as the undaunted way she met his eyes. So she was not the innocent she seemed. He looked at her long and deep before leaning across the table and taking her face between his hands. She had the type of looks that maturity would further enhance. While she touched his heart in a way that no one else ever had, he still viewed her as a prize to be won rather than as a woman to be cherished. 'You must trust me.' As he spoke, he believed in his own trustworthiness, promising himself he would not let her down, also knowing he would move heaven and earth to have her.

That night Kate lay sleepless in the large canopied bed, keeping nervous vigil with gas light and rosary—praying was impossible but the act of running the beads through her fingers was comforting. Not knowing what to expect and trying not to imagine the worst, she wondered would she ever again experience joy, have fun or laugh unrestrainedly with Louisa. Eventually dawn crept through the windows.

Captain Palliser's expression at breakfast was inscrutable and his behaviour throughout the day impeccable. He hired a carriage and brought them sightseeing—he was a knowledgeable guide and there was much to see from the grandeur of Government House to the teeming crowds of the Borah bazaar. Public opinion was in favour of government borrowing for public works, and the same attitude was endorsed by *The Times* of India, with the result that Bombay was a hive of building industry. To the haunting sound of violins, he proved himself a sophisticated host; he had reserved the best table in the mezzanine area of the Russian Tea Rooms, and Kate, watching the changing blue of his eyes, was lulled into a false sense of security. Meanwhile Miss Carmody, nodding in time to the music, rode high on a wave of optimism.

That night when the captain came to Kate, a cat-lick figure blurring among the rippling shadows, she was half-asleep. In silence he hauled back the thin coverlet and lay down beside her, his shoulder touching hers.

She held her breath for so long that she thought her lungs would burst.

Since seeing her he had turned on the spit of desire, hot and sleepless, taunted by thoughts of her moonlight skin and the softness of her body. He touched her in the expert way he had long perfected, which made women's bodies sing and their skin scream, and when he felt her silvered response it was almost too much to bear. Turning to this girl, who through no fault of her own had taken over his life, in a swift tear he divested her of her nightgown, and with one hand tangling around the back of her hair he drew her to him with the force of pent-up frustration. His love was rough with more need than tenderness. He had not wanted it to be that way but it was all he knew. As he suspected she was untouched.

Next morning when Miss Carmody looked at Kate she knew. Kathleen's eyes held an expression that had not been there before, a bruised suggestion of sadness and experience. Gone forever was the untroubled, confident gaze of youthful innocence. Overnight her charge had truly come of age.

In an unexpected epiphanic moment of acceptance, Miss Carmody knew that she would never experience love. It hollowed her out to acknowledge that her fantasies were over, her dreams worthless. She would never share her life with a poet, a major, a captain or any of the men who crossed her path. She would never hold her own baby or have a child of her own to love. The hope that had burned eternal within her for more than three decades had up and left. But she consoled herself, she was lucky to have Elmwood and her young ladies.

Captain Palliser used his contacts and money to facilitate the necessary travel arrangements and to organise some too fashionable and too brightly coloured gowns for Kate. Despite the devastating news of the war escalating, compounding all sorts of scary rumours that were confirmed with Paris falling to the Prussians, their journey back to England passed without incident.

Miss Carmody was almost able to persuade herself that she was their travelling companion, and Kathleen and the captain the married couple the remainder of the passengers took them for. Sometimes together and on more occasions in the company of others, they played rubbers of whist, which Kate invariably won; tried their hands at games of chess at which Captain Palliser excelled, and danced innumerable waltzes during their short stay at Shepheard's Hotel. While at sea, even after the nights of passion, Kate crept out of bed early and came on deck to watch the waves and the pattern of clouds in the pre-dawn light.

★

It was spring again when the *Scully Seal* docked at Folkestone. Miss Carmody left behind her last lingering thoughts of India, and occupied her mind with plans for Elmwood—her endless calculations confirmed that within a year the school could be operating at a profit. With the arrival of the first of her young ladies, complete with fussing parents and excessive baggage, her home had come alive, its very walls reverberating with the potent presence of youth. It was only now that she was returning that she realised how much she had missed her life in London. She raised a pale face to the wan February sunshine and breathed deeply of the English air.

Kate was not looking forward to facing her father's displeasure at the marriage that was not and her impending divorce. Tempered by the necessity of returning to England, she had become shamelessly ambivalent about her relationship with the captain. He was kind to her and while initially she had been more scared than flattered by their intimacy, he was a skilful lover and to her amazed horror she had come to enjoy the physical side of their relationship.

When the skies were blue and sunny, she believed God understood her actions, but in the dark of the night what had appeared to be a practical solution became a horrendous decision framed by the flickering flames of hell. She felt as if she were living with a permanent hole in her soul. Although the captain possessed her, he never owned her as she kept a part of herself to herself. However, she wished she could recapture her innocent past, that life could go back to the way it had been, even the Lenten fasting and cold of Elmwood, and her father's decision-making were preferable to what she had become. Her belly knotted with terror for the unknown future.

'Perhaps I'll come with you to Elmwood?' she whispered to Miss Carmody as they stood at the rails of the vessel watching the docks of Folkestone hove into view.

'You can't. Aren't you and the captain to wed?' Miss Carmody's shoulders moved uneasily under her sensible grey plaid cloak. That was the persuasion that had bought her compliance, and she voiced it on every occasion.

'I won't stay long, just a few days until I can sort out things with Papa.'

'Yes, what about me?' Captain Palliser teased catching up on them and with his hand proprietarily cupping Kate's elbow, they stood together waiting to disembark, to all intent and purpose three old friends, laughing and joking as though they had not a care in the world. They were wearing their public faces at which they had grown expert: Kate smiling, the captain gallant, Miss Carmody the catalyst. An observer would be clueless about the intricacies of their relationship.

Standing at the South Dock, well out of sight, Major Charles Kelly squared his shoulders and wondered. There was something conspiratorially illegitimate about the trio's inclusiveness. He was dressed in a sombre suit of charcoal grey. Out of choice he would have favoured the impact of his military uniform but in the circumstances he considered inconspicuous discretion to be the better option. At the time, already disturbed by the contents of Mrs Montgomery's telegram, and being without personal funds, he was both intrigued and relieved to receive the telegram from Captain Palliser requesting permission to accompany his daughter and chaperone back to England, assuring expenses would be met by him.

He had made it his business to find out the name and estimated date of arrival of their ship, and he also knew that two cabins had been booked in the name of Captain C H Palliser. Further investigations had both impressed and unnerved him. The captain came from a wealthy military family and his army career, spanning almost two decades, was exemplary, proving him to be a man of action used to being in command.

This was a situation that required wary treading. The major had lived his story for so long that he almost believed he had served in battle action during the Sepoy Rising. He had no real claim to his hero status, or his title, as his 'military' career had been in administration. Craving a life of adventure and lacking the diligence of his father to study medicine, he had joined the East India Company and was posted to Lahore. He enjoyed colonial life and the socialising that went with it, but soon discovered that men of action rather than the deskbound were more sought after, and so began a minor dishonesty that grew into a major deception. After the Indian Mutiny, the regiments of the East India Company Army were absorbed into the British Army and the company was replaced by the India Office, where Kelly rose to the rank of chief adjutant and accountant officer in Agra. His adventures had taken place in his head and he had become expert at managing his pretence. His story would not stand up to the scrutiny of a man like Captain Palliser.

Looking at his daughter and the captain coming down the gangplank followed by Miss Carmody, his brain raced. The intuition that had served him well over the years supplied the answer. Like Miss Carmody, he too knew his daughter's status. How could she? In his relief at what seemed a viable solution to get her back to England, how could he have been such a fool? But it wasn't his fault. It was Miss Carmody's. What the hell was she doing while Kathleen was being taking advantage of? She was the reason for this debacle. Despite sending Kathleen halfway around the world to be married, he had still thought of her as a child. But not anymore. She had turned out too beautiful for her own good—no wonder the captain was enamoured. She was quite gorgeous with that perky red bonnet and matching gown, which showed off her figure to excessive advantage.

He sighed deeply, unsure of his next move. He had received a long, complaining letter from Mrs Montgomery about the abuse of her hospitality, and the expenditure involved in hosting the wedding ceremony and dinner, all of which he had ignored. He was still not clear what had happened to justify Mr Newton's reactions. Despite his urgent entreaties, Mr Newton was refusing to withdraw from issuing the decree nisi.

The major had never forgotten the night Kathleen was conceived and the wild abandon of his wife Flora, which to his chagrin had neither been repeated nor referred to again. The traitorous doubt began its wriggle that perhaps his younger daughter had taken after her mother. He would never have such worries about Mary Pauline: she had a sensible face and sensible brown hair. He shook his head as though to banish such thoughts. He had failed his beloved daughter and in doing so had also failed the wife he had so loved.

For every and yet for no reason, he remembered the

year the rains were late—at the time they were still stationed in Lahore, and a shutter banging in the middle of the night announced the arrival of the monsoon. Loving its vitality and the imperious way it made its entrance, he had risen from his bed to savour the cool swishing, the subsidence of the date palms and to watch the way the gold mohur trees raised their heads as though listening. Kathleen, clutching her doll, was on the veranda before him. Frederick and Mary Pauline had no such sense of adventure.

'Shush, listen.' She spoke as much to him as to the doll, although it was the doll she shook into submission.

Through her eyes and ears, he watched her as she watched the garden become a jungle: frogs croaking, crickets out-voicing them, and the other myriad of shrill-voiced things singing in the heaving eternal monotones that was India. For his daughter there was no awareness of the rotting matting, perspiring furniture or multiplying of cockroaches. The monsoon was forever etched into the two of them on the veranda and the singing frogs below in the garden. And he had swung her high, emulating her joy.

'Papa, Papa.' Unimpeded by the uneven cobblestones, she came running towards him, arms outstretched—the way she did as a child when she was dressed in layers of white and constantly scampering from her ayah to him. He caught her as he used to, enclosing her in his arms. If he had the strength he would have swung her high. She hugged and kissed him soundly on both cheeks. He held her at arms' length. She was safely back. And she was crying.

The captain had not anticipated being met by the major. He stood bemused at the quayside, not knowing what to make of the emotional reunion between father and daughter. Throughout his philandering he had encountered the occasional irate husband but he had never before had to deal with a father. Indeed, once he had received the major's telegram, he hadn't given him another thought.

Major Kelly placed his arm protectively round Kate's shoulder. 'I'm obliged to you, sir.'

Kate was washed with wave after wave of relief. Her father was here. Everything would be all right; he would make it so. Whatever the debacle of the wedding and impending divorce, he need never know about her and the captain.

'Come, Kathleen,' Major Kelly said. 'There's a train due shortly. And you too, Miss Carmody.'

The captain moved in front of him. 'Don't you remember you gave your daughter into my protection?' He gave a little laugh—a man-to-man laugh.

They looked at each other, bantam cocks shaping up for a fight.

'She's coming with me.' The major straightened to his full height and tightened his grip on Kate's shoulder.

Captain Palliser had no wish to become involved in vulgar confrontation while standing on the South Docks. He had been out of touch for so long that the family's considerable commercial interests urgently needed his attention. He had rushed business in Delhi to return to Agra for the wedding. His mother had written several demanding letters and an irate telegram from his steward had been waiting for him in Cairo.

As he debated the pros and cons of the current situation, he knew that generations of Pallisers would not have achieved their continuing financial and commercial successes if business had not come before pleasure. It was beholden on him to continue with the family priority of looking after their investments. He needed to get to his London office as quickly as possible. There would be plenty of time later to sort out his private life.

He drew Kate's gloved hand to his lips and kissed it. She remained statuesquely curved within the arc of her father's arm and refused to meet his eyes. 'I shall call on you within a few days.' He was purposely vague as to whether he was addressing father or daughter.

Chapter Seven

Since his return to London during the summer of 1869, Major Kelly had comfortably lodged with Mrs O'Connor, a widow from County Kerry. Deciding it was in the best interests of all concerned to keep Kathleen within sight until he had sorted out her future, he negotiated a keen price for a small room for her.

To Kate's relief, her father did not ask the awkward questions she had anticipated, although from his closed expression and air of preoccupation she suspected he was pursuing his own enquiries. But she was too relieved to be back in a safe environment to concern herself overly with her father's strategies.

As soon as she was properly settled in, Kate sent a note to Louisa asking her to call. She received an enthusiastic reply by return and Louisa arrived the following afternoon. She was fashionably turned out in deep burgundy and carried a small matching muff. When she saw Kate she burst out crying and threw her arms around her. 'Oh, isn't it awful,' she sobbed. 'I can't believe it.'

Kate eased out of her embrace and stepped back. She had never known Louisa to be so upset. 'What is it? What on earth has happened?'

'Haven't you heard?'

'No. Heard what? Tell me, you're frightening me.'

'Miss Carmody is dead.'

It took Kate a few moments to absorb the information. 'She couldn't be. She travelled down on the train with us from Folkestone and Papa organised a carriage at Charing Cross to bring her to Kensington. She was well, really well, and looking forward to getting back to Elmwood.'

'Did you know the school was closed down while she was away?'

'No, I didn't. Why?'

'Lack of money, I think. At least that's what Mama says.' Louisa dabbed at her eyes. The honourable Mrs Caufield was known for being thoroughly informed on all matters concerning her family.

'How did she die? She wasn't that old. And she wasn't ill.'

'Do you remember the little Irish maid?' Kate nodded. She remembered Dolly well and with great fondness. 'She found her dead in her bed.'

'Poor Dolly. What an awful discovery to make. How is she?'

'Well. That's another story. She has disappeared.'

'How do you mean, disappeared?'

'Took some of her clothes and vanished.' Louisa shrugged. 'Everyone is looking for her. People are saying...'

'Saying what?'

'Well...that she must have had something to do with her death. Otherwise she wouldn't have run away.'

'No, Louisa! Dolly wouldn't. You should know that. The only reason she's missing is she is scared. The poor thing. I hope she's all right.'

Kate found it difficult to believe she would never again

see the person with whom she had gone through so much. Despite her faults Miss Carmody had been kind to her, and circumstances had drawn them close, particularly on the voyage home. 'Papa and I planned to call but we hadn't got round to it yet.' It was a visit Kate had worked hard at avoiding, suspecting that when her father had time to weigh up the pros and cons of her situation, he would wheedle information from Miss Carmody that she considered best left unspoken. Tears of remorse flowed unchecked at her selfish preoccupation. It was the first time she had cried since learning of her betrothal to Isaac. Of one accord, the young women came together again, putting their arms around each other, and standing close with their bodies swaying in unison they comforted each other.

Kate drew Louisa into Mrs O'Connor's minuscule parlour. Miss Carmody's death had left her in an invidious position: she was the only person who knew what had happened during their voyage out, their time in India and the return journey, and for Kate there had been comfort in that. Now she had nobody; nobody knew her story. Her determination not to speak of those months became an immutable sentence of secret building on secret. She couldn't bear the overwhelming feeling of isolated loneliness that settled on her like a pall. Did Louisa even know she was in the process of being divorced? She thought not; she had written a hurried note from Aden saying little more than that she was returning to London.

Kate wanted to tell all, to spell out the circumstances and the reasons for her decisions, as much to share what had happened with Louisa as for her to try to make sense of it for herself. So much had occurred to colour her history and make her the person she was. It was more than she felt able to cope with. 'Have you heard my news?' she tested.

Uncharacteristically Louisa paused before replying, 'Well, yes. A little, I think.'

'A bad little, I suppose?'

'Well, not really a good little.'

'If I tell you—try to explain all that happened—will you just listen and promise not to judge me?'

'Oh, Kate, of course I'll listen. Who am I to judge anyone? You're the bravest, most courageous person I've ever known.'

Kate began tentatively, gradually gaining confidence, telling her story in sequential bursts, including her muddled emotions, but avoiding the intimate details of her relationship with Captain Palliser, and finishing with 'I'm sure honesty with Isaac was the correct course of action but it has ruined me.'

Louisa listened avidly; her stroking of Kate's hand was soothing, although she had no solution or comfort to offer. Her words too were tentative. 'You did what you thought was right at the time, but perhaps you were overly scrupulous in confessing about the captain. You know what men are like and after all at that stage, nothing had really happened.' Kate detected sensible echoes of her mother.

Louisa came and sat on the floor, resting her head against Kate's knees. It was the way Miss Carmody's young ladies relaxed during musical evenings at Elmwood. 'I hope you don't mind, Mama and I have discussed you. People are talking and it must be really hard for you.' Louisa did not say that much of what Kate had confided was known or guessed. 'Mama says time is a great healer and people have short memories. Eventually they'll forget.'

'I hope so.'

'What are you going to do?'

'Papa hasn't said.'

'Now that you're married, and with a husband, do you still have to obey your father?'

'I'm not sure that I have a husband. There's been no contact from him. I don't know what's going to happen, except it looks as though he's going ahead with the divorce.'

'Have you seen Captain Palliser?'

'No. Not a word from him either.'

'Do you think your father is keeping you apart? That would be so romantic, like in a novel.'

Kate jumped up and her voice was sharp. 'Don't be ridiculous, Louisa. My life is not in the least romantic, it's quite horrid. I don't know anything and that's the worst part.'

Louisa was instantly contrite. 'Oh, I am sorry. I don't mean to be frivolous but I don't know what I can do or what you can do.'

'It's all right, or it will be, I suppose.' Kate had no idea of how to make her life better except she knew she had to try. As for her dreams of freedom and choice, they had vanished. 'That's enough about me. Tell me all about your dashing admirers.'

Louisa dropped her eyes. 'There is only one and he's rather special.'

'I am so glad. He's lucky. I presume he's suitable husband material?' Kate stood with her elbow on the mantel and even managed a smile as she spoke. It was a question Miss Carmody's young ladies considered to be of prime importance, with 'suitable' translating to sociably acceptable and from an adequately moneyed family. Knowing Louisa's mother, Kate was certain he was.

'Yes, he is. He's quite wonderful. We're announcing our betrothal next month. The family has estates in Yorkshire, although John is attached to the embassy in Paris. Mama is worried for us as the city is so unsettled.'

'You'll be the perfect wife for a diplomat. I believe the worst of the troubles are over in Paris and they certainly will be by the time your wedding arrangements are in place.'

Louisa played with the braid trimming on the sleeve of her jacket. 'May I ask you something?'

'Yes, of course. Anything.'

'You have to promise to answer.'

'If I can.' Kate grinned mischievously, and for a brief moment the turmoil of her life took second place. The answering game was frequently played at Elmwood.

'Did you do *it*?'

Kate may have hoped to avoid that question but she should have known better. It was not in her nature to lie, certainly not to Louisa. She stalled, 'What do you mean?' She knew precisely to what Louisa was referring. *It* was a subject that like love received much uninformed coverage at Elmwood.

'You know. Being intimate with somebody. What was it like? Did it hurt? Were you afraid?'

'That's more than one question.' Kate closed her eyes and for a poignant instant relived this *it,* wishing she had been equipped with even a little knowledge. 'Yes, it hurt the first time—my mind as much as my body. It's a dominant act and I was afraid I'd no longer belong to me but that didn't happen.' Kate paused, collecting her thoughts. She could not bring herself to admit, even to

Louisa, how she had felt her body had betrayed her in its physical response to the captain. 'I think it could be special, Louisa, very special with the right person. Nobody ever told us that, and it's something we should know.'

'Is your Captain Palliser that special person?' Louisa had such a soppy, romantic look that Kate burst out laughing.

'No, Louisa. He most certainly isn't.'

'But why…?'

'I can't explain now.'

If the true nature and reasons for her relationship with Captain Palliser became public knowledge, Kate knew that her reputation would be even more tattered. It was one thing being sent home by a husband after a few hours of unconsummated marriage; it was quite another becoming a kept woman to fund that return journey.

'But you'll wed?'

'I shan't. I most certainly won't.'

Louisa's eyes widened and she brought her hands to her lips. Her mother had stated that no matter what had or had not happened between the captain and Kate, she was compromised, and when she had made the pronouncement while presiding over the tea tray, she had not known the full story.

Kate had spoken too soon and too definitely. That evening her father joined her in the parlour. He closed the door and stood advantageously looking down on her. 'Kathleen, I need to talk to you.'

She put aside her book. 'Yes, Papa.' Her uneasy feeling was back in force. After talking to Louisa she had been fired with bravery and optimism that by some miracle her future would be favourably sorted.

'I've been in discussion with Captain Palliser…'

Kate's anger rose and she burst out, 'You never said!'

'No, I didn't. You've caused enough damage and confusion.'

There was nothing to be gained by remaining passive. 'Me! Damage? Confusion? What about him?'

'We are not talking about Captain Palliser. We are talking about you. Your reputation and your future.'

'We're not talking. You're doing the talking. You appear to be the only one allowed to talk. And my future is mine. Not yours.'

'Behave yourself, young lady. It may not be my future, but your behaviour is affecting our whole family. Just as well Mary Pauline is married.'

Kate snorted.

'Please remain quiet and listen. As even you with your radical ideas must be aware, you cannot re-marry until your divorce comes through. I'm advised on good legal authority that could take the best part of a year. It appears Captain Palliser is reluctant to make a final commitment to you until he is aware of the outcome of your divorce.'

'I don't want his commitment. I don't want anything more to do with him.' She stood up, stretching to her full height and tossed her head.

Charles Kelly groaned. Negotiating with Palliser had worn him out. The man wanted Kathleen to live with him, without even a formal betrothal, while waiting for the divorce papers. He had negotiated as keenly as possible in circumstances loaded against him—Palliser's only weakness, as far as he could ascertain, was his feelings for Kathleen, which he took to be genuine, although being a man of the world he wondered how long the infatuation would last.

Long enough to have Kathleen wed, he hoped, and considered there was a better chance of that happening if he kept proposed bride from proposed groom. While his adversary had negotiating advantage, he had bargained well and now instead of gratitude he was getting a bellyful of grief from his daughter.

'You'll wed him if he asks. In the circumstances, he's your only chance. You don't have any choice.'

'I won't.' Kate's determined resourcefulness had begun with the falling apart of her marriage, even though or perhaps *because* Isaac had never been a husband to her. The pain of losing what she never had rankled. She had coped with an excess of grief and despair but no self-pity. A veneer of gentility sustained her but she would not go gently. She bared her teeth in a smile of someone starved beyond hunger.

Major Kelly played his trump card. 'Some people would consider your behaviour warrants time in Bethlehem Hospital.'

Kate looked aghast. Confinement at the Bethlehem Hospital, better known as Bedlam, was a threat held over recalcitrant daughters by mainly male relatives who believed female disobedience to be a moral weakness leading to madness. The stories of such incarcerations were spoken of in hushed tones.

Frightened as she was by her father's threat, Kate tossed her head. 'I do have a choice. I won't wed him. No matter what you or anyone else says.' Grabbing her book, her wrap trailing, she swung from the parlour, banging the door behind her.

Her father's sigh was exasperated. He did not know how to handle Kathleen; he never had. But he knew that fiery women with opinions had no place in modern society. He wanted this business done with. Why would she not conform? He was in the middle of negotiating a sweet deal on a gentleman's property in Conisbrough in south Yorkshire, and there was a widow of some substance and good looks he was growing increasingly fond of. He feared for the success of his plans if Kathleen's shenanigans became public knowledge. Perhaps Mary Pauline could talk sense into her.

When Kate visited her sister at her home at Hill Road in St John's Wood, she was stifled by the narrowness of her all-enveloping domesticity. Polly presided over the tea table with the aplomb of a woman two decades older, as she cut, buttered, jammed and greedily ate slice after slice of bread.

In the three years since her marriage, she had become plump of body and positively matronly in mind and attitude. Nobody mentioned in her hearing that she had not yet produced a child, although her apparent inability to carry her babies for more than a few months was a frequent subject of discussion. People wondered at the state of her marriage, as Augustus Hervey was a man who was vociferously enthusiastic about wanting a large family.

'Papa has told me a little of what happened.' Polly leaned forward as though afraid of being overheard. Her voice, more censorious than caring, invited details and clarification.

'Has he?' Kate would not make it easy for her sister.

Polly dabbed at her lips with her napkin. 'In the circumstances, you are fortunate that Captain Palliser wishes to marry you.'

'Well… .' Kate tossed her head. 'As I told Papa, I don't want to marry him and I shan't.'

Polly leaned forward again. 'Kathleen, listen to me.' Her voice dropped to a whisper. 'None of us can do as we truly wish.'

'No, you listen. If men can, why can't women? I've always wondered about that. It's not right that we don't have a say in our lives.' Kate made no attempt to lower her voice; if anything she raised it a few decibels.

'As women we've never had a say…'

'Yes, we have. Don't you remember Mama telling us all about the Irish Banshenchas?'

'Bless her. What a lot of nonsense she filled our heads with. She was as bad as Poonam with her constant talk of the power of Hindu goddesses.'

'It wasn't nonsense.' Kate thumped her fist on the table. 'Derborgaill, daughter of the King of Ossory, had six husbands, all chosen by her. And that was five centuries ago. So women had a say in their lives then, a big say. And as for Poonam's goddesses, they were powerful entities and lived according to their wishes and values.'

'Well we don't have such choice.'

'We should.'

'Oh, don't be ridiculous. Everyone knows women can't manage their own lives.' Polly gave up and jammed another slice of bread. It was unlikely Kathleen would ever change. Although she was pale with deep shadows under her eyes and had eaten virtually nothing, she was as outrageous as ever.

'My clothes have come at last.' There was no point pursuing the rights and wrongs of choice with Polly. Her wedding gown and the blue sari were missing but she had sunk her face into the sensuality of Butterfly's robes and under things. 'Fashions in India are very different from London's.'

'Well, as we all know, you like being different.' Polly's smile took the sting from her remark.

Mrs O'Connor handed Kate a note.

'When did this come?' She didn't recognise the writing.

'It was on the floor inside the hall door this morning.'

Kate slit open the envelope with her index finger and drew out the sheet of writing paper. She glanced at the signature at the bottom of the page. Louisa's mother.

Why was she writing to her? As she read the terse words she knew life could not get worse. The honourable Mrs Caufield was sure, in the circumstances, Kathleen would understand that in the best interests of her daughter's future it was more appropriate if she and Louisa had no further contact.

Kate was not sure when she first became aware that her body felt differently—perhaps it began with vague feelings of sickness and tiredness, which she put down to the upset of her life, and of recent days her clothes appeared somewhat tight.

However, she did remember the specific moment when Mrs O'Connor, with a look of concern and a primping of lips, asked, 'Are you sure you're all right, child?'

'Yes, of course. Thank you.' Kate was more irritated than grateful for her concern.

Mrs O'Connor, who prided herself on calling a spade a spade, followed her from the breakfast table to the water closet in the backyard. Kate emerged white-faced and gagging. 'You're not all right, sure you're not!'

'No. I feel quite ill. It's the carbolic and the smells.'

'God help us but that's nothing to do with it. It's not ill you are.'

'What do you mean?'

Mrs O'Connor had a sharp pair of ears and an ability to cobble nuances into facts. She knew more of Mrs Newton's situation than her lodgers realised. The infatuation of the handsome captain for the beautiful bride was all over London. As for the bridegroom, a man passing up on his marriage rights, as it was said, was, in her opinion, not a man at all and rightly deserved to be the butt of all the sniggering talk and jokes. 'When was your last blood flow?'

Kate was so appalled by the question that she was stunned into answering. 'I don't know. I can't remember.' Nobody had ever even hinted at that hidden aspect of her womanliness; such things were not mentioned in genteel society. 'Why?'

'Try to think.' By Mrs O'Connor's reckoning, Mrs Newton was about four months gone, and she should know as she had carried eleven of her own, most of whom she had delivered herself. She had lost track of the number of babies she had brought into the world for family and neighbours.

Kate so hated the inconvenience of her monthly blood that she *should* remember. Yes, of course. How could she have forgotten discovering her pantaloons streaked with blood on the train journey from Agra to Bombay? 'It was in January. Why?'

God help her. Mrs Newton had no idea what was happening to her but she would pay the consequences of her actions for the rest of her life. Mrs O'Connor robustly spelt it out and marvelled at the stupid innocence of the gentry; servants could not afford such gullibility.

Eyes wide and face pale, Kate had asked, 'What shall I do?'

Mrs O'Connor's kind heart bled for the young girl. 'First you must tell your father.'

'I couldn't. I can't.'

'You have no choice, you have to.' Knowing it was a matter to be dealt with immediately, she insisted Kate accompany her to the parlour where the major was working on his papers.

The major looked up irritably. 'What is it?'

'We need to talk to you.' It was Mrs O'Connor who spoke.

'Not now.'

'Yes. Now.' Kate stood in the doorway and announced, 'I am with child.'

Major Kelly took the news with a sharp intake of breath and a feeling of horror. This was beyond his worst nightmare. From Mrs Montgomery he knew, without doubt, that Isaac Newton had not laid claim to his bride. He said nothing to Kathleen because he did not know what to say. It was left to Mrs O'Connor to offer small comfort to a dry-eyed Kate.

Chapter Eight

Captain Cornelius Harold Palliser was bored in the extreme by Mr Charles Ashburnham Kelly's attempts to secure his daughter's future. He thoroughly disliked the man and his falseness, and he was taking a Machiavellian delight in throwing in outlandish obstacles to their negotiating process.

Despite his negative reaction to her father, Kathleen occupied a considerable portion of his thoughts. He could not believe how much he missed having her around. In quiet moments he found himself reliving incidents of her liveliness and warmth, and smiling at her outrageous opinions and beliefs, but most of his time was fully occupied with the complexities of family business, and while he was enjoying catching up on various social events around London, they had lost much of their gloss.

After her father's outraged reaction, he had dismissed the idea of having Kathleen live with him, decided the ideal solution would be to set her up in lodgings close by, and when her divorce came through it would be time enough to make up his mind about marriage.

He preferred not to imagine his mother's response to such a match, which would mirror that of his highly placed extended family. His relations were of one determined voice that he should marry 'appropriately', as they termed it, which he knew translated into a virgin from a moneyed family whose sole purpose would be to provide heirs for the Palliser lineage. He imagined with horror living out his life in the company of a plain-faced, simpering miss with a dutiful attitude. That was not the life he envisaged.

When Mr Kelly called unannounced to his rooms in Piccadilly on Tuesday morning, he was in thoroughly bad form. A gentleman would know better than to be this persistent; he hated being pressurised—his mother and relatives on one hand and Kathleen's father on the other. He tossed aside the visiting card and told his footman to inform his visitor that he was unavailable. That afternoon Kelly sent a note inviting him to dine at the Café Royal on the following day. Captain Palliser ignored both note and invitation. In exasperation and for want of better amusement, he agreed to see him when he called on Thursday.

When he entered his parlour he found Kelly, hands behind his back, looking out of the window at the bustle of people and carriages thronging the narrow streets.

'My dear, Captain Palliser, thank you for seeing me. I happened to be in the area.' Kelly talked smoothly but his eyes darted uneasily.

First lie, thought the captain, who wondered at the reason for the urgency written in every fibre of his visitor's being. He did not invite him to sit, nor did he call for refreshments. Legs spread, shoulders back, he stood by the fireplace of the gloomy, brown-toned room, which was crammed with items of too large furniture and dour paintings from the family estates. Facing his visitor he asked, 'And what can I do for you?'

'It's about my daughter.' Kelly, with his back to the window, moved from one foot to the other.

'Yes.' The one word was impatiently delivered: presumably a visit from this man would not be about anything else.

'I've considered the situation and have come to the conclusion that she should be with you.'

'Oh?' Captain Palliser wondered at the change of mind.

'Yes. I am willing to allow that, as long as you agree in writing to wed her as soon as her divorce comes through.'

The captain took a cigar from a box on the table and a knife from beside it. The nerve of the upstart. A little probing had shown that the pesky man was no more than an official in the Indian civil service, and had retired as Chief Adjutant and Accountant Officer. Who did he think he was—using the title of major, calling unannounced and making demands as though he had a right? With the skill of a surgeon, Captain Palliser cut a cross on the end of the cigar. Only then did he look directly at his visitor, and using the cigar to point asked, 'Why now?'

'It's for the best.' Kelly met his eyes too purposefully.

'For whose best?' Palliser had no intention of offering a cigar to his visitor.

'My daughter's of course. You've made no secret of your feelings towards her. As her father, I don't feel I have the right to stand in her way.'

'As her father and with her best interests at heart, I presume before you called here with your proposition, you spoke to her and have her full agreement?'

Kelly considered that the captain with his talk of having Kathleen's agreement was beginning to sound as ridiculous as Kathleen. 'In my experience young girls are incapable of choosing the right men as husbands.'

'Isaac Newton was hardly a felicitous choice.'

Kelly ignored that and determinedly continued. 'I'm sure Kathleen is fond of you and I've no doubt that in time she'll grow to care deeply for you.' He believed the only acceptable conclusion for his daughter's behaviour was that like her mother before her she had experienced a one-occasion aberration of passion. He had heard it said that a woman so roused was forever indebted to the man. 'I've heard women do with those who successfully bed them,' he stated tentatively.

Palliser recoiled from Kelly's vulgarity. It confirmed what he thought of the man but he decided against confrontation. He lit his cigar, puffed deeply and exhaled slowly. 'Allow me to consider your proposal.' Without looking backwards, he left the parlour.

That afternoon the captain called on Kate. He was disturbed by her father's attitude and apparent change of mind, and confused by the conflicting depth of his own see-saw feelings. He did not know what he wanted, except that he had a need to see Kathleen. He wanted to judge the situation for himself, although he had dismissed as insanity his previous dream of Mama and Kathleen breakfasting under the one roof. Hadn't he known for a long time that England was not large enough to accommodate his mother and himself on a permanent basis?

Too late Mrs O'Connor realised that Mrs Newton was not dressed to receive visitors, particularly this immaculately turned-out gentleman. These days her young lodger lived the life of a recluse. As she was not in the habit either of making or receiving calls, she paid little attention to her toilette, barely dressing and pinning up her hair haphazardly.

After watching the captain bend to take Mrs Newton's outstretched hand between his two palms, Mrs O'Connor withdrew, shaking her head. As she returned to her kitchen, she was smiling. Thanks be to the merciful God. That must be the father of the unborn child. He was obviously prosperous and good-looking too. What a handsome couple they made. She went about black-leading the range with a light heart, certain the visitor had come to put matters right—in her experience men, especially the gentry, found it difficult to turn their back on a child, particularly when there was the prospect of a son.

In all her born days she had never come across somebody as young as Mrs Newton who was so contrary, and who knew so precisely what she did and didn't want. But even she would have to change her mind about marrying—she couldn't be so foolish as to ignore the father of her child. Indeed if her antics went on for much longer, she'd have her own father in an early grave with worrying.

Kate passed her days and nights veering from panic to despair, unable to envisage what sort of a future lay in store. On her journey out to India to be married, she had thought she could never again feel such despair. How little she had known.

She looked at the captain, wide-shouldered and slim-hipped and smiling tentatively, and wondered how she had ever lain with him, ever shared such intimacy. He had taken advantage of her and if she had not given into fear and financial pressure, perhaps Miss Carmody would still be alive, although in all likelihood they could yet be stranded in Bombay or else making their way back to England via a series of insalubrious voyages. But she would not be in her current predicament.

'How are you?' he asked

'Well, and you?' she answered politely.

'Your father has been to see me...'

'I know. He told me.'

'He was with me again this morning.' Captain Palliser wondered at her dishabille, but found he was as enchanted with her earthy naturalness as he had been in Bombay.

'That I didn't know. What did he want?' she asked in a muted voice, scared her father had advised him of her condition.

'He suggested you live with me with the proviso that I sign an agreement to marry you as soon as your divorce comes through.'

She settled her expression into the passivity of lowered eyes and closed lips, but she was seething with anger. So her father was willing to condone publicly her becoming a kept woman, a mistress. He obviously hadn't said anything about the child. 'And how did you answer him?'

'I haven't. Yet.'

'Why?'

'I wanted to talk to you first.'

'I've been living here since we returned.'

'Your father didn't want me to contact you.'

'I see.'

'No you don't. He and I have been negotiating about you but I want to know what you want.' Now that he had

113

seen her again, he was overwhelmed by his feelings and knew he wanted her permanently by his side. He improvised madly. 'I've to return to India and you could come with me. We could marry when your divorce comes through. It would be easier for us there.'

Perhaps it would. But then anything would be easier than her current situation.

Her mind ran over various possibilities. If Captain Palliser knew about the child, he would claim rights to paternity, to which in law, she suspected, he was entitled. Despite her avowals to the contrary, during the sleepless hours of too many nights, she had considered the positive implications of marrying him and the benefits of being absorbed into a powerful family. While initially there would be talk and perhaps social ostracising, given time the harshest voices would gentle, particularly, she knew, if the child within her was a boy.

And now he was offering India. Returning to the land of the heart was appealing. In India, one surrendered to win, as she had done, breathing in the silence; recognising heart was king and a wiser guide than head. There she had been willing to make the best of a marriage that initially she had fought against. Kate thought of Poonam, philosophies and answers glittering in her eyes. For her, every heartbeat was a universe of possibilities with the power to transform fate. No matter how good or how bad the luck, Poonam believed life could be changed with a single thought or an act of love. 'Put one foot forward and then the other,' she would say with her lotus-blossom smile. 'Add consequence to the tides of good and evil that flood and drain the world; push brave hearts into the promise of a new day.'

Kate's head was full of pictures of India that lay below the surface of her consciousness: a young girl brushing forward the black satin of her hair; a mother sluicing water against her son's naked backside; an old man in a snow-white *dhoti* leading three goats with collars of red ribbons; a young man being shaved, surrounded by a laughing gaggle of children and skinny dogs; women wrapped in crimson, blue and gold, walking barefoot through the tangled poverty with patient ethereal grace. They belonged to white-toothed, almond-eyed men and gave birth to fragile-limbed children.

In the same breath of memory, she remembered the narrowness of colonial life: continuous gossiping afternoons, endless card games and the relentless digging of information and background on friends, enemies and newcomers alike, as well as the ridiculous preoccupation with gowns and the latest fashion.

Wherever she lived and however she lived, she wanted to be able to hold her head high and lead a worthwhile life. She knew she craved the impossible by wanting her innocence back and the child within her no more. But that afternoon she recognised that she had the choice she so craved. And, more importantly, she had the freedom to make that choice.

Slowly, weighing the facts, she made her decision. And it would be final. There would be no more thinking backwards and forwards. She would abide with what she chose.

She rose from the low chair, drew to her full height, gathering her wrap so that the captain would not be aware of her thickening waistline. Standing injected her with an immediate power, although as she spoke she was both gracious and dignified. 'I thank you for coming and I truly appreciate it. I hope you understand and believe what I am going to say.' She paused and took a deep breath. 'I do not want to marry you or to be kept by you. My father already knows this. I guarantee he will not trouble you again.' She took another deep breath. There, it was said.

'Was it only to get back to England that you agreed to be with me?' There was a mixture of vulnerability in the question and muted admiration for the bravery of her decision.

In one way it made Kate feel powerful and in another way sad, to be able to say, 'Yes. And you must have known that.' She would never tell him about his child growing within her and for whom she felt nothing but detestation. She would kill herself if she was forced into marriage. Despite her religious beliefs and the ever-lurking flames of hell, she believed there were worse fates than choosing the time, place and method of her own death.

As she touched the palm of her hand to the captain's cheek in a goodbye gesture, he reached into an inner pocket and drew out a small black velvet-covered box. 'I want you to have this.'

She recoiled. 'No, I cannot take it.'

He opened the box. Inside was a delicate, enamelled, butterfly pendant nestling against a curling silver chain. 'Please. I had it made for you. It's the Blue Peacock butterfly.'

She recognised it, and she remembered, but she shook her head.

During their season Blue Peacock butterflies swooped down to cluster on the lotus blossoms that lined the walls of the compound. With antennae quivering and wings wiggling, they covered the golden glory of the plants in shimmering silver. While waiting for the card tables to be set up on their last evening at sea, she had regaled Captain Palliser and Miss Carmody with stories of how Polly and Freddie and she would run at the butterflies, wanting to see the long skein of them rise and fly back over the walls to freedom.

Captain Palliser dropped the box on the mantel and left.

That night while the household slept, Kate slipped down the stairs to the kitchen. She lifted the lid of the range and dropped into the dormant flames her copy of *Lalla Rookh*. Magical as the verses were, they were too tied up with memories of Captain Palliser who had the audacity to point out to her the similarity between them and the lovers of the poem. With the long black poker, she stabbed the book deep into the fire and as the flames caught greedily at the pages, she was blinded by tears, grieving for Aunt Muriel, sobbing for the loss of the life that she might have had, crying for the unknown future she faced.

In a clean sweep, she planned to have the pendant join the book in the range—she had already passed on to Mrs O'Connor the gowns provided by the captain. In the end, she couldn't destroy the image of the butterfly, which was such a part of her childhood. She put the velvet box back in her pocket and wearily climbed the stairs to her small room.

'I've come to ask a favour of both you and Augustus.' Charles Kelly was not in uniform but with shoulders squared he was as military in attitude as if he were back in

India ordering the natives to his bidding. 'I am particularly appealing to your generous natures.'

He could not have chosen a worse time to call. On rising that morning, Polly had discovered, once again, that she was not with child. This time she had been so sure. Seeing the bloodstained sheets, Gussie had clamped his mouth tight and left for the bank without breakfasting. She ached with sadness and her ill humour was aggravated by severe stomach cramps that dragged pain down both of her legs.

'What's it now?' She made no attempt to hide her irritation. Her father, who behaved publicly as though he had the world at his feet, was frequently on the private scrounge for money.

'It's about Kathleen. There's a problem.'

'There's constantly a problem with Kathleen. Always has been. You're much too lenient with her.'

'Please, for this once hear me out.' He was not particularly taken aback by her outburst. He had become somewhat used to it. Ignoring her tight lips and refusal to meet his eyes, he traced the sequence of events pieced from what Kathleen, Captain Palliser and Mrs O'Connor had told him.

Polly could not believe what she was hearing. Her own sister. Her behaviour was worse than that of the actresses in the Theatre Royal; worse than the so-called heroines of any penny novel—not that Gussie permitted her to attend the theatre or to read such nonsense.

Her father sat back, relieved to have that over with. He was pleased at his level of fluency. Next he laid out the precise reason for his visit—there was no point in shilly-shallying. 'Will you and Gussie take in Kathleen?'

'Take her in? You mean have her come here to live with us?'

'Well...yes.'

'I cannot believe what you're asking.'

'She's your sister. She'd be company for you. You constantly complain you're lonely.'

Polly was outraged. 'How dare you! My husband wouldn't tolerate some bastard child sharing our home.'

Neither Charles nor Polly knew from where her newfound spunk had sprung. Charles reckoned Gussie was overly lax with his wife; whereas Polly put down her outburst to her delicate state. Her father looked off in the distance and after an uncomfortable silence took out his pipe and fiddled with it. Polly pretended not to notice. In the circumstances he did not feel it appropriate to light up. He gave her time to cool off before asking mildly, 'Will you even give my request some consideration?'

'I most certainly shan't.' Polly flounced her head and looked away from him, out the window at the garden, where she lavished time and love and it repaid with a riot of yearlong blossoms. How could her father be so insensitive? Had he any idea of the hurt and anguish his wild demand was causing her?

At that moment Polly hated her sister with a deadly hate. She who so wanted a child, conceived with difficulty and lost with ease. Her barrenness was all-consuming. Each time she heard of the birth of another baby it was like rubbing salt into her wounds. And Kathleen, who had no right to a child, was effortlessly having one. It just was not fair.

Part   Two

Chapter Nine

Kate turned the knob, pushed open the door and briskly entered the room. That morning she was a woman on a mission, but she was halted by the sight of her sister. No wonder the wet nurse was having such problems. Polly looked up from weaning her daughter with a start of guilt, which immediately stretched to a smile. She was a changed person since the births of first Isabel and now Lily. Despite the exhaustion of two children in under two years, there was a new lightness in her step, a kindness in her manner, and she had a ready smile and a pleasant word for everyone. She was a woman who was thriving on motherhood.

Gussie had been away, travelling on banking business for the best part of a month, but he was expected back within the next two weeks. During his absence time passed more quickly and pleasantly than usual.

Hill Road was a different place when he was not around, mainly because Polly relaxed, and her more laissez-faire attitude spilled over into the whole household. She no longer spent her days looking over her shoulder wondering what orders the servants had failed to carry out; neither was she constantly anticipating her husband's every need; nor fussing Cook about ingredients for the unimaginative food he insisted on; furthermore she did not have to be seen to concern herself about things he fretted over, such as his latest obsession with the colonies of tiny black aphids that had taken up residence in his collection of aspidistras. Such incidents profoundly upset Gussie and by osmosis created chaos for those around him.

Kate had developed the habit of moving quickly, performing tasks briskly and responding to situations instantly. If she did not act soon, it would be too late. She knew that if Polly picked up on her sense of urgency her mission would fail.

She sat down beside her sister on the sofa and absently ran a cupped palm over the baby's bonneted head. 'Have you thought any more about our visit to Paris?'

'I can't say I have. I don't seem to do much thinking these days.'

'That's understandable.' Although Kate had little sympathy for her sister's delight at motherhood, her absorption with domesticity, and her insistence that she was the only one capable of smoothing over the various household problems, she made a point of mollifying her. 'It will be easier to go while Gussie is away; you know he won't be able to bear the thought of you leaving him when he returns.' Kate constantly reinforced Polly with her husband's need of her. It was a kindly boosting of her sister's self-confidence, which, never robust, was rendered even more fragile by Gussie's constant demands, exhausting complaints and exacting standards. On this occasion, Kate was determined not to be swayed by Polly's excuses.

'Yes, he does not manage well on his own; he has continuous need of me.' Polly's voice was complacent.

'If I were a wagering woman, I'd bet he needs you for

more than merely managing.' Kate's comment was forceful. She forgave herself the white lie and pushed her dislike and contempt of Gussie to the back of her mind. If she could not persuade Polly to travel to Paris for just a short break, she felt it was quite possible that she would go mad. And then her father and Gussie would have just reason to commit her to Bedlam.

'I hope so.' Polly's voice held the smugness of a woman who believed marriage to be proof of being truly loved. 'I hate the thought of being without my girls, particularly this little one.' She hugged the baby to her fiercely. 'I'll miss her so.'

Kate had no compunction about leaving her daughter. No matter how hard she tried, or how often she held Violet to her, stroked her cheek or kissed her forehead, that special bond supposed to exist between mother and child was missing.

Courtesy of arrangements made in hurried and shamed secrecy by her grandfather, Muriel Violet M Newton was born in squalid lodgings in the small town of Conisbrough, with only a slatternly midwife in attendance. Violet's birth was the worst experience of Kate's life. She sweated in the cold of the room and felt as though all her organs were becoming creatures, tearing her apart so that they could have life.

Time passed. How long had it been? She had lost track of the hours but was kept occasional company by a pair of pigeons who came and went, their beaks cracking against the window and their silvery droppings dribbling down the glass. The pain had started at some time before dawn. Kate had watched watery, grey daylight creep over the rooftops. At some stage numbness took over, and when that receded the pain came back. It was a different pain, an intense pain of hopelessness.

She could feel the baby tunnelling headfirst into her, a bone and flesh extractor of her flesh and bone, a deepener of her depths. She imagined it swimming through her, falling into the stillness of a morning pond, water parting at its velocity. Now dusk was bruising those same rooftops. Time continued to pass. The pain rolled in and out, its tunnelling intensity increasing until Kate was sure she would be riven in two. She imagined the baby's face but she didn't want to see it. She wanted it gone from her, unborn. She did not want to be mother to this child.

She watched the ceiling and listened to the cracks against the window as she and her child rolled towards each other. The midwife shuffled at the end of the bed. Kate caught a whiff of carbolic and felt the child surging, rushing. She pushed and pushed again and again, playing out the macabre dance of birth. One more time and the head came out. She put down her hand to touch its slippery wet velvetiness. Soon it had to be over. She took a deep breath, amazed she still could. After more pushes than she thought possible, the child tumbled into the world. The midwife took over. Kate was left empty and released at owning her body again, and as she was luxuriating in the mess of soiled sheets the child squawked weakly, then the sounds of its arrival grew in strength.

The midwife placed the swaddled bundle of her daughter on Kate's belly. Kate looked down at the tiny face, all pink and creased, the hair a matted fuzz and her eyes blindly searching. If there had to be a child from her union with the captain, Kate was glad it wasn't a boy.

'I know how you feel, Polly. Of course we'll miss the

children but we're blessed with Hopkins,' Kate encouraged. 'She must be the best nursemaid in London.'

'I hope Gussie doesn't feel excluded,' Polly worried, off on yet another tangent. 'Perhaps we should ask him to join us.'

Gussie accompanying them to Paris was the last thing Kate wanted. He had the dubious distinction—without even trying—of being able to ruin the most pleasant of occasions. 'I doubt it. He is his own man and as you know he doesn't like France or anything French. He is so delighted with the children. I'm sure he wants you to have a holiday...' Kate trailed off.

Such falsehoods were unworthy of all concerned. Polly may have hidden from reality by determinedly remaining cocooned in her own special baby-and-husband world. But she wasn't a fool. It was her business if she chose to make the best of life with a pompously tyrannical man who considered it a wife's duty to be constantly available. Kate prayed her sister would never learn of Gussie's overtures to her, which she repelled with ill-concealed disgust, and in the process knew she had made an enemy for life.

'Yes, he is delighted with his girls, isn't he? Although I'm sure he and his mother would have preferred boys, particularly second time around.'

Polly's voice was both proud and humble and Kate wanted to lash out verbally. Even the slightest hint of that boy-god attitude enraged her. She had seen enough of it in India to last a lifetime. It was everywhere, and even as a child—and particularly as a girl—she had been exposed to the attitude.

The incident that still haunted her was visiting Poonam's cousin who had given birth to a daughter. On a hot airless morning a week before her eleventh birthday, they journeyed to the distant village by wagon drawn by an ancient buffalo. On arrival they climbed down into the thin swirling grey dust and hordes of staring people. Poonam was the centre of attention with all interest directed at her feet. Her feet were bare, extremely small and decorated with silver toe rings, bought from the local bazaar, in a gesture of independent femininity.

The shock of coming in from the outside brightness to the dark chaos of the tiny shack caught at Kate's throat— the earthen floor, cockroaches coming out from the walls, scattered cooking pots, and smells of stale food and fresh blood. The baby lay on the table wrapped in a sheet of bright yellow. Its lips were moving but no one paid it attention. Kate reached out and touched its neck, which was warm and throbbing. She had the strangest feeling that she knew the child, and she felt a deep longing to protect it with a talisman blessing or a kiss of acknowledgement. She never understood from where that knowing and longing came, but she could feel the infant's loneliness. It was loneliness of an extreme and incurable variety, the sort of loneliness that as an adult she had come to know and learned somewhat to cope with.

With the flat of her hand, Poonam had pushed her forward towards the turbaned man with the curling moustache and cold eyes standing at the back of the shack. He looked over her head as though she wasn't there. When Poonam poked her between the shoulder blades, Kate brought the palms of her hands together a few inches from her chin and bowed her head in respectful greeting, as she had been taught. There was no reaction from the man but Poonam kept up a run of rapid Hindustani, touching Kate's shoulders and hair, running her hand down her face. After what seemed an age, his lips moved, revealing a narrow scary space between his teeth. Kate, her heart thumping and her hands clammy, ran back outside.

The mother's howls of entreaty and Poonam's noisy sobs trailed after her as she stood in the hot dust, clenching and unclenching her fists. Kate did not know how she understood the implication of the small bundle carried out by the turbaned man, although the keening wails of the village women confirmed it. On the journey back, Poonam was silent but Kate saw the story written in her face. From what she had learned from Tarun during the short time she had been back in Agra, the barbaric tradition was still going on with baby girls being left to die or killed at birth by fathers and uncles.

After all the miscarriages and the three nightmare days it had taken on each occasion for her to give birth, Polly did not deserve the disappointed comments of Gussie and his mother as Kate, eyes flashing, had angrily informed them during the long drawn-out hours of the last birth, knowing no matter what she said or did, in their eyes she could not be any more *persona non gratis* than already she was.

While living on Polly and Gussie's charity was far from an ideal solution, Kate knew but for them her fate could be so much worse—the novels of the time were full of the dreadful lives of unmarried mothers, and even worse, their stories were covered in cold facts by the newspapers. She owed her sister and brother-in-law an unpaid debt of gratitude.

Only hours after Violet's birth, as Kate lay wondering at her future, her father had burst into the room, waving a sheet of paper. 'Your decree nisi has been granted.' Before she could comment, he continued, 'From next month you and the child will be living at Hill Road.' Kate often wondered how he had persuaded Polly and Gussie to take them in. But he was plausible in putting forward various reasons and was used to getting his own way. In the circumstances she had no weapons of argument.

Instead of creating a further chasm between them, the birth of Violet had drawn the sisters close—closer than they had ever been. Polly could not have loved her niece more if she had given birth to the child herself, and in less than a year she was holding her own baby. Without it ever being put into words, Kate sensed Polly understood and did not judge her lack of maternal feelings. They continued with the charade of Kate being happy in motherhood, and to give her her due, she tried. But how could she succeed? Each time she looked at her daughter she was reminded of Captain Palliser. As the years had gone by, she came to accept and make the best of her life, although she never lost hope that some sort of a happiness miracle lay around an as yet elusive corner.

'It hasn't been easy for you. You really want to go to Paris?' Polly asked gently.

'Yes. We could go next week. Say Tuesday. Shall I pick up the rail and ferry tickets?' Kate's voice, in contrast to her dark thoughts on girl children, was light.

'I don't know. I'm not sure.'

'Let's get the tickets anyway. If we decide against going, we can always sell them.' There was little chance of a re-sale and Kate knew that Polly's parsimonious nature would not allow a pair of first-class tickets, train and boat, London to Paris, to go to waste. She left the room hastily before her sister had time to re-gather her thoughts.

Chapter Ten

The hotel, situated on a narrow cobbled street in St-Germain-des-Prés, was small and quietly luxurious. Kate shook herself in delight, beamed widely and took deep breaths of vibrant Parisian air. After the drudgery and dullness of years, life had taken an unexpected turn for the better. She would savour every minute. Animation. That was the word that best described what she was feeling. She was in the city where everything and anything was possible; where neither she nor her reputation was known. Her past was in London and for the duration of their stay she determined that was where it would remain. Her cheeks glowed and she gave a little hop, skip and jump of joy.

The wrought-iron balcony of their third-storey room had clusters of trailing scarlet geraniums. Kate leaned out over the balustrade, admiring the ancient delicacy of the buildings, and last night she had stood enchanted at the way the streetlamps made soft explosions of green in the trees.

Judging from the variety and elegance of the parading fashion, as well as being safe for un-chaperoned women, the area was stylish. Young matrons wore slim-fitting tabliers in delicate pastels and with the perkiest of matching hats; men sported frock coats with contrasting collars, Ascot ties and top hats; even the small dogs prancing along on their coloured leads were chic. A laughing girl in a knee-length blue dress with a pink sash rolled a hoop with the dexterity borne of long hours of practice; and there was a man wearing a rakish cap pedalling out of sight on a bicycle. Kate had heard that French women had taken to cycling and she planned to take a bicycle ride before returning to London.

She breathed deeply again and offered a brief prayer of thanks to the God she frequently railed at for deserting her. 'Polly, come and look, it's wonderful.'

'In a while,' came the disembodied voice from inside.

Kate stepped back into the room. Polly, skirts spread out on either side of the chair, was sitting at the bureau with an open writing case. 'Surely you're not catching up on letter-writing?'

'Of course not,' Polly laughed. 'This won't take long. I'm writing to a few more of Gussie's contacts; after the trouble he went to, he'll be upset if we don't use them. If we're to have a social life in Paris, we'll have to let people know we're here.'

So far Gussie's contacts had proved ghastly: taking tea with the elderly Mrs Pavely in her stifling hot, too heavily furnished apartment on the previous afternoon had been a penance, but that dreadful lunch with grumbling Mr and Mrs Osborne and their pack of yelping Pekinese was even worse.

Kate collapsed onto the sofa and crossed one leg over the other. 'Honestly, Polly, I'd prefer to remain in the hotel than to sit through more of that sort of socialising.'

'You're not used to being with the right people.' Polly's

tone was the mildly censorious one she used to pacify Isabel. 'Don't worry. I'm well used to managing the complexities of organising a social life. It's a pity you're so seldom included on our friends' guest lists.'

Frequently Kate was more than happy not to be, but she felt a kindly comment was called for. 'I fear you're right. It's so long since I've socialised that I've lost the ability.'

'Nonsense, you've always been the more outgoing. Outrageous, as Papa frequently said.' Polly paused and left down her pen. 'Don't you remember when we were children how you were always telling me that we could do anything we wanted? You almost had me believing it.'

'That was a long time ago and much has happened in between.'

The following day an unexpected and unusual invitation arrived with the post. Polly was not impressed, but Kate was—at being invited to view an exhibition of paintings at the Académie Julian. 'Artists,' Polly sniffed. 'Painters, particularly. They're not worth socialising with.'

Perhaps not, if like Polly you were interested only in the world of commerce, banking and politicians occupied by your husband, but Kate thought spending time with artists would be exciting. She enjoyed the little she knew of art and she still dreamed some day of taking lessons in painting. 'Oh, let's go. We have to. If only for the experience.'

'You and your experiences! I'd have thought you'd have had enough to last you a lifetime.'

From the time Kate and Violet had come to live at Hill Road, Polly had never once referred to Kate's past. She even went to the extent of behaving as though her niece had been conjured up miraculously by some form of immaculate conception. Kate attributed Polly's repartee to the enchantment of Paris, but it wasn't to last. Like a talisman, Polly touched the cameo brooch at her neck. It was a present from Gussie to mark the birth of Isabel, and she was never without it. 'Gussie wouldn't approve of us attending such a function.'

Kate grinned. She wanted to say to bloody hell with Gussie; she hadn't thought of Freddie and his swearwords in an age. She tossed her head. 'Well, I plan to go. I'll go alone, if necessary. I shall take a carriage to the Académie and back.' Forestalling Polly's further objections, she added, 'And I shall be quite safe.'

'You certainly cannot wander around Paris on your own.'

And so the matter was settled. The following afternoon at five o'clock a hansom cab drew up outside the hotel. Some thirty minutes later, Kate in Butterfly's green silk and Polly in an unbecoming shade of yellow arrived at the Passage des Panoramas.

The place buzzed with creative life. The reception was held in large, glass space with swooping white walls enhanced by an evening sun spangling light and shadows. A trestle table covered with a red chequered cloth was crowded with bottles of wine, glasses, chunks of bread and wedges of cheeses and pâtés. Worktables were piled with paints, brushes, pots, canvases and the general paraphernalia of a working artist. Two uncomfortable-looking armchairs, three rectangular tables and an upright piano were jammed against the walls.

'What are we doing here? This is most inappropriate.' Polly looked around and sniffed at the dozens of framed and unframed, finished and half-finished canvases that covered every inch of the walls and were stacked on the floor. There were still lives of fruit and flowers; picnics *en plein air*, sunlight dappling water and landscapes that Kate wanted to step into, as well as solemnly grouped family gatherings.

Nobody came forward to greet them. Kate hoped Polly would not make a fuss and draw attention to them, or even worse, insist on leaving. Just being there, soaking up the atmosphere was so exciting. She gave a sigh of envy mingled with wonder, trying to image the marvel of living daily surrounded by such creativity. As she turned, her attention was caught by movement to her left. A beautiful young woman with milky skin and pale golden hair, wearing an elaborately trimmed rose pink gown, was laying a slender hand on a man's arm.

It was the broodingly handsome man who captured and held Kate's attention.

He had dark, floppy hair curling to his collar; slim wrists and long narrow hands. While he was slender, he gave off an impression of vitality that reminded her of the tiger she had seen as a child—beautiful, coiled and ripping with energy. She couldn't have been more than six years of age when she had stood still and fearless under the banyan tree in the corner of the compound, watching the animal's lithely sinuous, almost lazy movements on the branch above her. Slowly it had uncoiled, dropped to the ground and gracefully sloped off. There was a similar elegance in the way the man extricated himself from the woman. His cream linen jacket set him apart from the military men in their uniforms and the bankers in dark pinstripes with whom she was familiar.

A gentleman in a frock coat and a watch chain straining

against his large belly materialised from behind Polly. With a little bow, he presented her and Kate with glasses of red wine, and clapping his hands he called for attention. When the buzz of conversation had somewhat abated, he spoke: 'Please welcome our special guests, Mesdames Hervey and Newton from London.'

As Kate was smiling a general acknowledgement to the assembled group, she was aware of the man watching. Slowly he moved forward, until he was standing directly in front of her, and never taking his eyes from hers he raised her hand to his lips.

For an immeasurable hiatus blink of time, Kate felt there was between them a fusing of their psyches, an insight of total understanding. It could have been an hallucination, a result of too much loneliness and imagination, but its intensity was such that she was sure he had to feel it too.

'I am Jacques Tissot and you are most welcome to Paris.' In tone and resonance, it was all a man's voice should be— perfectly spoken English with just that hint of French. If accent had a colour his would be a warm chestnut.

Kate felt sure that everyone present must feel the air crackling between them. But when she looked around, nobody was paying them attention. The other guests were socialising—admiring the exhibits; chatting in small groups—more French voices than anything else; laughing; flirting; sipping wine; mopping up the creamy runs of Brie with crusty bread. Polly had moved towards the back of the atelier with the watch-chain man in attendance.

Kate did not know what to say but she discovered there was no need to say anything. She felt extraordinarily at ease. Monsieur Tissot was still holding her hand, which felt warm and comfortable.

'So, Mrs Newton?'

'So?'

'So? I don't know that I should ask you.'

'Ask me what?'

'I have a very important question.'

'Are you going to ask this very important question?'

'Where is your husband?'

She should have known but it did not stop waves of disappointment engulfing her. Why should Monsieur Tissot be any different from the other men and women of the times? It always came down to 'husband'. No matter where she was, or whom she met, she was known as the surgeon's divorced wife, with a bastard child by another man. In London society her reputation invariably preceded her. She often wondered why she had allowed herself to be overruled by her father's insistence that she keep Isaac's name; after all it had been rightfully hers for only a few short hours.

As she answered, it was her turn to look Monsieur Tissot in the eyes, to watch for his reaction. She had learned to be brief and to the point. 'We are divorced.' How many times had she said those three words?

He smiled. It was a smile that spread from a widening of lips to a crinkling of eyes. '*Dieu merci*. That's wonderful. I am so glad for me and for you. For us.'

It was the first time Kate had come across such a response. She was used to blatant lasciviousness—men openly wondering at her sexual availability, or their eyes slithering from hers in an indelicate rush to move away as though she were contaminated. She found herself smiling up at him. He was tall.

'How long are you staying in Paris?'

'Nearly three weeks.'

'So little time. We have none to waste.'

She shivered; fingers of deliciousness ran up her spine. She knew precisely what he was implying and yet she did not know how she knew.

The protocol of the times required that she ask coyly what he meant rather than reply with banter. She ignored protocol and chose the latter, laughing up at him. 'And how, pray, do you propose to implement this non-waste of time?'

'I have my ways to which I shall introduce you—if you will permit me?'

Kate believed she could read his soul in the softness of his brown eyes, and her answer too was soft. 'I shall give this permission my deepest consideration.'

'You and I shall lunch together tomorrow, and in the evening I shall escort you and your sister to the Comédie-Française. The opera *Carmen* by Bizet is playing.'

She liked the confident way he issued the invitations, and answered formally. She had never had occasion to master the art of flirtation. 'Thank you. Your invitations sound delightful.'

Monsieur Tissot, who had not expected such a straightforward acceptance, resorted to the practical. 'You are familiar with *Carmen*?'

Kate was not but she had read the reviews in *The Illustrated London News*. Despite the reviewer being less than kind about the production and principals, she would like the opportunity of making up her own mind. He laughed when she told him, and, nodding solemnly, he looked at her with approval. 'I suspect you frequently make up your own mind and, no doubt, the minds of those around you too.'

The sky was indigo, the fading light apricot and the stars were beginning their tentative emergence as Kate and Polly journeyed back to their hotel. The pavements of Montmartre were thronged with noisy revellers and sedate families, old and young, pushing and jostling against each other; the cafés were crowded, with their light, music, wafts of food and wine and bursts of laughter spilling out to the street.

Kate was silent. She had never experienced anything like the strands of silky, fluttering feelings that Monsieur Tissot evoked. To hold onto them, she wrapped her arms around her body, hugging to herself what he said and hadn't said, the laughter in his eyes, the curve of his lips, his hand gestures. What were those lines of poetry, she wished she could remember—something about it being better to have loved and lost than never to have loved at all? Why was she thinking of that now? No doubt if Poonam were with her, she would point to the activities of the gods.

'You're very quiet.' Polly broke the silence.

'I was thinking. It was a good entertainment, wasn't it? Did you enjoy yourself?'

'Surprisingly so. I am glad we went. You were right.' Polly leaned impulsively towards Kate and touched her knee.

'We have an invitation for a performance of *Carmen* tomorrow evening.' Kate kept her voice light.

Polly was on immediate defensive. 'We have? Who has invited us?'

'Monsieur Jacques Tissot.'

'Oh,' Polly's nose wrinkled. 'That man you were talking to? Have you accepted?'

'Yes.'

'It received poor reviews.'

'We should judge for ourselves. I certainly shall. I understand despite the reviews, tickets are scarce.'

'What does Monsieur Tissot do?'

'He's an artist.'

Polly shrugged and lapsed back into silence, playing with the toggle on her jacket.

Kate ached for her to comment. Eventually she could stand it no longer. Keeping her voice casual and thankful for the gloaming of the cab, she asked, 'What do you think of him?'

'Who?'

'Monsieur Tissot.'

'I haven't given him any consideration. Gussie has no time for art or artists. And I've never heard of a Tissot painting or a Tissot exhibition.'

Kate said nothing. Her mind was swirling as to how she could escape from her sister to fulfil her luncheon engagement.

Chapter Eleven

As it happened, next morning when Polly woke, she was thoroughly out of sorts. She walked up and down the room clasping her head between her hands and moaning softly.

'What's wrong?' Kate rose up from the bedclothes on an elbow, her nightgown slipping over one shoulder. She had been awake for much of the night, lying quietly beside Polly, just breathing and thinking of Monsieur Tissot, consumed in equal measure by happiness and fear of the unknown. She offered little prayers that everything would be all right, and it was dawn before she drifted into a deep, peaceful sleep.

Polly was deathly pale. 'I have a dreadful headache. From that cheap red wine, I shouldn't wonder. Gussie would never allow the serving of such an inferior quality.'

'Shall I ask the concierge to fetch a doctor?'

'No.' Polly came to sit on the side of the bed. 'I am sorry to ask but could you possibly occupy yourself this morning? Perhaps if I lay down for a few hours in the quiet, with the room darkened, the pain might go. At what time is Monsieur Tissot calling for us?'

So Polly was coming to the opera. 'He'll let us know,' Kate improvised. 'Please don't worry. I'll be fine. There's so much to do in Paris. I shan't disturb you—not even for luncheon.'

Polly's simple gratitude and her unconditional acceptance gave Kate a brief pang of easily dismissed guilt. She could not believe her luck. As she dressed, she was back listening to Poonam's soft voice telling how the past reflects eternally between two mirrors—the bright mirror of words and deeds, and the dark one, full of things not done or said. It was as though Ganesha, the laughing Hindu elephant, symbol of good fortune, was smiling down on her, encouraging her joyous deceit—without doubt Polly's headache would increase in intensity if she knew of her plans.

A quick glance and a gay smile in the looking glass confirmed to her that she was as suitably turned out for lunching with an artist as was possible, given her limited wardrobe. This was such an excitement. Having refused Monsieur Tissot's offer to send his carriage or to escort her in person, he had given her detailed directions on how to reach his apartment.

Drawing on her gloves, she turned right on leaving the hotel, smiling in anticipation of the stretch of happy hours before her; nothing would ruin this glorious day. She had allowed plenty of time to peruse the many tiny exclusive bow-fronted boutiques that lined the streets, and even had Polly been well, Kate would have chosen to experience such a jaunt alone, as she loved lingering and savouring new places and sensations at her own pace.

She stopped at a window where a pale grey satin high-heeled boot was displayed to advantage on a cushion of crimson crushed velvet, and was awed by its simple elegance; further on a dainty midnight blue hat with floating organza streamers sat on a light wooden stand. Although mostly she favoured plain over elaborate, she was taken by the glorious swatches of glimmering sea green ruffles in another window. Not that she wished to possess what she was seeing. She was not acquisitive; looking in admiration was pleasure enough.

Across the narrow street was a window filled with jars of brightly coloured boiled sweets and wedges of toffee in glass dishes, as well as slabs of chocolate displayed on sheets of golden paper. Kate had a great fondness for chocolate, but this would be a gift for Polly. As she turned the knob and pushed in the door, a raucous green parrot announced her arrival from behind the bars of his cage, screeching 'entrez'. The chocolatier, an elderly man with twinkling eyes, emerged from behind green velvet curtains decorated with jingling brass bells. As he weighed a portion of chocolate, he kept up a fast-speaking commentary, little of which Kate understood, although her nodding and smiling seemed to satisfy him. He executed an elaborate scarlet knot on the silvered gift-wrap paper and ushered her out with a gracious bow.

The sun was dancing angel rays on the pavement and Kate could not believe how much time had passed and how lovely its passage had been. Moving with a shyly sensual grace, she was unaware that she was the subject of many turned heads and second glances. Although not fashionably turned out in the accepted Parisian sense, she possessed an indefinable presence that was beyond beauty and style.

In the end, as she pulled on the bell chain of Monsieur Tissot's home in rue Bonaparte, she was no more than a fashionable ten minutes late. The heavy gate was answered by an elderly retainer, dressed in dusty black, and so stooped that she wanted to offer him her arm for support. However, he appeared agile enough as he led the way through the cobbled courtyard where a fountain bubbled silvery notes of water behind a screen of weeping willows, bordered with purple pansies and yellow-eyed daisies.

The doorway was narrow but the hall into which she stepped was an Aladdin's cave of brightness and light— white marble floors, carved golden pillars and crystal chandeliers. The old man knocked on a double door of heavy mahogany with an elaborate brass frieze. It was opened so promptly, by a footman in red livery, that Kate decided he must have been standing in wait. She felt a giggle rise in her throat, which she suppressed by blinking her eyes and swallowing hard, a technique perfected at Miss Carmody's. She could not remember when last she had thought of giggling. Looking at a point over her shoulder, the footman bowed low and gestured her to follow him across another expanse of marble.

Jacques Tissot appeared at the top of the curved staircase, and, as he came down towards her, his movements were so light and graceful he seemed to float.

He took both of her hands in his. 'You are most welcome.'

She smiled and nodded.

'I was afraid you wouldn't come.' In daylight his eyes were even softer and kinder.

'You should have known I would.' She answered fearlessly, as though any other course of action was inconceivable.

Deep within him, he had, although he had feared to believe it too intensely as that might be tempting fate.

Despite her limited experience of men, Kate knew Jacques Tissot was different from other men who had crossed her path. While Father Mathew's spiritual influence lingered, and she remembered him with fondness, he no longer intruded into her thoughts. She had mostly succeeded in relegating her ex-husband Isaac Newton to the back of her mind. Her father and Gussie could not be so easily dismissed, but she had adopted a method of working around their foibles. Captain Palliser was impossible to forget. He was with her daily, embodied in his daughter, who had inherited his blond colouring and broad shoulders. The cold chill of overwhelming sadness rose within her. No. She would not travel to those memory places inhabited by the captain and attended by Violet.

Jacques Tissot's home and sophisticated way of life were more sumptuous than anything Kate had experienced. But she was so used to her father's false claims and half-truths that she would not have been too surprised—although she would be disappointed, if they turned out to be less than they purported. She wondered if ever a life could be lived in transparent honesty and overall goodness.

When they sat to table, the meal was served by a black footman extravagantly dressed in ruby-coloured brocade. Again she wanted to giggle at the delicious improbability of it all. Her body sighed with pleasure. The wine was white and light and the food delicious: perfectly chilled *vichysoisse*, followed by a delicate *sole meunière*, then Camembert cheese. Over the meal they covered a wide range of subjects. He listened to Kate's opinions and theories, actively wondering what she thought about this and that, including the Franco-Prussian War, the work of missionaries in India, and the abiding power of Hindu gods.

For his part he talked of 'the cultural landscape', insisting that France and Russia were the giants standing on tiptoe and attempting to shake hands over the head of their large common enemy—Germany. 'France isn't just Europe's cultural superpower, it's the most fashionable country on the map, the world's style-setter and mode-maker. Even the Russian bear—bluff, boorish beast that he is—feels his loins stirring at the thought of Mademoiselle France.'

As they finished off the meal by peeling fresh peaches and apricots, she ran the pads of her fingers over the fruits' blossoming skin, threw back her head and laughed her deep rich laugh at his metaphor. She was as intrigued by the scope and range of the dialogue between them as she was at being treated as an intellectual equal.

Demitasse coffees were served in the salon on a low table, and when the footman withdrew, gently closing the double doors, they were alone, sitting opposite each other on matching couches of golden brocade.

'So, Mrs Kathleen Newton?' Jacques stretched out long lean legs, linked his fingers and clasped his hands behind his head. He was a beautiful specimen of manhood.

'So?' She sat upright, shoulders sloped, hands clasped lightly in her lap. Smiling. Willing time to stand still. She wanted nothing to change so that she could hold forever the essence of the atmosphere between them. She had waited for this man and for this day for all of her life. This, without doubt she knew, was love.

'Tell me about yourself. I want to know everything. As far back as you can remember, back to when you were a little girl.'

She put a hand to her throat. 'Now that I've told you

about the gods and missionaries, there's little else to tell. Please let's not go into the past.' Panic rose within her. She would have to watch her words because she was tempted to reveal all, to spill out her story from her heart, so that he could know everything. But experience had taught her caution. She could not risk destroying the relationship that hovered so tentatively and delicately between them.

Jacques was confused by her quivering reaction. Despite her air of innocence, surely she could not be that sheltered? After all she was a divorced woman. And with her poise and beauty she must be used to the effect she had on men. But he couldn't be sure as he had never been in love.

Despite his grandmother's prediction that he would experience a great love, in the quiet of night he often wondered if he was capable of this grand ardour that could consume his artist friends, take them from their paints and easels and into the realms of passion. As time went on, he sadly and reluctantly decided he was not. He was nearly forty years of age. Up to the previous evening he had lived only for his art.

From boyhood, as surely as he recognised that he would never follow in his grandfather and father's commercial footsteps, he recognised his destiny lay in being an artist. He felt the call of oil in his bones; his fingers ached to caress brush and canvas. The subjects of pictures quivered on the horizon of his mind as he wandered the docks at Nantes, sketching the rigging of the tall ships; or greedily watching the entrance and exit of sumptuously dressed women to the theatre. While he knelt in church as well as praying for paternal indulgence of his artistic ambition, he visualised the pictures he would create, portraying the agony and ecstasy of Christ, Mary, Mother of God, living out her life in virginal exposure, as well as saints and apostles.

Despite the odds and family pressure, he followed his dream of studying in Paris, and enrolled at the École des Beaux-Arts, where he became friends with James McNeill Whistler, Edgar Degas and Henri Fantin-Latour. He fulfilled his assurance to his father of 'being as successful as you' by the expedient means of familiarising himself with the market, seeing an opening and creating and meeting demand with supply.

His timing was impeccable. Europe was going through a period of shifting change and values with the foothold of the upper echelons of society being challenged by a rising middle-class. The new breed of merchants and tradesmen who had the ability to generate real wealth wanted evidence of both the fruit of their labours and acknowledgement of their cultural awareness. What better way than a commissioned painting? Tissot's works depicting contemporary social scenes became as highly sought after as they were priced. With the proceeds he built a luxurious house near the Bois de Boulogne, one of the most sought after addresses in Paris, and furnished it lavishly. Tissot senior pronounced his pride in his son's marrying of artistry with commerce.

Realising the war would devalue property, he sold early and at a good profit. He planned to travel but wanted to keep a small pied-à-terre in Paris, and instructed his agent to find a suitable apartment. At first sight he fell for the impressive and private first-floor apartment in the *hôtel particulier*, set behind a high wall and an equally high gate.

While he was interested in Kate's every detail and wanted to know everything about her, he was willing to bide his time. He was used to achieving his objectives, but being inexperienced in matters of the heart he was unsure of how to proceed. While deciding, he removed a cheroot from a silver box on the table between them. 'Do you mind?'

'No. Of course not.' She was relieved to have the emphasis off her.

'Would you care to join me?'

Kate had enjoyed several surreptitious and not so surreptitious cigarettes with Freddie, and she considered it ridiculous that the pleasure of smoking was denied women. She sat up straight. 'Oh, yes, I'd enjoy that.'

He passed over the box, but eased out a slim black cigarette. 'Try this. I believe it will be to your liking.'

When he had lit it and she had inhaled with pleasure, she settled back into her corner of the couch and allowed the miasma of smoke to envelop her. In an attempt to lighten the atmosphere, with a wave of her hand she announced gaily, 'I could grow used to this.'

He answered seriously, 'I hope you will.'

She dropped her eyes and did not reply.

Once he had spoken the words, he knew he should have matched the light-hearted gaiety of her comment with a witticism. 'Do you and your sister have friends in Paris?' he asked in an attempt at conversational reprieve.

'Polly has contacts from her husband. We are sightseeing—monuments and museums...' Her voice trailed off.

'May I make arrangements to spend time with you?' He wanted to break through her defences.

She was on instant guard. 'Well, we are attending the opera together this evening.'

'Yes. But there is tomorrow and the next day and all the days until your holidays are over.' He leaned across the divide of the low table and reached towards her hands. Her withdrawal was almost imperceptible, and although he noticed, he ignored it and was in no way offended. '*N'aie pas peur.* And after that…?'

'You must understand, there can be no after. There's only this time.' Her voice wavered. Despite their intimacy she had always thought of the captain as Captain Palliser but already in her mind Monsieur Tissot was Jacques. What a perfect name it was.

The silence of the unsaid and the un-queried hung between them.

He would speak. 'I want you to know that my intentions are completely honourable.'

They were the words Kate most wanted to hear and yet they struck such a knell that she wanted to put her hands over her ears to shut them out.

'Will you tell your sister about us?'

'No. Most definitely not.'

'Why? Despite being an artist, my reputation is impeccable, and, vulgar though it may be, regarded to mention money, I am wealthy. "Suitable", I suspect, is the English word.'

'I don't doubt what you say…' She sensed a change in the status quo of their relationship, quivering on the horizon of her future. It made her nervous.

He was puzzled. Matters such as intentions, reputation and wealth, which so concerned most women, appeared to be immaterial to her. He wished he had more understanding of women. His voice took on a note of curiosity. 'How did you escape this morning?'

Kate explained.

'And what happens tomorrow?'

'I don't know.'

'Perhaps you will both take luncheon with me and I could…'

That was progressing from bad to worse. Kate raised her hands as though to ward off evil, and a terrible devastation it would be if Polly suspected Jacques was romantically interested. And it would be even worse for her to admit an interest in him. Polly and Gussie monitored men's attitude towards her with hawk-like intensity. 'Please no. That is not a good idea.'

Jacques did not understand the reason for her distress, but he was aware of it. 'Does she like painting? Perhaps I can invite her to an exhibition of work by Degas.'

'She is happiest sightseeing. I am the only one in my family interested in painting.'

'You paint?'

'A little. Someday I'd like to take lessons.'

Jacques raised his hands above his head, interlocked his fingers and placed his hands palms down on his head and smiled. '*Ne crains rien.* Trust me. I have a plan.'

Chapter Twelve

Kate was full of bubbling fun and laughter. 'Whatever about the wonderful extravagance of *Carmen*, wait until you see my masterpieces—I promise I'll present the first to you and Gussie.'

Polly said nothing but she nodded slightly and smiled weakly. Initially she had been far from pleased with the arrangement Monsieur Tissot had put in place for her guided sightseeing tour, but his determined charm was so persuasive that she was almost—but not quite—at the stage of believing it was all her idea. She shrugged off a sensation of unease about Kathleen's painting lessons; in all fairness she could not begrudge her the opportunity to have at least one of her dreams come true. Not that Kathleen complained, but her life had to be difficult. That she had brought it on herself, as Gussie frequently said, did not change the situation; nor did it change Polly's feelings towards her, which veered from sisterly fondness to an un-sisterly crossness at ruining the family's reputation, then back to awe at her ability to make the best of her life.

Last evening, prior to attending the opera, eyes wide with pleading, Kathleen had begged her to avoid discussion on personal aspects of their lives – particularly hers. Polly had readily agreed. She was relieved to know Kathleen was not interested enough in the French painter to want to confide in him.

Jacques and Kate stood side by side outside the hotel as Pierre Dupois, who Jacques assured was both a thorough gentleman and an accomplished guide, handed Polly into a stylish carriage. As soon as it moved off, Jacques cupped Kate's elbow in his palm, and seeming as one they strolled along the narrow, cobbled street.

'Where are we going?' she asked, not caring.

'Before bringing you to my studio, I'd like to show you a place that has always intrigued me.'

Now she *was* intrigued. Despite the early hour, the beggars were out in force, and, by the time they reached their destination, the June air was so stifling and the atmosphere of the narrow streets so full of decaying vibrancy that Kate was reminded of the back streets of Agra. Jacques told her that the area had been a canal in the 1300s, at the time of Dante's writing of the *Divine Comedy*, and while it had been covered over for centuries, on occasions it still pooled.

While the beat and pulse of everyday boulevard life were the main grist to Jacques's creative mill, he loved and drew inspiration from Paris's many pockets of history. He was particularly taken by this place's mood of decaying grandeur: the raddled frontages of the buildings leaning forward as though trying to see their faces in the water; the way pipes jutted from the dilapidated windows, and the constant dripping dribble of water from a lead gargoyle into a scummy fountain.

They stood silently, together, but each within their separate spaces of thought.

Kate was captivated with the place's tendency to evoke

powerful memories of the India she loved—temples, shrines, churches and mosques, thousands of bodies and hundreds of bazaars devoted to perfumes, spices, incense and flowering trees. Living was the worst good smell in the world and in this backwater street it was all around her.

Jacques, with his hands plunged into his pockets, caught whiffs of the sweet, sweating smell of survival, which was as much the opposite of despair as the sour, stifled smell of greed was the reverse of love. He had watched his contemporaries move from relationship to relationship, frequently have children, sometimes marry. He had been largely indifferent to the variety of women who were drawn like flies to the honey of his success: mothers in the marriage market for their precocious daughters; wives bored with their husbands, seeking thrills outside of their homes; the new breed of independent woman purposefully pursuing her own pleasure; and, of course, the ever-present prostitutes. On occasions he had succumbed to the dubious charms of all types of woman, knowing it was nothing more than a physical act of release, but afterwards hating himself.

Those thoughts were still running through his head as he watched Kate remove her bonnet and gloves in the hallway of his Parisian home. He must explain to her that this was not his permanent residence. But in the circumstances, and with her refusal to divulge anything about herself, or apparently to discuss a future beyond the next half an hour, it hardly seemed of importance. If the exercising of a lack of information, curiosity or planning was what it took to win her, so be it.

He brought her straight to his workroom, which was white and spare and full of northern light. With his footman's help, they had turned one corner into a small separate studio, complete with easel, workbench, palette, and a selection of paints and brushes, standing in a tall pottery vase decorated with geometric patterns in bright greens, scarlet reds and vivid blues. Kate picked up the vase, held it towards the light and ran her hands along its curves. 'This is wonderful. I love the shape and colours. I can't wait to get started.' In her enthusiasm she began rolling up her sleeves prior to putting on the saffron-coloured smock slung across the chair.

'Would you like to work on your own for a while?'

'Yes, of course. I shan't disturb you.'

'I didn't mean that. It was more to give me an idea of your style.'

'Hmm. Style. I'm not sure one exists yet. What are you painting?'

'It's what my critics will call a "social scene".'

'Critics?'

'Yes. They are the bane of my life.' He felt it inappropriate to mention that the sale of such paintings made possible his sumptuous lifestyle.

'You must be important to have critics.' She was already sitting at her worktable, beginning to sketch.

'May I see?' he asked after an hour.

'Not yet. Perhaps I'll have something to show you shortly.'

Jacques returned to his own composition. Yesterday he had been inordinately pleased with the work he had provisionally titled *The Ball on Shipboard*; today he was dissatisfied. Yet the riggings were right; he had been around boats throughout his childhood and could paint them and their components in his sleep.

His problem was the women—all proudly different in both expression and dress. And he wanted to change the lot of them to the delightful Mrs Newton. He yearned to paint her pale skin with its dusting of ridiculous freckles, the flecked green of her eyes, the curve of her rosy lips, the tilt of her nose, but most of all he wanted to capture the glorious chestnut of her hair tumbling about her shoulders. He itched to portray her on canvas. So why didn't he? She was so absorbed in her drawing that she was unlikely to notice. He wouldn't though because it would seem like an invasion of her privacy. Some day, he hoped, when he had her blessing and when she had allowed him access to her inner self, he would be able to paint her as often as he wished. Her profile was quite perfect.

Some time later she called, 'Would you like to see?'

She had completed several charcoal sketches. They were crude and lacking in skill but she had a basic talent. He liked her sense of pride in her accomplishment.

'Well done. Some of these are good. Will you paint one?'

'I think I need more practice.'

'Perhaps, like relationships, the acquisition of skill is continual.' He rested his buttocks against a worktable opposite and held her gaze. 'Why won't you talk to me about yourself?' His voice was jocose but he was serious.

Her shrug was casual but her insides were cramping and her voice was strained. 'As we have so little time together, let us neither look backwards nor forwards.'

Again he felt there had to be more than social reluctance to her flimsy excuse. When they first met, he had experienced what he was sure was mutual attraction. When he tried to progress it, she appeared to withdraw, and yet he was certain she felt for him. He trusted in fate, and, ridiculous as it seemed, after just a few minutes in her company, he believed he had waited all of his life for this tantalisingly beautiful woman.

'But surely that's up to us. I would like us to have a future.' Again he had moved up their relationship a notch further. It was too early to talk about a future but it was the truth; he had been reared to truth and honesty, and, wanting to state his intentions, he saw no point in prevaricating.

Kate dropped her head and would not meet his eyes. Her heart was beating fast and her mind racing. Could she take the gamble, go with her heart, tell him her story and hope for a future? It was probably too late. Perhaps, when he'd first asked, but if she'd done so, she felt it unlikely they would be together in his workroom. The more she knew of him, the more she recognised his integrity and admired his openness. She could not bear it if he turned away from her.

As though reading her thoughts, he said, 'There could be nothing in your past that would change how I feel about you.'

What he said rang sweet and true but still she could not, she would not dare to take the chance.

When she looked up her expression was tortured. It was difficult to believe this was the same woman who had laughed so happily and so readily such a short while ago. In his enthusiasm he was rushing her. He thought he must have been wrong in his previous assumption of her worldliness. Obviously she was a gentlewoman, unaware of the effect of her beauty, bruised by her divorce and leading a sheltered life with her sister and brother-in-law.

'Please, let us just enjoy now. We'll never have these minutes again.' She picked up a stick of charcoal and bent towards her drawing. Her fingers were short and capable and her nails clipped short.

He returned to his easel. 'When I was a young boy...' he began, looking over at her industry.

'When you were a young boy. Go on.'

'So you don't mind hearing about me?'

'No. Please do.'

It was a start, he supposed, wondering how best to proceed. Emotions had played no part in his upbringing. His father was a strict, undemonstrative man, as devout a Catholic as he was a commercially successful merchant and shopkeeper. He sent Jacques to board with the Jesuits at the age of five, to receive an education to groom him to take over the family business. The priests of the order were hard taskmasters who believed the man was made by the time the boy was seven years of age. They may not have prepared their young pupil for life in trade but they did instil in him a sense of Catholic religion and a code of morality, as well as ambition and the ability to access and to appreciate his own strengths.

But he wouldn't go into all of that. He'd tell her the fun family things, make her laugh—he loved her laughter. 'My grandmother was a true matriarch, ruling and controlling. My grandfather started the family business and when he died she determined not only to keep it going but to have it expand, which is where my father and I came in. Our lives decided for us by her.'

'What was the business?'

'Initially *Grandpère* was a trader; he started with one small stall in the marketplace and expanded to several before acquiring his emporium. *Grandmère* and he didn't talk about their humble beginnings, though everyone in Nantes knew, but he liked to portray himself as coming from several generations of prosperity.'

Kate was fascinated. Her father had a similar attitude of pretending to be what he was not. 'What did he sell?'

'In the beginning anything that would turn a profit, but before he died he settled on being a milliner—in the old-fashioned sense of the world.'

'Making bonnets?'

'Oh, those too, but primarily he saw himself as a purveyor of fancy goods.'

'How old were you when he died?'

'About four, but I felt I knew him intimately, because throughout her life *Grandmère* behaved as though he was still alive.'

'She sounds formidable, a woman of purpose—rather like my Irish grandaunt. What did she look like?'

'Small and plump with papery white skin, which smelt of lavender. Her hair was silvery and she wore it in an elaborate loop on the crown of her head. Each night she sat before her cheval with candlelight playing on its mirror, and when uncoiled her hair reached beyond her waist.'

Jacques's words were so visual that Kate could see the shadowy figure of his grandmother in the flickering light of her boudoir, and she had the strongest urge to reach up her arms, to shake loose her hair from the confines of its pins, and to let it tumble to her waist. Her breath caught in her throat and nostrils and her head was full of memories of loveless nights of passion with Captain Palliser. She wondered how it would be to lie with Jacques.

Polly returned from sightseeing flushed and happy; she was the enthusiastic sister whom Kate remembered from their childhood.

'Have we plans for tomorrow?' she called gaily from the doorway of their room.

This was unusual; Polly was not in the habit of consulting her. 'Not that I know.'

'How did your painting go?'

'Well. But it was more drawing than painting.'

'Will you continue?'

'Monsieur Tissot did mention it but I didn't like to commit.'

'Go ahead. I'll be all right with Monsieur Dupois. He has several more places on his list.' Polly remained on the threshold of the doorway, still half in and half out of the room, and Kate was aware of some sort of a whispered discussion in the corridor.

'Do you have preferences about dining this evening?' Polly's head came back around the door.

'I haven't thought about it.' That was not a word of a lie. Since meeting Jacques, Kate, who was so fond of her food, did little more than pick, and Jacques who also professed an abiding interest in eating was doing no better.

'Monsieur Dupois suggests we might like to dine at his aunt's home. She is holding a reception for some of the cast of *Carmen*.'

It was most unlike Polly to be interested in such an outing, but Kate answered, 'Why not? It sounds most agreeable. You go ahead.'

'Most of the family will be present, so we'll be well

chaperoned. I don't believe Gussie would mind in the circumstances.'

'I'm certain your arrangements would have his total approval.'

'What about you? Surely you'll be joining us?'

'Thank you, no. I'll dine with Monsieur Tissot. In the circumstances it would be impolite not to as he invited both of us.'

Polly looked dubious—Kathleen dining alone with a man? Over the years she had viewed at first hand the effect her sister had on men and on more than one occasion Gussie had hinted she was the kind of woman who enjoyed intimate relations. While Polly wondered how he could arrive at such a conclusion, she had never dared to ask. 'Have you told Monsieur Tissot about Violet?'

Kate shook her head vehemently. 'Of course not. Our interest is purely in art; Monsieur Tissot is so well informed.' The lie slipped out easily and Polly looked relieved.

While whispered arrangements were made in the corridor, Kate wrote a quick note and rang for a footman.

'I am interested to know how the lovely Mrs Hervey is getting along with Pierre. I hear on good authority that he is utterly enchanted with her.'

Kate burst out laughing. 'If only Polly could hear you.'

'Why? Surely she'd be flattered?'

'It's not like that.'

'So how is it? Explain.' Jacques would grasp at the slenderest of straws to understand this enigmatic woman.

'Well... .' How could she explain the nuances of her sister's marriage without breaking confidences? 'Being brought up in India, convent educated, married when she was seventeen, she doesn't think like that. She is devoted to her husband and would never consider having even the smallest flirtation.'

'Her loyalty to her husband doesn't prevent Pierre from being enchanted by her.'

In their attempt to divert attention from their feelings for each other, Kate and Jacques were animated in their discussion of the relationship between Polly and Pierre, but the air between them was thick with desire, their food was mostly untouched and their silences filled with longing.

Jacques had taken as a good omen Kate's note advising him that she would be happy to dine with him, and in her sparkling eye contact, heightened colour and liveliness he read promising evidence of her feelings towards him. He hoped he was right. 'I believe I am in love with you.' It was the first time he had spoken the word 'love' to a woman; he was gambling that Kate would be more responsive to straightforwardness than to an amateur flirtation.

As anticipated, she was and she responded without coyness. 'I believe I know, I feel it too and it's wonderful. Like nothing I've ever experienced. I'm deeply honoured.' She wanted to sing and dance and shout their love to the world, but of course she couldn't. 'Knowing you feel this way about me is enough.' It had to be enough. Her feelings for Jacques could go no further. She would have to keep a tight rein on her emotions.

'*Non, ma petite à moi.* It is not enough. Not for me, not for you.' Jacques's voice was low and insistent.

Kate fiddled with the stem of her glass. 'It is. It has to be.' In her intensity to make him understand, her eyes filled.

He reached for her hand. 'Please do not cry. Do I make you so unhappy?'

'No. I'm sad with joy.'

The air between them was more charged by the second. While Jacques's emotions were in turmoil and his passion riding high, his intentions were honourable. This was the woman he wanted to spend the rest of his life with. He would not compromise her, and that evening he had no ulterior motive but to let her know of his love; he wanted to express it but the decision had to be hers.

Had she met Jacques before her relationship with Captain Palliser, Kate knew she would have been guided by her feelings and accepted his love without question. Had life made her so cowardly that she would turn her back on the man of her dreams? She was sure of her feelings for him and she believed implicitly that he felt the same for her. So why was she hesitating? Behaving so indecisively? This was one of the few occasions in her life when she had the opportunity and freedom to exercise her choice. Now was, perhaps, her only chance ever to love and be loved. But she couldn't; she wouldn't. Bloody hell. What was wrong with her?

Chapter Thirteen

Kate and Polly spent happy hours wandering the streets, browsing Le Bon Marché, captivated by the perfumed confusion of the department store, raving over fistfuls of elaborate underwear, cashmere from India and pale chemises in materials as soft as flower petals. From the countertops there were whiffs of scent, sparkles of glass, whirls of bright and light colours with saleswomen enquiring, '*Mesdames, vous désirez?*'

The time Kate spent with Jacques passed in a leisurely flurry of tender talking, strolling the boulevards, drawing and painting, growing closer, getting to know each other better. Jacques exerted no pressure but she accepted and revelled in his love; sometimes for want of fulfilment she felt as though her head was about to burst. Polly's life was more intricate, as her expeditions of sightseeing involved complicated decision-making sessions with Pierre, regarding itineraries and travel arrangements.

As the sisters breakfasted in their room towards the end of the second week of their holiday, Polly's cheeks were flushed and she alternated between fiddling with the cameo brooch at her neck and crumbling the roll on her plate.

'Where are you going today?' Kate wondered what had her sister so fidgety.

Polly was usually without guile. But that morning her answer was uncharacteristically evasive and she did not meet Kate's eyes. 'I'm not sure; perhaps some galleries or maybe one of the parks. No doubt Monsieur Dubois will have drawn up an itinerary.'

Kate, having drained her *café au lait*, was liberally applying apricot conserve to the last of the croissants and debating requesting more. As well as being blissfully happy, she had recovered her appetite and was constantly hungry. The hotel footman, notable for little except his sullenness, arrived at their door with a note.

Jacques was waiting in reception. 'How are you, *ma chérie?*'

Impulsively she hugged him. 'I have never been better. And why wouldn't I?' She stood back, beaming happily.

'I couldn't wait to see you.'

She answered with the secret smile of a woman who knew she was well loved.

'It's a beautiful day. Perhaps we will take a trip down the Seine? That's if you agree?'

'It would be perfect.' It would remove her from the temptation of being alone with Jacques, her urge to throw caution to the winds of Paris and allow herself to love and be loved. She clapped her hands. 'Let me fetch my bonnet and gloves. Perhaps you will introduce me to the secrets of painting water?' she peeped out at him from under her eyelids. Her enthusiasm for art knew no bounds, and Jacques joked that he was quite jealous of how it consumed her thoughts.

'If your sister wishes, and if it pleases you, she may accompany us.'

'I don't know what she wishes but it doesn't please me in the least to have her accompany us.'

'I like a woman who knows her mind.' The fondness in his expression took the sting from his words.

Kate bit on her lip. Perhaps she should be less outspoken, more gracious. Sometimes she felt she had been rushed through young womanhood, and now the world was pausing to allow a place of incredible brightness to open its doors. But making her way through its loaded air was like pushing through waves. She and Jacques had too little time together to play games with social niceties. The majority of the people she'd come across had in their different ways disapproved of her strong will, outspoken nature and behaviour, but Jacques was smiling, his eyes twinkling, and he was nodding as though he not only understood precisely what she was thinking but thoroughly agreed with her sentiments.

Kate breathed long and deeply in an attempt to capture and hold the Parisian air of that morning. If only she could bottle the conflicting scents and sounds encapsulated in the perfumed linden-tree dust of iron-shod hooves ringing on cobblestones, as carriages, jaunting cars and heavily laden drays competed for space.

Below them stretched the pavements of the lower quay, glistening white in the hazy heat, and the cool smoothness of the grey-green Seine. Down the promenade a boy watered horses and a lavender seller plied her wares. In the middle of the river a commuter boat chugged past a barge, coloured posters gleamed on the *bateau-mouche*'s square roof. While they waited for the next boat at the small jetty at Pont Neuf, Kate noticed a child selling *boutonnières* from a heavy shoulder tray. 'Look, Jacques, that little one is so young.'

Jacques's face tightened. He called over the child and in a voice that boded no argument he bought the contents of the tray without haggling over the price: a few francs-worth of small white roses, petals adhering to each other from the early morning heat.

'Give the remainder away,' he urged the young girl, taking three buds and pinning them on Kate's shoulder. 'Go now, and come back to me when you have it done.' With a pat on her arm he sent her on her way.

They watched as she did his bidding, curtsying gracefully to each of the surprised recipients before explaining the situation with a nod back in Jacques's direction. When she returned with the empty tray and a tentative smile, he gave her a few more coins. 'Buy yourself a meal and go home for the remainder of the day.' His voice was back to stern.

'Why, Jacques?' asked Kate as the child scampered off, the shoulder tray thumping against her scrawny body.

He sighed. 'There are too many such children—educated in the ways of the world before their time. I try to do what I can but it's always too little. Doubtless she will be back tomorrow with another load of roses, and eventually she'll be on the streets without the roses. Regrettably, she's pretty enough to make her living without flowers.'

He wondered if Kate had children and thought not; there was nothing maternal about her, but watching the little one scamper out of sight he realised he could grow to like a child, particularly a child with Kate. Strange that, as, up to meeting her, he had no urge to bring children into the world.

Their small boat had a cheerful red and white striped

awning and they settled on the cushioned benches on deck. It was a perfect day with the slight heat haze clearing and giving way to stillness and jewel-bright colours; the sky was so blue that Kate felt she could taste it on her tongue. Despite the darker side of their encounter with the young girl, it was a day of happiness, a day of hope.

The lapping of the water against the side of the boat was hypnotic, as was Jacques's closeness. How safe Kate felt with him. How different he was to Captain Palliser—it was ironic really, as protection was what he had offered but failed to deliver, whereas Jacques offered nothing but love, but with it came the assurance of both protection and security.

There were few other passengers on board: just a young couple who looked profoundly serious and were deep in solemn conversation; an elderly man with a flat cap and a striped jersey chuffing on a pipe; and a harassed mother ineffectually entreating her three lively children to desist from hanging over the boat rails.

Jacques leaned towards Kate, took her hand and looked deep into her eyes. 'I love you more than I thought it was ever possible to love anyone. I want to marry you and take care of you for the rest of our lives.'

His words were sweet to her ears but they brought sadness to her heart. Oh, that life would allow her to be with him, to marry him. She had become adroit at sidestepping his plans for the future. Against the metronome of lapping wavelets, she answered, 'I love you too but I'm divorced. And as you know, the Catholic Church does not permit remarriage after divorce.'

He dismissed her reasoning with a flick of his wrist. 'Our Church is no different to other institutions. As long as the fee and contacts are appropriate, anything can be arranged.'

'Do you have that power?'

'Perhaps not me alone. But my family does.'

'And your family would do that for me?'

'Yes, because you're my choice. I will ensure they do whatever is necessary for us to be together.'

There was no point in pursuing such talk, which could bring nothing but heartbreak. She raised her face and smiled mischievously. 'I presume you believe I'm comfortably off? Perhaps you're marrying me for my money?'

Jacques had grown used to Kate's rapid changes of subject whenever he brought up the subject of their relationship. 'I hadn't thought about it one way or another.' That was a slight wavering of the truth. From the beginning he had been taken by her beauty, elegance and personality, but he wondered why she constantly wore the same green gown. While it complemented her shapely figure and suited her skin tone and hair, it showed visible signs of wear. As every woman he knew possessed several gowns, he presumed variety of dress to be an integral part of the female psyche, but with Kate he could not be sure as acceptable social practice did not apply to her. 'In our ignorance, we bachelors presume all divorced women are well provided for.' He clapped his hand on his knee and threw back his head in an uproarious laugh. 'And penurious artists are particularly susceptible.'

'This divorced woman is not provided for. Comfortably or otherwise. I live in London by the grace and favour of my brother-in-law.'

Jacques stored up that nugget of information. Much as

he would like to add to it and to question her further, he wouldn't. There would be plenty of future occasions to acquaint her with that titbit of coincidence.

Next morning a note in Jacques's scrawl requested that Kate accompany his footman.

'Where are we going?' she asked from inside the landau. The footman shrugged. She had seen the gesture before—it was his way of not answering, but he did it with such panache that Kate felt nothing but amusement. After half an hour of manoeuvring the pair of whites turned into rue de la Paix and drew up outside the House of Worth.

Everyone knew of the House of Worth: not only had the Empress Eugénie given Charles Frederick Worth's creations her seal of approval, his clothes were frequently pictured in *The Illustrated London News* and Kate had heard that certain wealthy American women came to Paris twice yearly to buy their whole wardrobes from him.

She and Jacques had several discussions on the influence of painting in the modern trend of *en plein air*. As she had admired his social scenes of elaborately gowned women, she presumed she was about to be educated in the art of capturing in paint the tawny nap of velvet, the smoothness of silk and the intricacies of trimmings.

Jacques, stylishly turned out in a lightweight black jacket and a silver-grey Ascot, held in place with a large luminous pearl, waited in the marble foyer. He held her hands and kissed her cheeks in greeting. 'We're going to see some of the season's latest fashions.'

White-gloved bellboys, ornate in red and gold livery, brought them through the foyer to the first-floor balcony, which was strung like a latticed necklace between the marbled necks of fluted columns. Kate's eyes soared up the cathedral heights, a further two floors and more receding into a vaulted glassy distance.

The stimulation of conversation on a diversity of subjects with Jacques and the time she spent at her easel, as well as the essence of Paris, had expanded Kate's mind and opened it to opportunity. When she returned to London she planned to visit Harrods, which had mannequin shows, and even Hyde Park should be a source of ideas and artistic inspiration. Her dull life could have its own moments of excitement, and perhaps she would become accomplished enough to carry out magazine illustrations. The thought was deliciously exciting.

They were led to an area of mirrored walls, glass chandeliers and gilt chairs sitting on a rich deep green-coloured carpet. Monsieur Worth waited. Champagne was produced, amber bubbles in bowl glasses, and Monsieur Worth raised her hand to his lips. Wait until she told Polly.

Jacques drew the couturier to one side. With elegant gesticulations and glances in her direction, he was obviously making his requirements known. Kate loved watching Jacques interact—he had a natural way of getting on with people and an ability to bend them to his will in the nicest, most gracious way.

The first mannequin wore a tea gown of sapphire blue silk trimmed with a large pink rose at its waist. Her movements were poised and she displayed the gown to its best advantage.

'Do you like it?' Jacques whispered. He knew blue was Kate's favourite colour and considered the rich undertones of this would both appeal to her and complement her glowing natural colouring.

Kate's eyes shone. The gown was beautiful in its simplicity, but she thought it would be difficult to capture from memory. She wished she had known to bring a pad of paper and a pencil.

Next along the slender strip of carpet was a ruby red walking suit of voided velvet, with jacket and overskirt gently draped to accommodate the bustle. It was worn to equal advantage by a different mannequin. Jacques leaned in towards Kate and again asked, 'And do you like that one?' The previous afternoon he had a private meeting with Monsieur Worth and had made a selection of the garments he wished to be shown.

'Oh yes. I want to reach out and touch it.'

Monsieur Worth, who was watching proceedings, motioned the mannequin in their direction. When Jacques grasped a fold of material between thumb and forefinger, Kate followed suit, bending her head to the material. He was right: that shade of red was perfect for her.

There followed a patterned silk evening gown in shades of emerald green merging to jet black, with a generous décolleté and lavish crystal beading.

As Kate wracked her brains to remember every detail, Jacques searched for appropriate words. While he had no experience in such matters, it was important to him that she should accept his offer in the spirit in which he was making it. In the end he spoke from the heart. 'Kate, *ma toute belle*, I wish to make you a present of those gowns. They enhance your beauty and come with all my love.'

Kate reached for his hand, touched it lightly and said, 'Thank you. They are almost too beautiful to wear.' Jacques's gesture was so unlike the farcical, absurdly modish outfits presented to her by Captain Palliser, given not for her pleasure but to shine on his arm. By consenting to Jacques's gift, she had broken yet another of the codes of behaviour that had been drummed into her since childhood. But it made little difference, as no matter what she did, she knew that her life could never revert to being socially acceptable. And even if it were possible, she could not, she would not sacrifice any one of these moments of perfect happiness for the sake of achieving a life of respectability.

Before that day was out she had broken the greatest of all taboos.

Their embrace in Jacques's golden hallway was spontaneous and as natural as day following night. When they stood back from each other with expressions of joyous wonder, Kate was flushed and smiling; Jacques was smiling too but there was intent in his gesture as he put his arm round her waist. When she leaned into him and rested her head on his shoulder, he took it as a signal of her acceptance. He led her up the curved staircase to a bedroom of gauze curtains, soft comforters and cool stillness.

Theirs was a slow and gentle journey of exploration, without a past, without a future, with just the richness of the present. Every nuance and change of mood from light to dark passing between them brought them closer. She was driven by an all-encompassing wave of love, which once released swept her uncontrollably along. His arms were strong and his kisses tender. Although she was sure he would be a skilful lover, the gentle passion and mastery with which he took her came as a shock. Hungry for her, he held his passion in check until she was satisfied.

'I love you,' he said as he gave himself to her with a potency that made her shudder.

Kate felt as though the last years of her life had evaporated in a waft of misty time. She remembered the ancient Sanskrit legend that spoke of a destined love, a karmic connection between souls fated to meet and collide and enrapture one another forever. Lying across Jacques's chest with her lips close to his ear, she whispered, 'The loved one is instantly recognised because he is loved in every gesture, every expression of thought, every movement, every sound and every mood that prays in his eyes.'

In acknowledgement, Jacques closed his eyes and wrapped his arms around her. After a time, he eased her from him, raised himself on an elbow and looked down at her. 'Tomorrow, *ma belle*, I shall send a telegram to this mysterious whoever is responsible for your welfare; then I shall tell my family and after that we shall visit them in Nantes.'

She sat up, horror-struck 'You can't. It is not possible. You must know that.'

'You belong to me now and I refuse to compromise you.'

'I belong to myself and I am compromised. It's a glorious compromise and I love every minute of it. Don't let's ruin what we have now by thinking of the future. That'll have to take care of itself.'

Wearing the deep flush of her feelings and the smiles that kept breaking out around her lips, she touched his thickly arched eyebrows, ran the tip of her index finger across his eyelids, down his nose, tracing his lips, the indent on his chin and finally the lobes of his ears, slowly imprinting each movement on her mind. For as long as she lived she would never forget the feeling, texture and sensation of his face.

The Parnell family were highly thought of throughout Paris: people with political inclinations knew of Charles Stewart's passionate work for Irish tenant farmers. From childhood, he and his nine siblings had stayed with his uncle in his apartment on the Avenue des Champs Elysées. A decade previously, Jacques and he had struck up an unusual but cordial friendship.

'Perhaps,' said Jacques to Kate as they strolled to a reception in Parnell's honour, 'it was because neither of us had women in our lives.' He gave Kate's hand, which was resting on his arm, an affectionate squeeze, and she returned his touch with a caressing gesture. Despite the heat of the evening, she felt cool and elegant in her tea gown. A frivolous hat perched high on the back of her head, its silken streamers drifting round her face in the sunny breeze. On her feet she wore the soft matching slippers that Jacques had suggested Monsieur Worth make for each of her gowns. But she was still trying to make sense of Polly's outburst.

When the gowns had arrived at their hotel, in their distinctive black and gold packaging, she had no choice but to offer an explanation to her sister. 'They're a gift from Jacques.' She said it quietly, knowing her words laid bare the depth of their relationship. Polly turned around from the mirror where she was dressing her hair. Momentarily, her eyes widened in astonishment and she threw up her hands before bursting into tears. Shoulders slumped, face buried in her palms, she sobbed wildly. Kate dropped to her knees and put her arms round her. The cause of her distress had to be more than new gowns. Polly had a vast wardrobe. 'Please don't be upset. They're only gowns. How can they cause you such grief?'

Polly raised a tear-streaked face. 'It's not them. It's just...'

'Just what?'

'We're having a wonderful time, aren't we?'

'Yes, of course we are.'

'But we have to go back to London.'

'Yes. We do.'

'And this will all be over.'

'Yes.'

'I have done a most awful thing.'

Kate could not imagine Polly doing anything awful— but then their ideas of awfulness were diametrically opposed. 'What did you do?'

Polly raised a tear-stained face. 'I allowed Pierre to kiss me. And I liked it so much that I kissed him back. And he made me a gift of this.' The words tumbled out in a childlike burst while Polly rummaged under the bodice of her gown and pulled out a handsome silver filigree locket on a fine chain. 'I wasn't going to tell you... . Wasn't going to tell anyone, ever.'

'Well,' said Kate as pragmatically as she could manage, with her head reeling at Polly's disclosure, 'perhaps if I'd received such a beautiful gift that could be hidden away, I wouldn't have told you about my gowns either. Are you fond of Monsieur Dupois?' she asked with some trepidation, still remembering Polly's sharpness when she had enquired about her marriage happiness all those years ago.

'Yes.' This time there was no hesitation in Polly's answer. 'We love each other dearly.'

'What will you do?'

'Return to Gussie and our daughters, of course. More than anything in the world, Gussie wants a son.'

The reception for Parnell was unexpectedly informal. But the apartment where it was held was stylishly decorated; its walls covered in delicate grey *toile de joie* depicting rural scenes of haymaking, fishing and picnicking; its floors herringbone parquet and its windows lavishly dressed in royal velvet. The chic guests included a sprinkling of minor royalty as well as diplomats, politicians and people from the world of the arts.

Sipping from a glass of champagne, Kate thought how wonderful it was to be on Jacques's arm, to belong to him and him to her. 'I find the security of certainty so comforting,' he had said on the previous evening, and she hadn't answered because she knew the certainty he was talking about did not exist for them.

Parnell was an imposing black frock-coated figure with reddish-brown curling hair and beard. 'More international than Irish in attitude,' a slight man with greying hair and a monocle commented. From her father, Kate had built up an erroneous impression of the Irish as a race more prone to amiable foolishness than international statesmanship. Parnell's attitude disputed that. Growing up in India had been educationally restrictive, Miss Carmody's school had not been much better, and her current life was even more so. She had allowed the breadth and possibilities of learning to pass her by.

Parnell stood with his elbow resting on the mantel of the marble fireplace, holding the floor mesmerised with his passion as he spoke of his dream of founding an Irish National Land League. His aim was to help tenant farmers and to abolish landlordism.

'Surely the peasants need landlords?' asked a red-faced gentleman.

'It depends on the landlord.'

Kate remembered her grandaunt's letters, which frequently took the form of a diary in their descriptions of her stewardship attitude towards the care of her tenants: the visits, provision of food and medical attention when they were ill; encouraging the children to learn to read and write; pointing them towards a better life, promising times would change. Interspersed in Aunt Muriel's writings were stories of abuse, rack rents and the penurious living conditions of tenants from other estates.

'Mr Parnell is right. It does, indeed, depend on the landlord.' Kate spoke without thinking.

A ripple of interest ran around the room. She was the most beautiful and elegantly gowned woman present. Heads had turned at her entrance and everyone wanted to know who she was and why she was there. Such women were not expected to have opinions, their role was seen as purely decorative. She had not intended to speak or to find herself the focus of attention.

'And what do you know about it?' It was the red-faced man.

Kate looked at Parnell. With a nod he gestured her to answer. She lifted her head defiantly and jutted out her chin, the way she had done from childhood when making a point. 'Perhaps not as much as people who have lived for decades in Ireland, but enough to know the way my grandaunt handled her tenants.'

'Where were her estates?' The question was belligerently asked.

Kate kept her voice calm. 'She lived in County Wexford.

Her family were land granted in Cromwellian times, and as it is frequently said they became more Irish than the Irish themselves, even to the extent of marrying locally and becoming Roman Catholic. She loved Ireland and the Irish with a passion and she saw caring for her tenants as her duty and role in life.'

'Did you live with her?' Parnell's voice was authoritative and his personality was all-encompassing.

'No. I was brought up in India. My grandfather was a doctor there and my father his only child. My grandaunt is dead now but she taught me much about Ireland through our correspondence.'

As Kate stepped back, there was a spontaneous burst of applause, but it was Jacques's look of pride and approval that meant the most to her.

Kate spent that night with Jacques 'Every day of my life, I will be with you,' she told him next morning, tracing his eyebrows with her forefinger. She would remember the times they spent together: theirs was not only a short relationship, but one whose memories had to be consumed in sips to get her through the long, lonely years that lay ahead.

Those years happened sooner than either she or Polly anticipated. Mr Parnell's reception and impassioned speech were covered by the London *Times*, and not complimentarily either: the British establishment found it hard to justify Parnell's passion for Irish tenants, particularly as it regarded him, a Protestant landlord, as an establishment figure. The attitude reported by the paper was that politically he had sold out to Irish rebellion. In a final paragraph the reporter concluded that Parnell's philosophies were endorsed by a Mrs Kathleen Newton, who claimed Irish ancestry and was currently holidaying in Paris with her sister Mrs Augustus Hervey.

The telegram that arrived from Gussie together with their escort back to London was succinct. They were to return immediately, and under no circumstances were they to discuss the matter with anyone. Polly was reduced to a paroxysm of fear, and in an instance her newfound happiness and confidence deserted her. Their escort was Gussie's latest secretary. He was an impassive young man who insisted on their presence while he oversaw the chambermaid's packing of their luggage. His presence did not stop Kate writing a brief 'goodbye' note to Jacques and parting with the last of her francs to the surly hotel footman for delivery. Within thirty minutes their carriage was en route to the railway station.

Polly was in such a state that Kate sublimated her own feelings of devastation at leaving Jacques. 'It will be all right. It was I who spoke out. Gussie will not blame you for what I said. You weren't even present,' she assured with a confidence she did not feel.

'He will blame me. You do not know him as I do.'

Chapter Fourteen

The nursery at Hill Road was situated under the eaves. If the novels of the time were to be believed its angled corners and small square windows could be regarded as romantic, a perfect hideaway for fun happenings and a nurturing place for dreamy stretches of childish imagination. But there was nothing fanciful or dreamy about the Hervey nursery—the wooden floors were pockmarked; the wallpaper was stained where damp had seeped through the roof valleys; and the furniture, such as it was, had long since lived out the best years of its life.

From halfway up the stairs Kate could hear the screaming and thumping of her daughter. Isabel and Lily seemed to have been born placid and obedient, but Violet had a temper. For a few moments Kate stood, watching unobserved through the half-open door. Hopkins, her rosy face rosier than usual, was standing over Violet, who was lying on her stomach on the floor, thumping at the wood with her little fists, shouting, 'No!'—her most frequently used word of recent months.

'Come on, now. There's a good girl,' Hopkins cajoled. 'Get up and finish your porridge.' Kate never ceased to marvel at the nursemaid's even temperament, her lack of obvious favouritism towards her charges and the endless patience she brought to her work.

There was another thump from Violet, a raised head and an extra, 'No!'

Hopkins squatted down beside the child. 'Get up. Now. Please. This minute.' She was scrupulously polite and her voice was authoritatively measured. Isabel and Lily, sitting strapped in, side by side in high chairs, paid no attention to the tableau.

'No. I want my papa.'

'Well, that is something you cannot have.' The nursemaid leaned forward, caught Violet under her arms and firmly hoisted her to her feet. Then with the palm of her hand in the centre of the child's back, she pushed her towards the small table. By craning her neck, Kate was able to see the large blue and white striped bowl out of which stuck the handle of a spoon, but her mind filled with images of Captain Palliser. It wasn't the first time Violet had asked about her father, and Kate knew it wouldn't be the last. Soon enough someone would consider it their duty to tell her, or being Violet, she would find out.

Hopkins sat the child on the wooden bench, and arms akimbo stood over her. 'I want you to eat this now.' The words emerged calmly from her narrow lips.

'No.'

Kate, still unseen in the crack of the door, dithered. She considered the English disciplining of children irrelevant. Children would eat when they were hungry, sleep when tired, clothe themselves against the cold; in other words they would learn to do what was necessary to survive, she'd seen it throughout her time in India.

It was immaterial to Kate whether or not Violet finished her food. Her visits to the nursery were rare, her relationship with her daughter so non-existent that she dismissed as ludicrous the chance of them ever becoming close. She considered it in the child's best interests to leave her rearing to the nursemaid. Hopkins had been assiduously vetted by Gussie.

Hopkins bent down, caught hold of Violet's arm and shook her. 'Eat,' she demanded. As the child, mouth wide open, bellowed in outrage, she shovelled the porridge into her, but Violet, ever determined, was having none of it and pushed it down her chin with her tongue. Hopkins stood motionless as Violet scowled into her bowl. All of a sudden the child grabbed the spoon from the nursemaid and began ladling the porridge into her mouth. After a few ladlefuls, she dispensed with the spoon and with her plump little hands scooped it from the bowl and crammed it into her mouth, pushing, swallowing as fast as she could in panicky, gulping motions. In an equally brisk movement, she vomited all over the little table.

By then Kate had retreated down the stairs.

Kate stood by the window, feeling the charged air of a storm brewing. Watching as it broke, wave upon wave of wind battering Polly's flower garden. Pausing. Beginning again, punctuated by splintering cracks of thunder.

As the four walls of the room closed around her, she opened the glass doors and stepped onto the pathway, her arms wrapped protectively around her body. A grey curtain of light revealed the trees' wild careening and the lawn strewn with debris—branches, twigs, leaves and dead blossoms. It was not yet raining but the calm, like hers, was deceptive—deep down it was raging and there was no break in the clouds.

A particularly angry burst of thunder took her by surprise and was followed by driving rain. As she dashed back inside, a pencil-thin dagger of lightning lit up the sodden lawns and dripping hedges. Another bolt of lightning danced gaudily and a crack of thunder rose like the crescendo of an orchestra gone mad.

Absence had strengthened Kate's feelings for Jacques. In an effort to hold onto and cherish the memories of their time together, her movements and conversations had become slower and more deliberate. He was constantly in her thoughts, and some nights when she woke his presence was so potent that for a glorious instant she believed he was lying beside her.

As the storm quietened, so too did her resolve. She knew what had to be done. She had to make plans for what lay ahead. Gussie's tolerance of her presence, already stretched to its limit since their return from Paris, would be forced to stretch further. As she had promised Polly, she had done the *mea culpa* for both of them. He had received her explanation in silence, her words and demeanour were stalwart and positive but missing the penitential tone he favoured for even minor misdemeanours. By unspoken consent, the subjects of holidays, the city of Paris or even the vaguest reference to culture had never since been mentioned in his hearing. Polly had reverted to a nervous and fragile shadow of her Parisian self.

Trying to acclimatise to her changing circumstances and making sure she was as strong in resolve as was possible in the circumstances, Kate waited a few more days before approaching Gussie. She chose a morning when he had been relatively amenable during breakfast. Giving him some ten minutes to settle, she followed him to his study and knocked on the door. When there was no reply, she turned the knob and entered. He was sitting behind his desk with its bundles of papers scattered in all directions.

He looked up from reading the newspaper. 'I'm busy.'

'I am sorry if I disturb you. I just need a moment.'

'I'm constantly disturbed with domestic problems.' Gussie continually complained of lack of time but Kate seldom saw him constructively utilise the huge amounts he had at his disposal. 'What do you want?'

His brusqueness curled Kate's stomach. To face him she had worked up a resolve of steel and she could not, she would not back down. 'There is something you need to know.'

'Well. Go on. Stop shilly-shallying.' His voice was abrupt. Kathleen was his dream woman, his hidden passion, and her presence in his home both unnerved and titillated him. As well as being bowled over by her beauty, he was awed by her apparent fearlessness and self-sufficiency. He had been instrumental in her coming to live at Hill Road—Mary Pauline had been vociferously against it. But he saw it as an opportunity for the realisation of his fantasy. Kathleen would be forever indebted to him and he was sure his seduction would be only a matter of time. How wrong he was. Instead of being grateful, from the beginning, she had repelled his every overture with mocking disdain.

She moved from foot to foot but held her head high and placed her hands across her belly. 'I am with child.' As she spoke her vision grew fuzzy, her voice seemed to come from a long way off and she held on to the rope edge of the corner of the desk for support.

Gussie's face turned a dark shade of puce and his pale blue eyes popped. He braced his hands on the arms of his chair and stood up. 'You are what?' he thundered, and Kate was glad of the protective barricade of the desk.

'I am with child.' There was no further elaboration required.

'When did this happen?'

'In Paris.'

'In Paris?'

'Yes.' She kept looking into his eyes; she would not bow her head or give him the satisfaction of dropping her voice.

'Do you know who the father is?'

If Gussie had wanted to shock Kate, he succeeded, and she knew he would not be the first to ask the question. She managed to answer calmly. 'I met somebody and I love him dearly. We love each other dearly.'

'And where is this latest lover of yours now?' As high and mighty as she appeared, she was still not above behaving like a whore.

'He lives in Paris.'

'Will you be joining him?' he raged, imagining her in fierce abandonment with this unknown lover.

'No.'

'Does he know he is to become a father?' He bet she was carrying a healthy son.

'No.'

'May I enquire when you plan to acquaint him of your situation?'

'I don't.'

'Ah. So I presume you expect me to provide a home

for yet another of your bastards?' By God, he would make her pay.

Kate had no answer to that because other than taking her chances on the streets, she had no option but to continue living at Hill Road. As her father had not thought to inform her, much less invite her to his wedding, and she had not even met her stepmother, it would be pointless to seek help from him. Anyway his previous manipulations with Captain Palliser remained all too fresh in her mind.

Nor did Kate consider letting Jacques know of his impending fatherhood, much as she craved throwing herself into his arms and spending the next months under his protection. She would not ruin his memories of their relationship by acquainting him with the truth of her life. Unlikely as it seemed, deep within her was the karmic certainty that somewhere, some time, somehow when the time was right they would meet again.

'I demand to know the name of the father.'

'You won't learn it from me.'

'Is my wife familiar with your sordid affair?'

Gussie on the warpath of hectoring answers from Polly was the last thing she needed; God knows she was fragile enough. Kate's answer was unflinching. 'She knows nothing about it.'

'And where was she while you were disporting yourself like a harlot?'

Kate wanted to slap Gussie's fat face to wipe off his lascivious expression. She could imagine what was going through his mind. She was aware of the salacious way he watched her when he thought he was unobserved, but in her vulnerable situation there was nothing to be gained and all to be lost by such a gesture.

'Well?' he roared.

'Polly was sightseeing,' she answered quietly, hoping her sister wouldn't be drawn to the room by Gussie's loud voice.

'I suppose next you will tell me it was Leonardo da Vinci who impregnated you.' Gussie used sarcasm as a weapon when he was stuck for words.

There was no answer to that except an incredulity that Gussie, who was vocally contemptuous of any form of culture, had even heard of da Vinci.

'That's all I wanted to say,' Kate said as she left his study.

'And it's damn well enough.' His bellow followed her down the hallway.

'I believe I'm with child,' Polly said, her voice heavy. She sat down beside Kate on the garden bench where the late September sun was casting long shadows on the yellow and bronze chrysanthemums, now in full heady bloom. It was such an unexpected announcement that Kate was lost for reply. She had said nothing to Polly of her condition, nor apparently had Gussie, which unnerved her as she had fully expected him to use it as a weapon of verbal sarcasm.

'Congratulations, Polly. You must be pleased. Are you all right?'

Polly nodded. 'I hope it will be a boy this time.' Her voice was barely audible; the shadows under her eyes were deep and her pallor pale and unhealthy.

'So do I, for your sake. But all that matters is that you and baby are well and healthy.'

Now was the ideal time for Kate to share her news about her baby, whom already she loved deeply, but as she reached for her sister's hand, Polly whispered, 'I'm so frightened. I wish it would go away.'

She threw herself into Kate's arms and sobbed until Kate began to worry for her sanity. All she could do was hold her close, stroke her hair and make soft murmuring sounds of reassurance. 'I'm sure Gussie is pleased.' If he was, the news hadn't softened his mood.

Polly lifted a tear-stained face: 'I haven't told him.'

Polly's reliance on Kate grew with each passing day. She was ill, poorly and fragile in both mind and body, from the late hour she rose in the mornings to her early departure to bed in the evenings. Eventually Gussie noticed.

'What is wrong with you?' He looked up from his plate of cheeses as for the third evening in a row she excused herself immediately after supper.

'I believe I am again with child.' She turned an ashen face to him and her voice was the faintest of whispers.

'Well, well, and about time.' Gussie remained seated at the table, his chair pushed back and his hands laced across his ever-expanding belly.

In his strutting delight at imminent fatherhood, his manner towards Kate became aggressively dictatorial, insisting she take over the running of the household and nurture Polly during the coming months. When Kate finally told Polly she was carrying Jacques Tissot's child, her sister scarcely registered that they would be having babies within a short time of each other. Where was the vivacious woman who had drunk the delights of Paris and been so joyously happy?

Kate knew that happiness lay within each person's realm, but she also knew from personal experience that certain people had the power to spread unhappiness. Gussie was such a person; he brought no joy to Polly or to anyone else's life, and he drove the most placid of people to distraction with his fussing and constant demands, all of which escalated during Polly's pregnancy. .

Then the unthinkable, but probable, happened—during the third week of November Polly lost the child that Gussie insisted was their son. During the days that followed she was inconsolable, keeping to her room and emerging a pale wraith of her former self. Even Lily, who was at the chuckling, dimpled stage of toddling around and lifting plump arms for hugs and cuddles, brought her no comfort.

Kate blossomed and glowed throughout her pregnancy. But at Gussie's insistence her lying-in was in hospital. During the three hours she spent giving birth, she could not be sure whether the child within her was crawling towards or away from her, but her excitement at meeting Jacques's child acted as anaesthesia to the pain. Near her time of delivery the contractions became remote and muffled like the peal of the bells of Notre Dame.

In the dimness of the church, a flare of candles marked the statue of the Virgin Mary. Kate had sunk to her knees and listened to the immense stone silence, hollow and reverent, an urn for music, a receptacle for her prayers for Jacques's happiness, and her cry for the forgiveness of her sins.

Outside Jacques and she looked up. 'Shush,' he said. 'Listen.'

'What do you hear?'

'The bells ringing out your name.'

She had laughed at him.

'*Non*. It is true. When lovers are together, the bells peal out the loved ones' names. Can't you hear?'

Arms entwined, they had stood, bodies touching. In the booming echo she believed she had heard the elongated sounds of Jaaacques, Jaaaacques and Jacques.

His arm tightened around her. 'I hear Kathleeen, Kathleeeen and Kate,' he whispered into her hair.

During the birth she heard the distant echo of 'Jaaacques, Jaacques, Jacques', and felt his presence. The midwives came and went, going about their ministering, but they were reduced to insignificance.

Kate's bonding with her son was instant. Immediately he was born, she insisted on the midwife laying the slimy morsel, warm and slippery, on her breast, and she knew the meaning of unconditional love. Red and wriggling, the child was heat enough to sear straight through her skin and mould to her ready heart. She held the warm skin bundle close and after examining the tiny boned head and pink ribbed face, she refused the services of a wet nurse. 'Cecil George. Child of mine,' she murmured.

Over the months that followed, during which Polly lost another child, the depth of Kate's feelings of love for her son somewhat alleviated her grief for Jacques. Although she never stopped thinking of him and loving him, equally she never doubted that her decision not to involve him in her life was right, and each night she prayed to God to keep him well.

In a matter of months she had identified the curve of Jacques's eyebrows, the slant of his nose and the taper of his fingers in Cecil. She spent hours looking at her baby lying in his bassinette, marvelling at his tiny hands raised on either side of his head, his fingers curled like new fern fronds and the inverted-comma dimples in his cheek.

Chapter Fifteen

As Kate stepped over the threshold of the nursery, Violet launched herself across the floor and hid her face in her mother's skirts. She was closely followed by Isabel and Lily, who clutched at Kate.

'Mama, come and see what I've done.' Violet shook loose her cousins and dragged Kate over to the table to see a drawing of a square house with a peaked roof, four windows and a door.

'That's good.'

'Me too, me too,' went Lily, offering for inspection a series of scribbles.

'You're too small to draw, isn't she, Mama?' Violet was scrupulous at all times in ensuring she drew her mother's attention away from Isabel and Lily.

'Very good too,' Kate pacified her niece, before addressing Hopkins. 'Get Cecil dressed, please; I'm taking him out for a while.' She planned to walk down the road to post a letter to Freddie. His letters from the Punjab were full of the colour of life and living. She had come to accept that the cloak of her past was cut from patches of feeling, that everything had its cause and its meaning, and nothing was wiser than failure or clearer than sorrow. But still, day by day she survived and she took pride in that.

'In this cold?' Hopkins's tone was disapproving.

After the sleet and snow of the previous weeks, when the whole family had been imprisoned by the weather, Kate could not wait to be out in the fresh air. 'He'll be cosy in the perambulator.'

'Please, Mama, may I come too?' Violet did not whinge, she asked directly.

'And me too,' went Lily, who constantly fought for inclusion in Kate's rare treats or outings, although Isabel never asked.

'Not today, perhaps another time.' This 'another time' was a constant refrain. Kate found Violet's company trying in the extreme, and, whenever Lily was included, the girls' bickering was constant.

The low sunlight of February glimmered off the powdery pathway as Kate pushed the perambulator down Hill Road and onto Abbey Road, which was quiet as usual. With the exception of Sundays, when they attended the service in the local church, the residents of St John's Wood were rarely seen out and about. She enjoyed looking into their houses, imagining the lives of the owners and wondering what it would be like to be mistress of her own home.

She took the turn to the right, walking the few hundred yards down Grove End Road to the intersection of Circus Road and Hall Road. A slim-figured man was standing at the post box. His shoulders were thrown back, his feet apart and his arms hung loosely. He was hatless, his hair curling to the collar of what looked like astrakhan fur on his dark topcoat, and although he was sideways to her, she had an impression of a moustache. When you loved somebody you saw them in the strangest and most unlikely places.

Whenever Kate was confronted by a likeness of Jacques, as frequently she was, she allowed herself a few moments of luxuriating that it really was the flesh-and-blood him. Invariably, then, swirling memories of the past engulfed her: Jacques standing before his easel, his talent bringing canvas to life; sitting on the golden couch, swirling a glass of amber liquid; hand proprietarily cupping her elbow as they walked the boulevards; and best of all making love, body fitting against body, taming loneliness with each other's presence.

She was on the point of turning around the perambulator so that she could point out the person to Cecil, tell him that handsome man over there was just like his father—she often whispered her secrets into the tiny pink shells of his ears—when the figure turned and began walking towards her. She knew that way of moving better than she knew herself. She watched mesmerised as he came near enough for her to see the widening of his eyes; almost catch the gasp of his breath and watch as his mouth stretched to a tentative smile.

Incredulity, joy, amazement, disbelief, she did not know what she felt. She wondered would she faint.

The man took a few more steps towards her: 'Kate? Is it really you?'

She stood, staring at this person who should have been across the English Channel in Paris. Cecil was forgotten. But as soon as she was filled with the certainty of love doubt crept in. Was it really Jacques? Or was she hallucinating? Seeing him as she had constantly during those first weeks back in London, throughout her confinement and after Cecil's birth? From out of nowhere her doubts multiplied and intensified, tumbling over each other. Could she believe what was in front of her, what her eyes were telling her?

'Kate,' he said again, as though speaking her name consolidated her presence. 'I can't believe it.'

'Neither can I.' Doubt dispelled, she was both laughing and crying, and as if she had not scandalised the district enough, she moved close and put her arms round him. Despite the stiffening muscles of his response, he felt better than she remembered, better than in her dreams.

After what could have been either a long or short length of time, he withdrew, held her at arms' length and looked at her in a solemn, puzzled way. 'Why are you here? What are you doing?'

'It's where I live, with my sister. Don't you remember Polly?'

'Yes. But I didn't realise it was here.'

'And you?'

'I've been living in St John's Wood for some years.'

'Where?'

'Just a few hundred yards from here. In Grove End Road.'

Kate thought of all the times she had walked up and down the road and felt she should have sensed his presence, known he was near.

At that point Cecil gave a gurgle. Jacques looked into the perambulator: 'Hello, and who are you?'

Kate's heart beat so fast that she thought it would leap from her throat. How could she answer but to tell the truth, the whole truth and nothing but the truth? Her story should have been told to a clamouring of cymbals but the only sounds were the rumble of carriage wheels and the clop, clop of horses' hooves. 'This is Cecil George—Cecil.

He is our son. Yours and mine.' As she spoke, she looked deep into Jacques's face. She needed to read his expression, to know his reaction.

Jacques opened his mouth; then crimped it shut. A small vein pulsed in his temple.

As she did in times of crisis, Kate stood straight, chin out, refusing to lower her eyes, and she fought against fidgeting with her hands, although she bit on the side of her lip.

When Jacques and she had first met, there had been that instant fusing of psyches, which later they spoke of with delighted awe. On this occasion there was no renewal of that fusing; if anything it was the opposite—Jacques withdrew. He had always been transparent to her. She could read his emotions like a book. Now she wished she did not have that ability because she recognised his bewilderment and hurt. And he was due for more.

He appeared to take her announcement about their son impassively. His questions were calmly spoken and flat in content. 'It must have been difficult for you. How did you manage?'

But he was struggling with his emotions. He had been devastated at Kate's abrupt departure from Paris. It had taken months of dragging himself from the depths of a breakdown, followed by a period of depression, to get back to painting. He had tried, without success, to put her out of his mind. Eventually, for his sanity, he had come to accept that not only had she left him but she had also chosen the manner of her leaving. It was only as he relived the hours they had spent together that he was able to acknowledge the implications of her refusal to look to a future. He had not expected to see her again. Now that he had, her impact on him was as powerful as ever. His feelings for her ran through him like floodwater. But he would not succumb. He had to protect himself. He could not, he would not, allow himself to love again.

Jacques's attitude was not what Kate expected. Her sham of a marriage, divorce, lover and daughter—the secrets she had insisted on keeping from him seemed ridiculous and unimportant. No matter what the outcome of this meeting, unexpected and unplanned as it was, she wanted truth between them. In for a penny, in for a pound, as her mother used to say.

'It was difficult, very difficult.' She answered his questions. Drawing a section of her lower lip between her teeth, slowly she released it. 'But I had the advantage of having been through a similar experience.' Her stance was straight and her voice true.

'What do you mean?' His voice was sharp, his body poised on alert, tuned to her every nuance.

'Because I already had a daughter.'

His face sagged in hurt and disappointment. It was his turn to bite on his lip, to glance away from her and to ask in a scrupulously polite voice, 'May I enquire her age?'

'She's nearly five.' Kate kept her eyes on his face.

'May I further ask—are you married?' Politeness can be a deterrent to reality and this was one such occasion.

'No. I'm not.'

'Were you ever?'

'Yes, but it only lasted for a few hours and I do have a decree nisi.'

'So that was true.' There was something in his voice that she could not quite identify. If it were Gussie she would have had no trouble in classifying it as sarcasm, but irony was not part of the Jacques she knew. She feared he was about to walk away.

Little stabs of relief pricked at her when he said, 'We need to talk.' His voice was cold with hurt as he fought against his feelings. He needed to keep control as much as he wanted to get to the core of the truth. He looked up and down the quiet road. 'Come for tea tomorrow at half past three. Number 17. And bring your children.'

As she watched him cross the road, had she not pinched her left hand with her right thumb and forefinger, she would have believed she'd dreamed up the encounter.

As Jacques walked back to his house, his head was filled with the vision of a face with the palest of skin, a dusting of freckles and a cloud of chestnut hair, and his desperate urge to capture her on canvas.

Violet listened warily as her mother asked Hopkins to dress her in the red velvet outfit, new boots, to ringlet her hair and to have her ready by three o'clock. She was a child of many crushed dreams but still she hoped.

'Are we going out, Mama?' Her voice was cautious.

The previous night Kate had spent sleepless hours, watching oblongs of moonlight on the floor while worrying about visiting Jacques. In the end she had risen from her warm bed, thrown a shawl across her shoulders and seen dawn creep over the chimney-stacks of London. When she and Jacques had met how could she have foreseen the future? How could she have known the direction or intensity of their relationship? Was it so wrong to seek happiness? Experience had taught her to be economical with the truth, and now she hoped the same truth—full-blown—would set her free.

'Am I really going out with you, Mama?' There was incredulity in the child's tone.

'Shush, Violet. Give your mama a bit of peace.' Hopkins had picked up on Kate's edginess.

Kate would prefer to visit Jacques without Violet but she did not have that choice. 'Yes. We're going for a walk to enjoy the sunshine because it's such a beautiful day.'

That sounded good to Violet, but as always she wanted more. 'Where are we going?' When her mother did not answer, she tried again. 'Is it a secret? I love secrets.' Violet was a talker, full of questions and demanding of answers. She jigged excitedly from foot to foot, but stopped when she realised Cecil was included in the outing. 'Must he? Does he have to come too?' Kate's look silenced her, though her spirits rose again on realising her cousins would be remaining in the nursery. They were playing with their dolls. She had never owned a doll.

As she waited in the hallway beside Cecil in his perambulator, 'without moving', as Hopkins had instructed, Cook came up from the kitchen and Violet overheard Hopkins say her mama was behaving most oddly.

Cook asked in what way.

'She is in a right state. Excited and flustered,' said Hopkins. Violet ran the word 'flustered' around her mouth; she liked words. 'Fixing her hair. Dressing up the young ones in their best. All for going for a walk, now I ask you.'

Cook touched her nose with her finger, whispered something and they both laughed, leaving Violet certain Mama's 'state' must be connected to their outing. She hated hearing her mother discussed and, with childlike logic, she justified movement to where Cook was standing beside one of Uncle Gussie's horrid plants. She put her hands behind her back and stuck out her tongue as far down her chin as it would go. Cook took a swipe at her but Violet moved too quickly for it to connect, and she was back standing immobile when Mama came down the stairs looking just like Mama, without any fluster.

Violet's ringlets bobbed and her boots squeaked as she walked, holding the side of the perambulator. 'Where are we going?'

'Oh, do be quiet. You're such a bothersome child.'

As soon as the words were out, Kate was contrite; spoken words could not be retracted. She tried hard to hide her lack of maternal feeling from Violet, and although she suspected she was not successful, it was not in her nature to be hurtful. 'I'm sorry. I shouldn't have said that.' She stopped pushing and looked at her daughter, so small, trying so hard, and pleased with so little. 'Forgive me?'

'Yes, Mama, of course.' Violet's voice was smooth, without emotion.

Outside the gates of number 17, Kate took several breaths. The scariest part of the visit was having no idea of its outcome.

'Why are we stopping here, Mama?'

'We're making a call and it's our special secret.' Kate hoped Violet was as into secrets as she and Polly had been.

As children, the Kelly sisters had been privy to a multitude of suitable and unsuitable secrets. Swearing them to silence on pain of unspeakable punishments from a variety of gods, Poonam introduced them to the dark and light sides of Indian superstition and culture. Whether terrified or elated by the imprint of their experiences, their lips remained forever sealed.

Kate pushing the perambulator, with Violet holding onto its side, walked up the curved driveway, which wound through neatly clipped lawns edged with box hedging. In the distance benches nestled under spreading trees, and lawns and shrubs stretched as far as the eye could see. If the grounds were so peaceful now, how glorious they would be in the full bloom of summer. They were as quintessentially English as was the immaculately turned out maidservant who answered the door. 'Good afternoon, Mrs Newton? Mr James is expecting you.'

Mr James?

The maidservant, carrying Cecil, led the way, followed by Kate holding Violet's hand. The library into which they were shown was thick with burgundy velvet carpet and curtains, and its walls were covered with the wild green meadows of William Morris design. Light skated off the polish of marble busts, mahogany shelves and leather bindings, and glinted in the gilt tooling of the books. There were two deep armchairs and a sofa in front of the fire.

Jacques rose from his seat. 'You're welcome.' He shook Kate's hand, and, hunkering down, he did the same to Violet. 'And you must be Violet. How pretty you are.' The child dropped her head and smiled slightly while looking up at him from under her eyelids.

While Kate was taken aback at the formality of his greeting, she was relieved by his reaction to Violet and her response to him.

The maidservant remained standing in the doorway holding Cecil, her expression of indecisive bewilderment betraying her lack of knowledge of children.

Jacques addressed Violet: 'And who's this?'

'That's my brother. He's nearly one whole year old and he's named Cecil. He can sit up and he can crawl too but he's too young to walk properly.'

'How lucky he is to have a big sister like you.'

Violet shot him an ecstatic smile. 'Please, sir, may we sit down?'

'Most certainly, how could I have forgotten my manners? Perhaps you'll take tea with me?'

'Me too?' Violet's eyes were wide with excitement.

'You especially.'

'You may put Cecil on the floor,' Violet said to the servant. 'Have you any toys?'

'No, miss.' Carefully the maid placed Cecil on the floor at her feet.

Violet looked amused. 'Please bring him up beside us. He likes company. Babies do, you know. Do you even have spoons? Sometimes he plays with spoons.'

'I'll ask the housekeeper, miss.'

As Violet settled on the floor beside Cecil, Kate's heart was thumping: she was both scared and exhilarated, and yet she felt quite incapable of functioning as Jacques looked from Violet to Cecil with an expression she could not fathom.

Jacques was equally unsure of how to handle the situation. Up to yesterday, the life he had clawed back after the devastation of Kate leaving Paris owed all to retreating behind highly disciplined, organised hours and total reliance on the catharsis of painting. From early boyhood he had been used to physical upheaval and lack of stability, and he had learned to use it to creative benefit.

During the unrest that followed the Franco-Prussian war and his involvement in the Commune, he moved to

London where he had held his first exhibition a decade earlier at the Royal Academy. Realising the city's potential as a source of wealthy patrons, he changed his name to James. His paintings of contemporary social events and conversation pieces became as profitable in England as they had been in France. They made him so prosperous that he was the envy of more critically revered painters like Édouard Manet and Edgar Degas.

The maid returned pushing a trolley with triangular sandwiches, sponge cake oozing strawberry jam, tiny scones with a jar of clotted cream, and finger biscuits, as well as linen napkins, china cups, saucers and plates and a silver tea service—an English afternoon tea. In her right hand, she clutched a selection of spoons, which she placed on the floor beside Cecil.

Violet sat in the corner of the couch beside Jacques.

The maidservant addressed Kate. 'Excuse me, madam, Cook wants to know if the children will come to the kitchen?'

Violet's eyes dropped and before Kate had a chance to reply, Jacques said, 'Thank you, Jane, but they will remain here. Please be kind enough to bring a glass of lemonade.' He draped an arm round Violet, 'Do you have lemonade on special occasions?'

'I don't know.' Violet's voice was muted; she was not used to being included in special occasions.

As Kate sipped tea, Violet ate heartily and chatted vigorously, addressing herself to Jacques who listened courteously as she expounded on Hopkins, the nursery, her dislike of porridge, her brother and her cousins. Finished talking and eating, she went to the window. 'May we go out?'

'Certainly,' Jacques replied. 'I was about to suggest it. Perhaps you would allow Thomas to show you the chickens and the puppies and I do believe there are fish in the pond.'

'I'd prefer you to come with me.'

'No. You must go with Thomas and Cook will mind Cecil in the kitchen while I talk to your mother.'

'I won't go without you, I shall stay here.' Her tone bordered on petulance.

As Kate was on the point of insisting, Jacques said, 'Either you go with Thomas or you go to the kitchen. It is your choice.'

Kate willed her daughter not to throw one of her tantrums. To her amazement, Violet looked to Jacques. 'Do I really have to?'

'Yes, you do.' His voice was firm and without irritation but it boded no argument.

'Then I will go with Thomas. To the chickens and the puppies.' She tossed her head. 'I don't like fish.'

Kate and Jacques sat without speaking.

Her glance birdlike, she looked at his hands and tried not to remember the pleasure they'd given her.

He watched her profile and again wished he had painted her.

Each waited for the other to break the pall of silence.

Eventually it was she who spoke. 'So you are now known as James?'

'Yes. Since I've settled in England.'

'So you've left Paris?'

'Yes, except for the occasional visit.' He would not tell her that when he went back he could not bear to retrace the steps they had taken together.

They were not the words either hoped for.

'My change of name and place of abode is not what we need to talk about.'

'It's not. You're right.'

He remembered her habit of taking deep breaths when she was nervous.

She took a particularly deep one. 'I owe you an explanation—hundreds of explanations; I have so much explaining that I don't know where to begin.' Kate kept her voice steady.

'Yes, you do. Begin at the beginning. But before you start I want you to know that in Paris there was nothing you could have told me that would have changed my feelings for you.'

Kate noted his use of the past tense and accepted the past was a place that could not be revisited, although she wondered if love could be salvaged. Even if he ended up hating her, she would tell him everything. 'I didn't tell you the whole truth, but neither did I lie. From the first minute I saw you, even before we were introduced, I think I loved you. And then I loved you too much. More than I thought possible to love anyone.'

Jacques too noted the past tense.

She explained her childhood: her father pretending to be a fighting man in the British Army, and her mother's silent condoning of the image he presented. She told him about Louisa and losing her friendship; her marriage to Isaac, rejection and Catholic guilt, and the circumstances of Captain Palliser; her father's betrayal; the fear of finding herself with child, her refusal to marry; how Violet was a daily reminder not only of the captain, but of the depths to which she had sunk. There was her gratitude to Polly and Gussie for giving her and her children a home. She finished by telling him that the memories of their time together gave her the strength to carry on from day to day. 'I'm glad to have the chance to explain and I hope you accept and believe what I've told you. I adore Cecil. Because he is the child we made out of love.'

Jacques considered he was immune to the foibles of human nature, but Kate's revelations stunned him. No woman should have to go through such a life, especially one that involved masquerading as respectable middle-class. Such a situation would never happen within his family; it wouldn't happen in France either—as a race the French had an inbuilt integrity that he found lacking in the English. But her own father? His instincts cried out to trust her, to enfold her in his arms and keep her with him forever. But his intellect urged caution and he had learned to be wary, to be dubious of trusting his intuition. Her story had the ring of truth. But she had left him and Paris without a word. He stubbed out his cigarette—he had chain-smoked during her recitation. 'Thank you for telling me. I appreciate how difficult it must be for you.' His voice was scrupulously polite.

Just then Violet came tumbling through the doors, her face flushed with happiness, ringlets awry, the red velvet dishevelled and her boots muddy. She was holding a puppy of indeterminate breed. 'Please, please may I have it?'

The mood between Kate and Jacques was broken.

'It's your puppy. Thomas said I have to ask your permission to keep it.' Violet drove home her request.

'The puppies are too small to leave their mother. For the present, they must remain here.'

'Well, then I shall have to come and visit.'

Without a trace of a smile, Jacques said, 'That is a decision that cannot be taken lightly.'

Chapter Sixteen

Arms waving and ringlets bobbing, Violet performed a defiant dance of freedom on the front doorstep. She stopped as Thomas turned in the gate. 'Thomas, Thomas,' she called running up to him. 'Have you brought the puppy?'

Thomas was dedicated to his master and he had brought the function of serving him to a fine art: as well as being a precise carrier-out of orders, he operated as a general factotum. He was skilled at performing a variety of tasks, none of which involved children. He had been instructed to deliver a note to Mrs Newton and to wait for a reply, if requested. That was what he would do. His tone and features were expressionless, as he answered, 'No, Miss Violet. I haven't.'

'Why are you here so?'

'I have a note for Mrs Newton.'

The child held out her hand imperiously. 'That's my mama. I'll give it to her.'

'Better not, miss.' Thomas was glad children were not part of his remit.

'Wait here so,' Violet told him. She dashed down the steps, into the house through the back entrance, up the stairs from the kitchen, along the hall and into the small morning room where her mother and aunt were working on their embroidery frames.

'Mama, Mama. It's Thomas. He has a note about the puppy. And he won't give it to me. You've to come and read it. Now. This minute.'

Despite Kate's anxiety, Violet had turned out to be as good as she and Polly were at keeping secrets. Her daughter didn't mention their visit to Grove End Road, although at every opportunity in her special *sotto voce* whisper she nagged about going back to see the puppy. As Kate felt she was in a limbo of uncertainty and with nothing to report, she hadn't told Polly about Jacques. She spent her days and nights on wondering tenterhooks, unsure when, or indeed if she would hear from or see Jacques again. The advent of Thomas and his note threw her into a dither.

Polly put down her frame and before Kate had a chance to divert Violet, she caught hold of her niece by her two arms. 'What are you talking about? Who is Thomas? What's all this about a puppy dog?' Violet's eyes widened in dismay, she was so devastated at breaking Mama's secret that for once she was caught short for words. 'Answer me. Immediately.' Polly's voice was sharp.

Violet looked to her mother. 'It's nothing, Aunt Polly. I made a mistake, that's all.'

Before Kate could begin to explain, there was a knock at the door. It was Cook, holding a note, and with curiosity etched in every line in her plump bob of a curtsy. Kate opened the envelope and read the contents. 'Thank you. There is no reply. Violet, please go to the nursery.'

'But Mama!'

'Go. Now.'

Polly had returned to her embroidery and was calmly

threading her needle with white silk; she had almost completed the last daisy that bordered the edges of the linen tray cloth.

'I've something to tell you.'

Polly jabbed the needle into the satin stitch petal before looking up, her attitude and expression were not conducive to secret-sharing, and when she spoke her voice was weary. 'What's it this time, Kathleen?'

'The note is from Jacques Tissot.'

Life had numbed Polly to such an extent that she gave no indication of surprise, or exhibited no curiosity as to how or when her sister had met up with Jacques. 'So he's in London.' She executed a meticulous stitch. 'Are you seeing him?'

Her reaction prompted Kate to tell her only what was necessary. 'I don't know; I'm not sure about anything except that he wants to call on Gussie.'

Polly stabbed the needle so hard into the linen that it missed her thimble and drew blood on her forefinger. 'Why?'

'He didn't say.' Kate touched Polly's shoulder gently. 'When I know, I'll tell you. I can't talk about it now. I hope you understand.' Jacques's note said little other than he had arranged to call on her brother-in-law the following evening. The tone of the message was without affection: indeed she wondered why he had even bothered to inform her.

Polly snipped a piece of thread with her small silver scissors. 'Nothing surprises me about you.'

Kate, arms clasped behind her head, lay on her small, creaking bed. Its comforter was shabby and the sheets threadbare; the washstand had seen better days and the jug and bowl, with their improbable pattern of blue roses and pink daffodils, were chipped. Her few clothes hung in the small walnut wardrobe. It was the only place she could call her own and be undisturbed. She had retreated there after Gussie's favourite supper of boiled mutton. She had no wish to be visible until she was summoned to the study, where the meeting was taking place, but in anticipation she had tidied her hair, washed her hands and pinned a brooch at the neckline of her blouse.

Punctual as ever, she heard Jacques arrive at the appointed time. As she settled down to wait, nervously she pleated and re-pleated the navy serge of her skirt, and it was with a heavy and confused heart that a short time later she heard the sounds of his departure.

The next sound was Gussie thumping up the stairs. His footsteps paused briefly outside her door before continuing along the corridor; after that came the muffled anger of his raised voice, followed by a long spate of silence. As she had given up hope of hearing what had taken place between the two men, and was on the point of undressing for bed, the door of Polly's room banged closed. Gussie's footsteps came back along the corridor. This time they paused. He knocked on her door. 'I want to see you in my study now.'

Kate could not even begin to imagine what had taken place between Jacques and Gussie or why Gussie was summoning her at this late hour. She presumed it boded no good. When she entered the small study, with its heavy mahogany furniture, Gussie was pacing up and down. His face was flushed and there was anger in his every stride and in his voice. 'I forbid you to have further contact with that Frenchman.'

Gussie had disliked Jacques on sight. His animosity was in no way alleviated by the several glasses of vintage sherry with which he had fortified himself prior to the meeting; nor by Jacques's graciousness: thanking him for caring for Mrs Newton and his son; as well as stating his wish to put matters right.

'You'll reimburse my expenses?' Gussie had asked. His face was redder than usual and the blue of his eyes paling with intensity. After receiving Jacques's note, on making some discreet and not so discreet enquires, he had been surprised by both the painter's wealth and social stature.

'Naturally, let me have your account. I shall also be making a yearly payment to Mrs Newton for our son's education and upkeep. Now, I would like to talk to her.' The timbre of Jacques's voice was even.

'My sister-in-law has no wish to see you. She asked me to tell you.'

'As you wish.'

If Gussie had hoped to spark a reaction from his visitor, he was disappointed. Realising he was out-manoeuvred by civility, he had rung for Monsieur Tissot to be shown out. In thoroughly bad form he had adjourned to his wife's room with a list of complaints about her running of the household. He concluded by forcing himself on her, trying to imagine it was Kathleen lying passive and frightened.

'Do you understand?' Gussie demanded of the composed woman in front of him. 'If you insist on seeing him again, you will leave here. Like that captain of yours, your Frenchman's intentions are dishonourable.'

She inclined her head. While she did not believe what Gussie said about Jacques, she did not know what else to believe.

★

A few days later, Thomas, with strict instructions from his master on the importance of secrecy, delivered another note to Hill Road.

Shortly afterwards Kate slipped out, unobserved, to walk the short distance to Grove End Road. She picked her way disconsolately through the least of the mud in her second-best pair of boots. Jacques's note, asking her to call, as there was an important matter he wished to discuss in person, was too polite to nurture expectation. But she was returning to Grove End Road in the bleak hope of explaining, trying to make him understand her reasons for being less than open with him in Paris.

Jacques received her in the library. Again he shook hands formally—he was becoming more English than the English themselves—and instead of sitting down, they stood facing each other in front of the fireplace. The warmth from the fire was comforting through the serge of Kate's skirt; her heart was beating wildly, but she would not drop her guard or let her feelings show. The Jacques she had known in Paris had been warm and affectionate; she did not know how to handle this cool, aloof and unemotional James.

If only she could have known—Jacques's stance and attitude were a protective veneer. Having passed confused and largely sleepless nights ruminating over Kate's story, with the facts going forwards and backwards in his mind, he was exhausted. He had parsed, analysed and tried to understand Kate's actions, but he had not been able to reach a satisfactory answer. He still didn't know what to think or do.

He stood with legs spread, shoulders back and hands folded across his chest. She had been everything to him, as he had believed he was to her. Any hopes he had begun to entertain for a reconciliation were dashed at her refusal to see him when he had visited her brother-in-law. But he kept remembering Paris and the way she had lain across his chest and run the palm of her hand over his face, whispering of the connection between souls that are fated to meet and collide and enrapture one another forever.

He justified this meeting by persuading himself of the necessity of telling her personally of the financial arrangements he was putting in place for their son, and the annual income that would guarantee her independence. But quite simply he had wanted to see her again. Now that she was here, he did not know how or where to begin, and, remembering her lack of interest in money, he worried about her reaction to his bequest.

In the end the decision was taken from him. Kate could no longer stand the silence. She was remembering her unwavering certainty that she and Jacques would meet again. They had met but had not reunited. Everything had gone horribly wrong. She felt as if they had been deserted by the gods. Perhaps those same gods could do with a little human intervention? She had nothing left to lose by speaking out.

With parched, hard-breathing mouth and shaking limbs, she said, 'I want you to know that leaving you was the hardest thing I ever did.' She clamped her lips shut and willed her legs to steady. It was said. If she had not spoken then, she would have turned and run from Jacques and his beautiful house forever. In her shabby skirt, worn boots and proud demeanour, she stood strong and powerful.

'And yet you did?'

'I had no choice. Gussie sent an emissary to accompany us back to London with strict instructions that we had to leave immediately.'

Having met her brother-in-law, Jacques did not doubt her explanation of the situation. 'But you left without a goodbye.' His expression had softened but the hurt was evident in his voice.

'No. I did not, of course, I didn't. I wrote you a note.' Her voice was hesitant as she searched to remember the details. 'And I gave that footman the last of my francs to deliver it, you remember the unhelpful one?'

Relief washed over Jacques at her explanation. When Kate had failed to turn up at their rendezvous that noon, he had called to the hotel only to be told by the concierge that the ladies in the company of a gentleman had departed for England. *Non*, there was no message. He had gone through the ensuing days and nights, weeks and months in a blur of disbelief.

'I cannot believe you thought me capable of that.' Kate's hurt made her the aggrieved one.

Certain moments in life are in another tense: they are going to become. Jacques did not know how to reply or how to finish with recriminations and reproach, but for them to move beyond this impasse he knew he had to. During the dark hours of recent nights, despite his insistence to himself of the contrary, he knew he was as enraptured with Kate as he had been when they first met; he was as enchanted by her personality, sense of pride and beauty as he was by the dichotomy of her Catholic religion, divorce and motherhood—his fallen angel. 'I didn't know what to think. If you had trusted me, perhaps, all this could have been prevented.'

'When I knew I could trust you, it was too late.'

He threw caution to the winds. 'I still love you; I've never stopped loving you. What's the point in pretending otherwise?'

'And I've always loved you too.' She spoke the words solemnly but her heart was singing.

He took a hold of her hand and looked deep into her eyes. 'What do you want to do, Kate? Suppose your decision concerned only you, what would you do?'

'Never leave you.' The end of the past and the shape of their future lay in her words, but once they were out she feared she had been too forward.

He bent to kiss her hand. 'Before moving in here, *ma petite à moi*, would you object to returning to Hill Road to collect our children and your belongings?'

'I'm happy for you,' Polly whispered, her heart breaking. Kathleen's happiness was another nail in the coffin of her own dreams. Pierre had wooed her with soft eyes and words of love, and for the first time in her life she had felt beautiful and desired. 'But do get married. It can be arranged and it'll stop any talk.'

Kate laughed gaily. Never again would she have to eat boiled mutton and onion sauce. 'Everyone must be talked out about me. There's nothing more to say.'

'Oh, they'll find plenty,' Polly assured. She would never have reason to look as radiant as her sister but then she did not have her courage to fly in the face of accepted social convention and to believe in her right to happiness.

'I'm ahead of my time,' Kate frequently said, and Polly would smile rather than contradict her. There was no point, as Kathleen refused to accept that women were not, or would never be equal to men. Polly believed that pigs would fly before women had control of their lives, or choice of husband.

'Don't you remember, I tried marriage once and didn't like it?' Kate threw back her head and laughed and laughed, grasping at her sister for support until, despite herself, Polly joined in.

Chapter Seventeen

When Kate moved in with Jacques she knew with the certainty borne of years of insecurity that she had finally come home, to the man she adored and who adored her. She loved the cosy grandeur of the house with its areas of luscious colourings and quiet places, and she enjoyed discovering the nooks and crannies of the grounds—the plots for growing vegetables, orchards, formal rose garden, lawns and shrubberies. Each morning and night she thanked her Catholic God as well as the Hindi gods and goddesses for reuniting her and Jacques.

Within a short space of time the timbre of their life was established. Kate spent endless hours watching Jacques as he worked; Violet, clasping the puppy, now named Lucky, was in and out of the studio, and Cecil, constantly good-humoured, pottered around with bundles of paint brushes.

The children had to be with them as Jacques's servants had not been hired to care for children. Violet, considering Thomas to be the keeper of the puppy, demented him with admiration, and he went to considerable lengths to avoid her. The cook-housekeeper, Charlotte Tong, a thin woman with a bun of steel hair and an enveloping white apron, liaised with Thomas about the gardens and outside work. Between herself and Jane Arthur, the other female servant, and occasional staff hired short-term, she ran an efficient household. But the strain of a new mistress, albeit a non-interfering one, and two, sometimes four children, was beginning to tell. She was reluctant to mention the matter to the master, who was a new man since the arrival of Mrs Newton.

On a particularly sunny June afternoon, Jacques stood back from his easel, wiped his brush on a rag, draped a cloth over work in progress, removed his paint-splattered smock and came over to where Kate was sitting. He held out his hands, drew her to her feet. 'Come, *ma chérie*. It's too wonderful a day to waste inside. Let's walk in the garden.' He scooped Cecil into his arms and gave him a hug, and when he saw the bleak look on Violet's face he bent down and gave her a resounding kiss.

'Poor child,' he whispered to Kate. 'We mustn't ever let her feel left out.'

'We won't.' Kate had developed a new love and feeling for the little girl who was thriving in the all-pervasive atmosphere of affection. She gave in to the spontaneous urge to gather her daughter to her, to hug and snuggle her face into her hair. The child responded a hundredfold by clasping plump little arms round Kate's neck and showering her with kisses before drawing back to whisper: 'Mama, may I ask you something?'

'Yes, sweetheart, of course you may.'

'Please can Uncle Jacques be my papa?'

Kate's breath caught in her throat as she battled to find an appropriate answer, but Jacques was not in the least perturbed. If anything, he appeared mightily pleased, as bowing from the waist he placed her two tiny palms in his slender hands. 'Yes, *ma chérie*, you most certainly may, and I am deeply honoured that you consider me for the very important role of papa—to you, the prettiest girl in the world!' The child's ecstatic smile said all.

Jacques threw himself into a chair, covered his face with his hands and groaned. 'No. I've had it. I'm exhausted. No more games for me today, or ever.' He had joined in a particularly robust session of hide'n'seek, a game the children never tired of playing. He tickled Violet who had jumped up on his lap. 'Go away, go and annoy your mother.'

He was happier than he ever thought possible: delighting in the constancy of Kate's presence, savouring the passion of their lovemaking, the intimacy of their unruffled domesticity, and the quiet hours spent in his studio were resulting in a prodigious output of paintings. On the few occasions when, at her urging, he visited the Athenaeum Club, it suited him that none of the members mentioned his private life; he knew from experience that time provided the solution for many a problem.

'No,' said Kate laughing. 'I refuse ever again to be annoyed.' She came to sit on the arm of Jacques's chair and ran her fingers through his hair. She too was happy beyond her wildest dreams, and not a day went by that she did not savour the joy of loving and being loved. On her first visit to Jacques's Parisian home she had wondered if it were possible to live one's life in true honesty and goodness. Now she knew it was. Jacques was that rare breed of man, thoroughly good and honest, and whenever the traitorous thought that she had little freedom or choice reared its head, she dismissed it instantly. 'How about you and I having a quiet cup of afternoon tea while the girls visit the fish.'

'What a splendid idea.'

'I don't want to see the fish.' Predictably that was Violet who still pestered Thomas, but whose feelings for her new papa bordered on adoration.

'Come on,' said Isabel. 'Otherwise we'll have to be minded in the kitchen, won't we, Aunt Kate?'

'You most certainly will,' Jacques answered.

As the girls exited, giggling and pushing and shoving at each other, Jane entered with a card on a silver salver. It was Johnny and Effie Millais calling. Since Kate and the children had moved into Grove End Road, Jacques had received few callers, and he was delighted to welcome his friends. Kate had enjoyed Johnny's company briefly in Paris and admitted to a curiosity about meeting his wife, whose life was even more colourful than her own.

'The house is beautiful, isn't it?' said Mrs Millais in her forthright way. She was small, dark and intense. 'It's neither French nor English—probably a combination of the best of both countries, don't you think?'

Kate agreed. The women had taken to each other immediately. 'Would you like to see a little more? The grounds are quite spectacular. And we could walk and talk.'

By then Mrs Millais had picked up on Kate's air of proprietorship and knew for certain that the gossip circulating throughout London was correct. She thought her either extremely brave or utterly foolhardy to be so open about her liaison.

When the women had left, Millais's question to Jacques was blunt. 'Is Mrs Newton actually living here?'

If Jacques was perturbed, he did not show it. 'Yes, she and our son and her daughter have moved in.'

Millais's dark eyes flashed. 'I didn't know you had a son.'

'Neither did I.' Jacques's delight was obvious in his broad smile.

'It's not done, you know, in proper society.'

'What's not done?'

'Having your mistress live with you.'

'Mrs Newton is much more than my mistress. She is the love of my life and the mother of my son and my Muse. You must know that. I was devastated when she left Paris.'

'I don't doubt your fondness for her but if you wish to remain part of London society you should set her up separately.'

Jacques shrugged. 'Your solution sounds rather ridiculous, so English—time-consuming and unnecessarily expensive.' He was laughing inwardly: he knew he had a reputation towards parsimony as he refused to spend lavishly on outside entertainment, although his domestic lifestyle was known to be so extravagant that it received considerable newspaper and magazine coverage both in France and England.

Ridiculous as the published article was, it was quite a coup to have Edmond de Goncourt, one of the most influential French critics, come all the way to London to write of footmen polishing leaves and champagne being served night and day in the Tissot household. Jacques knew his continuing success was the envy of his fellow-artists, many of whom in the changing times were struggling to eke out a living. Still as commercial as he was creative, he was pleased with any publicity that furthered sales of his paintings, though woe betided anyone who tried to intrude into his private life.

'If you continue with such an arrangement, it will be difficult for you to be accepted in polite circles, and Mrs

Newton certainly won't. You must look to yourself.' Thanks to his wife's insistence that he paint in a current, broader, more commercial technique than in the pre-Raphaelite style he favoured, Millais too was enjoying financial success. He had called as a friend to persuade Jacques not to turn his back on society. Having been the butt of whispering speculation herself, Effie was sensitive to the cruelty of the social scene.

Jacques's voice was polite. 'I understand your wife is not permitted to be in the same company as the Queen.'

He was seeing another side to his friend, who was blasé in ignoring the basis of his own marriage—he had fallen in love with Effie while she was married to John Ruskin, who was his patron. It was a strange situation and became the talk of London. Ruskin not only encouraged his wife to model for Millais but he had blatantly left them alone and unchaperoned, giving them every opportunity to commit adultery. But forewarned of Ruskin's Machiavellian scheme to cover up his own inadequacies as a husband, and to hide his predilection for pre-pubescent girls, Effie had out-manoeuvred him by being the one to seek an annulment.

And as if that was not enough of a scandal, there was the very public business of her having to submit to a gynaecological examination to prove she was still a virgin after five years of marriage. Millais and she had married the following year and produced eight children in quick succession, the two younger born when, rumour had it, she was well past childbearing age. In the circumstances, Jacques considered Johnny was hardly competent to lecture him on socially acceptable bahaviour.

'I'm more than aware that my wife and I are socially

restricted.' Johnny was utterly sincere. 'My friend, I beg of you do not make my mistakes.'

'Mrs Newton and I are not making mistakes. We can live without society.'

They were so blissfully engrossed in each other that they had no need of society. But Jacques's *raison d'être* was Kate's happiness and he knew how much she had enjoyed the social occasions they attended in Paris. He wanted her on his arm at London's literary and artistic soirées, receptions, theatrical first nights and parties. He was outraged at the stringent hypocrisy of the Herveys' Victorian morals, which had excluded her from having a social life, although after meeting Gussie he understood her lack of enthusiasm for being on the same guest lists as her sister and brother-in-law.

'I've an invitation from Lady Wilde, with a note wondering if the rumours are true,' said Jacques.

They were wandering slowly among the drowsy murmuring foliage, with him stopping to examine the buds of a white lilac, to check the drifting blossoms of a mauve wisteria, or to finger the scented leaves of the eucalyptus.

'What rumours?' Kate laughed, adjusting her shawl across her shoulders.

'I understand we're the subject of innumerable conversations. Would you be interested in giving the gossips some fresh ammunition?'

Kate was in no hurry to break the magic of their existence by facing the world, and yet she too remembered how good socialising with Jacques had been in Paris. She looked at him mischievously. 'Why not?'

As Jacques listened to the echo of the knocker, he wondered on this occasion which member of the Wilde family would be taking on the role of door-opening servant.

Invitations for the tea parties hosted by Lady Wilde were eagerly sought. Despite the gatherings being idiosyncratic and quite preposterous in their lack of attention to accepted forms of entertaining, even among the artistic set, she and her sons, Willie and Oscar, had cultivated an air of grandeur as well as thriving on their reputations as picturesque characters. Everyone knew they were as poor as church mice, and ran their rented house in the fashionable district of Chelsea without the services of a footman, or even, rumour had it, a housekeeper or maidservants. Guests could be announced by either their hostess or one of her sons.

That afternoon Lady Wilde was doing the honours. She flung open the door with a flourish. 'My dear boy, how wonderful to see you.' After a cursory glance, she ignored Kate, and drawing Jacques into the darkened hallway she reached up on her tippy-toes and with dangling strings of beads and pendants she kissed him soundly on both cheeks. He stood immobile, careful not to make a sudden movement: as usual she looked as though the slightest breath could disassemble her. Her black wig was topped with an imposing headdress of russet coloured brocade decorated with floats of netting and a large crimson rose; her gown in red and black was flounced in the style of the 1860s, and its bodice was too tight for her corpulent frame.

Lady Wilde favoured the gloam as she was not eager to exhibit either her wrinkles or her lack of staff. During the winter months the curtains were drawn at three o'clock each afternoon, the gas jets covered with red shades, and too few stubs of candles flickered in corners. She dismissed the untidiness of the house as romantic and saw poetry in its old staircases, twisting corridors and dim corners. Being a *grande dame* who craved a literary life, she could be depended on for flashes of rhetoric. She treated all her guests with respectful adulation, her assumption being that as they were in attendance, they were either already famous or on the point of becoming so.

When Jacques introduced Kate, Lady Wilde ooh'd and ah'd and widened her eyes as she ushered them into the small parlour, or salon as she preferred to call it. Kate, wearing a simple gown of sapphire blue with ropes of pearls at her throat, was looking particularly fetching. She stood statuesquely by Jacques with her elbow securely nestled in his palm. Everyone present knew Jacques and everyone presumed this had to be the Irish Catholic divorcee who had captured his heart, and who it was rumoured was the dominating force in his life.

Lady Wilde, clapping her hands for attention, announced as she always did, 'And this is Jacques Tissot, the artist from Paris.' She liked to give the impression that he had crossed the Channel specifically for her party. She ignored the fact that since coming to live in London he had changed his name to James. Despite her eccentricity Jacques liked her enormously. 'And this is,' and here Lady Wilde paused to get full effect from her announcement, 'this is Mrs Newton.' Now that their presumption was confirmed, a frisson of jealousy ran through the guests. How did Lady Wilde do it? How could she inveigle two of the most talked about and reclusive people in London to her soirée?

What an excitement. So this was the notorious Mrs Newton. She was even more beautiful than rumoured, and without an iota of shame. It was well known she already had a daughter from an affair with a captain in the Bengal Rifles, who had been so infatuated that on her wedding night he had whisked her from her bridegroom's arms. It was whispered that not only had she another child by Monsieur Tissot, but she and her children were living openly with him in the opulent luxury of his St John's Wood mansion.

And everyone knew how Tissot and Wilde had locked verbal horns. The guests stood around in squashed huddles, waiting for what had to happen, peering at each other in the dim light and knowing better than to drink the tea on offer.

Jacques considered circulating among and meeting the right people to be a necessary part of his career. He had firsthand proof of the benefits it reaped in the form of contacts, commissions and contracts. In the past, he had frequently found the whole process of ultra-graciousness and the extravagant flattery of socialising to be tedious. On many an occasion he would have preferred to remain in his studio painting. Having Kate by his side changed all that.

She had a way of raising her eyebrows that highlighted the dancing humour in her eyes. She found fun in the most ludicrous of situations, and had a healthy disrespect for what she termed 'nonsense', laughing her way around the pretentious preoccupation of the middle-classes with their fish cutlery and modern stemware.

Lady Wilde had come to London from Dublin for a few months to act as hostess, with the aim of furthering

Willie's career in journalism. She was aware of Oscar's newsworthiness and frequently inveigled him down from Oxford. Mother and her two sons were a potent trinity for publicity. She sailed purposefully among her guests, like a swelling canvas, as her son moved towards Jacques and Kate.

A passage of people cleared the way for Oscar. Everyone was intent on hearing the exchange between the two men. A few weeks previously Mr Wilde had announced in a stentorian voice that he considered the subjects of Monsieur Tissot's paintings 'over-dressed, common-looking people'.

Murmuring just loudly enough to be heard, Jacques had retaliated, '*Dieu merci*, I've always believed that even the uninformed are entitled to their opinions.' The precision of his remark in perfect, if accented English, had delighted the guests, grown in the recounting, and incurred Wilde's wrath. However, John Ruskin's comment a few days later dismissing Tissot's work as 'mere painted photographs of vulgar society' was more serious, as his every utterance carried critical weight. Nobody took into account or even wondered if Johnny and Jacques's friendship may have contributed to the scathing remarks. Yet, everyone purported to know of the scandal surrounding Ruskin's marriage to the current Mrs Millais.

For all the entertainment he provided, Oscar Wilde, with his flowing hair, ruffled shirts and cultivated air of nonchalance, could be tiresome with his posing and smart ironic one-liners. But that afternoon there was grudging admiration in his greeting. Like his mother, he had an uncanny knack of being able to predict and latch onto up-and-coming celebrities. Ignoring Kate, he held out his hand to Jacques. 'Monsieur Tissot. Congratulations are in order, I believe.'

Jacques disregarded his blandishment. 'Kate, allow me to introduce you to Mr Oscar Wilde. Mr Wilde, Mrs Newton.'

Oscar blinked rapidly before taking Kate's proffered hand, while Jacques's grip on her elbow tightened. He wondered what new devilment, as Wilde would say, was he up to.

'Aren't you interested to know why I'm offering you my congratulations?' Oscar Wilde's voice was raised in incredulity. He thrived on acknowledgement and praise and was not used to rebuff, no matter how politely executed.

Despite the Wilde and Ruskin comments, it was common knowledge in both artistic and social circles that Monsieur Tissot was riding high on the crest of several lucrative commissions, and his paintings were being lauded in some of London's most powerful drawing rooms. Aware of the positive effects of such rumblings, Jacques kept his voice light and tinged with amusement. 'No doubt you will not only inform me but also your mother's guests.'

'I understand Charles has been singing your praises around London.'

Jacques was astounded. Charles—typical of Mr Wilde to use his first name—that had to be Sir Charles Halle, founder of the Halle Orchestra. He was unlikely to be a friend of the Wilde family, so this was indeed a compliment. Jacques had recently completed a work depicting a recital by Halle's wife Madame Neruda. *The Hush* was a painting of which he was inordinately proud. He inclined his head in gracious acknowledgement and knew he had won a rather precarious victory.

Chapter Eighteen

W e should take on extra indoor staff. Charlotte and Jane cannot be expected to cope long-term without more help.' Jacques did not subscribe to the English habit of addressing servants by their surname.

'Violet and Cecil aren't that much trouble.' Kate protested with a moue of disagreement.

'I know. But Lily spends more time here than in her own home and Isabel has taken to visiting too.'

'The household always seems to run so smoothly.' Anxiously Kate asked, 'Has Charlotte said something?'

'No. Nothing like that.' Jacques slipped his arm around Kate's shoulders. '*Au contraire*, she is quite enchanted to be presiding over a family household. But she and Jane have to be overworked.' He used his final strand of persuasion. 'And you need a lady's maid.'

Her reaction was swift and definite. 'No. I don't. I haven't had a personal servant since I was a child in India and I certainly don't want one now. I manage well.'

'Wouldn't you like someone to dress your hair and keep your clothes in order?'

'I'd hate it,' said Kate firmly. 'I like doing my own hair and I don't have a wardrobe as such.'

'That's something we might rectify.' Seeing Kate's look

of defiance, he quickly added, 'Nothing wrong with your clothes but it would be fun and my pleasure to buy you some of this season's outfits.' Jacques loved dressing Kate in jewel colours but he also admired her independence, her reluctance to spend the personal allowance he had set up for her, her generosity of spirit and habit of buying thoughtful gifts for family, friends and servants alike. He returned to the subject of staff. 'An advertisement in the paper is probably the best method—unless you have other preferences?'

Kate was reluctant to take even the tiniest step that would change their routine, which happened each day with happy spontaneity. She sidestepped Jacques's regular suggestion that they consider marriage, by thanking him graciously, kissing him soundly and refusing so prettily. Much as she would prefer not to upset their existing arrangements, she realised that the smooth running of the household without additional staff was not a long-term option. Jacques required uninterrupted hours to paint; they needed exclusive time together and the children would benefit from some form of structured control. 'Let's look in *The Times* first, shall we? It will give us an idea.' She giggled. 'I've never hired a servant.'

'Well, don't you think it's about time you did? And if the newspapers don't work out, we can go to one of the servant registries.'

Her heart filled like a pool. When she closed her eyes she imagined her insides overflowing with happiness. Sometimes she thought she would burst with love; other times it all seemed too much.

The Times had several pages of both seeking and wanted advertisements.

'A good cook, middle-aged person, understanding the duties of the kitchen,' etc., 'and of course good references.' Too earnestly boring.

'A respectable young person looking for an engagement as a lady's maid, excellent needlewoman, hairdresser,' etc. More good references. Kate shuddered, she could see herself coiffed to within an inch of her life.

'A companion or nursery governess.' Another needlewoman, but with a passion for travel and good references. No.

Kate's eye was drawn to: 'A lady's maid understands her duties, good character, previous kitchen and general experience.' The address was DO, 15 Post Office, Charing Cross. That was promising; she favoured employing someone with a range of experience. Professional as Jacques's servants were, they were limited by their very expertise.

When she went to ask Jacques's opinion on the advertisement, he and Cecil were asleep, locked into each other on the couch. She stood for a moment enjoying the perfection of the picture and decided against disturbing them. Going to the morning room, she spread her skirts on either side of the chair, and sitting at her desk, feeling deliciously sensible and delightfully in control, she answered the advertisement, stipulating that references were required.

The young woman smoothed her dress over her hips, tucked a stray strand of hair behind her ear and clutched at her purse more tightly: the house and grounds were much bigger and looked grander than she had anticipated. But she would cope. Placing the advertisement in a newspaper had cost her 1d, but she considered it money well spent, as she had received more than half a dozen replies. This was the best address; she liked the wording of the letter and considered the position could offer her a chance to better herself. For a servant she was ambitious.

The time was long past to leave her present employment. Her mistress claimed to be too poorly to do other than spend her days lying on the chaise longue. The master, when he was at home, which was seldom, had started to behave as though she were his personal property. On the previous Sunday night he had tried to gain entrance to her room. She knew only too well the fate of servants so fancied, and was not about to become one of the number of such girls who walked the streets of London.

She took the three well-scrubbed steps down to the back door. The kitchen was a hub of warmth and redolent of the intense flavours of preparation, confirming that this indeed was a household of full and plenty. After a good half an hour of interview, the housekeeper led the way up the back stairs to the morning room. The light from the window played on the desk and cast a glow around Kate. 'It's the new help, ma'am. You asked to see her.'

With a thank you and a smile, Kate dismissed Charlotte, and, half-turning, addressed the young girl. 'Please wait. I'll be with you in a moment.' She had almost finished a letter to Freddie, which she wanted posted that afternoon. She had written several paragraphs on the introduction of street lighting to London—the newspapers were full of it—as well as describing Jacques and their life together. These days she had an abundance of happy personal news to share with him.

Finally Kate lay down her pen and folded the sheets of writing paper before tucking them into an envelope. Only then did she turn fully around. For a moment she thought she must be dreaming. She had often wondered what had happened to Dolly, knowing that being a lone servant in a house where a death under suspicious circumstances had occurred did not make for a good reference, and without one London was no place for a maidservant looking for decent employment.

Dolly's face stretched in a wide smile of delight. Miss Kate had been the kindest of all of Miss Carmody's young ladies, and she still had the linen handkerchief edged with lace that she had pressed into her palm the morning she left the school. She often thought of her and envied her married, far away in India. Try as she might, on seeing her again in this beautiful house, she was unable to compose herself into an expressionless, emotionless servant mien.

It was not necessary; Kate came across the small room, arms outstretched. 'It is really you, Dolly, looking for the position here?'

Dolly nodded.

Impulsively Kate caught hold of her arms. 'I'm so glad. You've obviously succeeded in gaining our housekeeper's approval and now, of course, you have mine. You have references?'

Dolly hung her head. When the word 'reference' had not been mentioned during her interview, she was sure she had got away without one. 'No. I don't.'

Dolly's luck, which had held out during the long months while Miss Carmody was in India, had run out on the morning after her return. Her mistress had been upset to the point of tears at news of the closure of her school.

Dolly was full of fear for her own future as she climbed the stairs with a breakfast tray laid with a cloth of crisp linen and the best china, holding a bowl of steaming porridge and a pot of tea. Calling a soft 'good morning' she placed the tray on a chest of drawers and went to draw the curtains, but something about the figure in the bed stopped her.

On discovering the body, cold and dead, initially she was rooted to the spot, although she recovered enough wit to make the sign of the cross on Miss Carmody's forehead, to close her eyes and to open the window so that her soul could begin its journey heavenwards. When she tried to think of what she should do next her mind went blank. She stood clasping and unclasping her hands, muttering Hail Marys. Through the mists of her panic she decided there was nobody she could turn to except Mr Wilberforce, the fat man with the tall hat from the bank who had allowed her to stay on in the house in return for keeping it aired and clean.

First she tidied the room, determined to leave everything right. It was while she was straightening out the comforter on the bed that she noticed the small glass bottle on the bedside locker. The writing on the label read 'Laud…' and a few more letters blurred beyond recognition. She put the bottle into the pocket of her apron, picked up the tray, closed the door firmly behind her and went downstairs where she slowly drank Miss Carmody's tea, cold now, but still with a power to course through her body.

She ran all the way to Mr Wilberforce's bank. After listening to her breathless story, he rang for a messenger to take a note to the metropolitan police station on the corner of Cromwell Road. On hearing the word 'police', Dolly's heart started thumping. In Dublin she and her family had known too much about the enforcers of law.

Seeing her distress, Mr Wilberforce was all kindness. 'Don't worry. All you have to do is tell the constable exactly what you've told me. Now be a good girl, go back to the house, wait for him and I shall call as soon as I can leave here.'

Dolly did go back to Elmwood, but only to pack her belongings. She was not going to wait around for anyone from the metropolitan police.

'What did you do then?' Kate asked.

'I got a bed in a hostel. After a few days, I got my present position as a parlour maid.'

'How did you manage that without references?'

Dolly hung her head again. 'I told madam I had been set upon and that my previous employers had gone to India.'

Kate smiled in appreciation of the innovation. Hard as her life had been she was protected by family and class. Dolly had been alone and forced to survive by her wits. 'Surely if you've been in the same employment for that length of time you're due a reference?'

'I may be due one but I shan't get it.'

Dolly had no choice but to explain her situation apropos of her present master, but she did not expect Miss Kate's reaction and burst of laughter. 'Men, they're the death of us. When can you start?'

'I'll have to serve out my notice.'

'Nonsense.' Since moving in with Jacques there was a happy decisiveness about Kate. She had developed the ability of decision-making by circumventing problems and getting to the solution. She waved a dismissive hand. 'You shouldn't have to face that man again. I shall send Thomas with a note explaining that you're taking up employment here immediately and he can fetch your things.'

The idea of having someone from her past was an unexpected bonus for Kate.

Dolly still carried that aura of not quite belonging, but during her stewardship of Elmwood she had developed a new competence and maturity. Left to her own devices, with just the occasional visit from Mr Wilberforce from the bank, she had drawn up a programme of household duties that would put to shame the most experienced and diligent of housekeepers in the grandest and most elegant mansions of the land. On Saturday evenings she traversed each room and, using a wooden framed slate and pencil, she wrote down the jobs to be carried out during the following week, her writing a personalised mixture of marks, pidgin English and Gaelic.

Each morning, no matter what the weather, she opened the windows for half an hour, the length of time it took to bake a loaf of bread and eat a bowl of porridge. She had developed a taste for tea from sampling the leavings from upstairs, and occasionally, as a special treat, she allowed herself a teaspoon of leaves from Miss Carmody's special tea caddy. After the first strong brew of the day, she harvested the leaves and dried them out on the kitchen windowsill for further use.

After breakfast she consulted the slate propped up on the dresser and tackled the jobs listed for that morning, which brought her to dinner time, when she ate slices of bread with a scraping of dripping. In the afternoons it was her habit to take what she called a 'learning walk'. Her favourite place was the South Kensington Museum with its ornaments from all over the world. Twice she treated herself to tea and a finger of shortbread in the Centre Refreshment Room, gazing in wonderment at the richness of the stained glass windows. She allocated the evenings to reading and writing—learning, as she called it.

'Come. I want you to meet your new master.' Laughingly, Kate added, 'Who I can assure you bears no resemblance to your previous one.'

Within a few hours, Dolly was settled into the household, with an annual wage of twelve guineas, an allowance for two gowns, a cape and four aprons and caps. The only sour note to her hiring was Thomas's reaction; he let her know that he was far from pleased at having to journey all the way to Charing Cross to collect a maidservant's belongings.

'Please, Violet. Tell me. I don't know it.' Lily's elbows were on the table, her chin resting in the heels of her palms.

'Well you should. And if you don't you'll have to learn.' Violet was competitive and held onto her every achievement.

'Will you help me, Isabel?'

'No, I won't. I've to read the whole of this page.'

'But how can I learn if I don't know?' wailed Lily.

Dolly came on the girls battling with headline copies and readers. Violet was chewing a pencil as she contemplated the loops of 'l's and 'f's; Isabel reading with little grunts, her plump finger with its non-too-clean nail picking out each word while Lily, her small freckled face scrunched in misery, pointed to a word on her page.

Dolly had never lost her appetite for learning. The

children at Grove End Road did not know on which side their bread was buttered. She wondered about her brothers and sisters, none of whom she had seen or heard from for years. She removed a few dead leaves from a slender-shaped vase holding heavy-headed blooms of blue hydrangea.

'That's nice,' complimented Isabel. 'Aunt Kate says it's in our nature to love flowers.'

Miss Kate liked the blue hydrangea, but they didn't last long in water and this was probably the final cutting. She must ask one of the gardeners to clip the best of the blooms, remove the leaves and hang them up to dry in the back porch. The petals would be papery but they would retain a faint bluish colour, even perhaps tinged with grey, which no doubt would have Miss Kate in raptures. Dolly fed from the happiness of her mistress.

'What does "in nature" mean about flowers?' Lily pursued.

'She's supposed to be doing her reading. Not talking about flowers.'

Miss Violet was a right telltale tattle.

'I can't. I don't know the words.'

'Allow me.' Dolly leant over the child. 'The cat sat on the mat.' She read the words fluently before supervising the dragging movement of Lily's finger under each word, which the child repeated slowly and painfully.

'Dolly, could you do this "f" properly?'

'No. But I'll show you.' Carefully Dolly guided Violet's hand and pencil along the slate, holding steady the curls of the letter. 'Now try it on your own.'

'I can't. My hand wobbles.'

As Dolly was repeating the process, Jacques entered the room. She straightened up, wondering at his reaction to this overstepping of her position. So far, as a master, he was proving himself to be almost too good to be true.

'Look, Uncle Jacques. Dolly is helping me with the headline. She helped me do the "f".'

Dolly need not have worried. Jacques was a firm believer in education. It was his idea to set the girls daily reading and writing tasks, and he planned to introduce sums within the next few months. The children would have to attend school soon enough and he wanted them to have the advantage of a good grounding in the basics. He was delighted to discover Dolly had an unexpected amount of education.

'Well done,' he praised Violet. 'And how was your reading today, Lily?'

'Not good but Dolly helped. Reading and writing are hard.'

'As are the best things in this life. Well done, Isabel, you're coming along nicely. And that, ladies, is enough for today. Put your books and slates into the cupboard and you are excused.' He turned to Dolly and courteously asked, 'Do you have a moment?'

After the girls had scampered off, he motioned her to sit opposite him. She did so, wiping at the back of her skirt, sitting centre chair and trying not to fidget. She was amazed at the civility of the household.

'Are you both a reader and a writer?' he asked.

'Yes, sir. I suppose I am.'

Jacques was curious. 'Did you attend school in Ireland?'

Dolly laughed at the idea of the likes of her having lessons in a school. 'No, sir. I taught myself while Miss Kate was in India.' As soon as they had left her lips, Dolly wished she could swallow back the words, particularly 'India'. The little she knew about Miss Kate's time there was from snatches of loose talk among the servants, which never had a chance to develop, as at the first sign of gossip Charlotte muttering about 'idle minds' found a chore for the gossip-monger. But Mr Jacques did not appear to notice her gaffe.

'I see,' he said. 'Well done.' He clasped his hands as though he was about to break into a clapping session.

Jacques's wish to paint Kate was fulfilled and he never tired of painting her. He painted her indoors and outdoors, in this gown and that gown, standing, seated, resting and active. During a particularly balmy spell of June weather, he had a specific idea for a portrait of Kate and Cecil. He wanted them dressed in white, in reclining positions by the pond.

Kate laughed at his optimism. 'But, Jacques, you know Cecil is unable to stay still for a minute.'

When Jacques planned a painting, he would not be diverted by the minor inconvenience of a moving child. 'You'll think of something,' he said airily, walking off whistling, whirling his walking stick. He had complete belief in her resourcefulness.

Kate was seldom without a book, passing happy hours absorbed in the works of Charles Dickens, Jane Austen and the Romantic poets. Sharing her passion with the children, she read fairy tales and nursery rhymes in her most theatrical voice—the more ghoulish Hansel and Gretel and Red Riding Hood were favourites with the girls, whereas Little Jack Horner stuck in the corner captured Cecil's imagination.

Her sessions of reading aloud were guaranteed a wrapt audience, broken only by gasps and laughs. But while posing for Jacques's latest work, Kate's reading didn't have the desired effect. Violet and her cousins showed their displeasure at not being included in the portrait by egging on Cecil to move about and pull faces. When Kate warned of the consequences of a wind change on contorted features, Violet taunted her brother with, 'Come on, I dare you and if you don't, you're a cowardy custard.' Cecil enthusiastically wriggled around, and stuck out his tongue as far as it would go down his chin, rolled his eyes and grinned like a gargoyle.

In desperation, when Kate switched to stories of the Indian gods of her childhood, she struck gold. Everyone's favourite was the elephant-headed god. 'Please can we have Ganesha?' one would start, and the others would take up the refrain, 'Yes, please, please.'

Jacques mouthed *merci* as he picked up his brushes while Kate began, 'When Ganesha's father, Shiva, returned to his home after being away for a long period of meditation, he did not recognise his son who was guarding the entrance to the house because his mother, Parvati, was bathing inside. In a rage, he cut off the boy's head.'

No matter how often the story was told, this was Cecil's prompt to jump up, wave his wooden sword and for everyone to scatter for fear of a beheading. Jacques laid down his brushes and watched with amusement, knowing there would be only the one dramatic interruption. After a few minutes of running and yowling Cecil returned to his position, sat placidly and Kate resumed, 'A hysterical Parvati insisted that Shiva return her son to her. Left with no choice, Shiva took Ganesha's body to Brahma. Who is Brahma?'

'The lord of creation,' four childish and one manly voice answered as one.

'Brahma told Shiva to place the boy's head on his neck to restore him to life. But the head had rolled away and was lost. The only way to save Ganesha was for Shiva to kill the first living being he came across and to place it upon his young son's shoulders. And that was?'

'A baby elephant,' everyone answered.

'And ever since Ganesha has had an elephant's head.'

Each time she told the story Kate was transported back in time. Happy as she was in the present, the call of her past was strong, and the lure of Bengal, Meerut, Kuman and Mangal Pandey seductive. Poonam's presence remained potent. Hadn't she indoctrinated her in fate and the power of destiny? Hadn't fate returned Jacques to her? And destiny brought Dolly back into her life?

'Finished, at last.' Jacques stood back from his easel on a balmy afternoon with a smile of satisfaction.

'Can I move now? Really move?' joked Kate who felt as though she had spent weeks in the reclining position. It was a work long in completion but joyful in execution and it had whetted her appetite to return to drawing and painting.

Jacques held out his arms and she went into them with the familiarity that comes from practice. Sunlight drifted across the canvas in which Jacques had captured the tenderness and harmony between Kate and her son. 'It's wonderful,' she whispered turning her face upwards to kiss him. 'What will you call it?'

'I'd like something different, as exotic as you, *ma chérie*.'

She laughed. 'I'm not in the least exotic.'

Jacques disagreed. But he knew no words of his would change Kate's opinion of herself, which she termed 'ordinary'. She had no idea of either her beauty, the impact of her personality or her sensuality.

243

She stood entranced, head cocked to one side. 'How about something simple and true, like *Mother and Child*?'

Paintbrush tapping against his lips, Jacques stared at the picture. After a while he said, 'If it's the truth you're looking for, how about, *Mrs Newton with a Child by a Pool*?'

Chapter Nineteen

As the carriage negotiated crowded Oxford Street, the sky was a crisp autumn blue. Kate marvelled at how in a few short years her life had changed. Loving and being loved was the best feeling in the world, and, with the added joy of painting, superlatives were inadequate.

When she'd brought up the subject of taking lessons, Jacques had been characteristically amenable, immediately putting down his newspaper. The 'theatrical furore', as so described in *The Times* reporting on the success of Gilbert and Sullivan's comic opera *HMS Pinafore* in New York, made for engaging reading but he was more interested in Kate and what she had to say. He was never too preoccupied to talk to her. 'I was hoping you'd want to paint again. Perhaps we could turn one of the small rooms into a studio.'

'I'd prefer to enrol for lessons in the Society for Lady Artists? I hear there are excellent teachers and it would allow me to express my creativity without being influenced by you.'

'Yes, *ma toute jolie,* that is a good idea and it would give you this independence and freedom you crave.' He smiled as he spoke.

Kate had jumped up from the table, scattering her napkin and rattling dishes. She went behind Jacques and threw her arms around him. 'Other than being with you, my darlingest, there's nothing I'd love more than to paint.'

The classes of the Society for Lady Artists were held at Great Marlborough Street on Tuesday, Wednesday and Thursday afternoons. Even during this, her second year, Jacques insisted on putting the small carriage at her disposal and having Thomas accompany her.

On one occasion, her annoyance burst forth. 'If I was a man you'd trust my judgement to travel on my own, and not try to smother me.'

Jacques had raised his arms in a gesture of incredulity and burst out laughing. '*Ma petite à moi*, I can assure you if you were a man, we would not be in this situation.' And then quietly with a look of tenderness that tore at her heart, he murmured, '*Viens que je te respire.*' She knew she meant the world to him. But the world was changing and she wanted to be part of this change. She also knew for then and for her this change wasn't to be. The matter of travelling by carriage, accompanied by Thomas was closed.

For nine hours each week, she moved exclusively in her own world of creativity, which both narrowed and expanded to an existence between her easel and a small worktable with a selection of paints and brushes. She was intoxicated by the smell of oils and spirit and canvas, invigorated by the other students' dedication and stimulated by their teacher's every utterance. Mr Rumple may have been small and insignificant-looking, as well as having a nervous tic in his left eye, but he was a giant among men when he spoke of brushstrokes, depth of oil or the merging of shades.

Kate was pleased that his concentration was on painting. Initially she was tentative in her dabbing of various shades of blue, but he encouraged his students to put paint on canvas instinctively. Stream of consciousness, he called it, and although she was flattered at the worthiness of his description, she considered it difficult to live up to, believing it sounded more like a phrase referring to a worthy poem rather than the work of amateur painters.

She was still fascinated by the exotic gods and goddesses of India and felt the pulses of Brahma, Ganesha, Lakshmi and Shakti beat within. But they lacked the all-enveloping security of the Catholic religion of her childhood, despite its restrictive attitudes and the scruples of conscience that still tormented her. While Jacques and she grieved at their Church's reaction to relationships such as theirs, gradually her God evolved into a gentle and loving amalgam of Catholicism and Hinduism. As her painting progressed, her dedication to her art became religious in its fervour.

As was his habit, Mr Rumple stood behind her looking over her shoulder as she painted a flat-petalled pansy: *pensée*, French for thought. Four bluish petals with a purple tinge and a golden centre, her flower was without stem or leaf. Frequently what she painted were not quite flowers, more designs for flowers as hieroglyphs or emblems, and while they seemed right at the time, later she wondered what drove her to depict them in that way.

Kate laid down her brush and turned around to face him.

'Good, good,' he said. 'Keep going. Don't allow me to interrupt you.'

'I can't. I don't feel comfortable with this.'

'Perhaps the time has come for you to look at the

variations and the possibilities of colour rather than hide behind one.'

Blue remained Kate's favourite colour. She loved its myriad of shades, thoughts and guises: azure, peacock, cobalt, indigo, ultramarine, cerulean, hyacinth. Jacques bought her a rust-coloured gown and a black velvet coat, and instantly she saw how the colours lit up and enhanced her skin tone and hair, but still she painted jugs of blue, some plain, more with intricate patterns. When she finished with jugs she turned her attention to water: oil-on-canvas islands, an unknown mainland glimpsed in azure mirrors, lake waters conjured up from a variety of blues.

There were so many blues to choose from. Washing blue, Reckitt's blue, bag blue, Paris blue, crown blue, dolly bags—such a lot of names for the small penny block endorsed by Queen Victoria's laundress. Blue blood; Kate liked the thought and wondered if her choice of Violet's name had anything to do with the old nursery rhyme, about 'roses are red, violets are blue'.

In Grove End Road she discovered artistry in the washing line of bed sheets—blue in their whiteness, enabling phantoms to be unlocked in the whispering breezes. As the wind blew they became visible with currents of brightness and shade whipping across their gusting. On blustery days, when the light shifted and creaked across their surfaces, the material came alive, like the whip and crack of a sail from one of Jacques's beloved boats. Later the thud of the smoothing iron taken from the fire had the sole purpose of making the bed linen crisp, and afterwards that same linen would fulfil its purpose by becoming crumpled and rumpled with use.

She began to assess everyday objects against specific

gravities of light and shade. There were different weights of oil paint to choose from, varying from the thick consistency of impasto on the nearly bare canvas to flimsy washes. Having acknowledged that Mr Rumple was right, her creativity with subjects, colours and textures began to know no boundaries.

Sometimes, she used backdrops and was influenced by the pink tinged sands of Jacques's painting titled *Seaside*, and his silvered reflections of the water in *Young Woman in a Boat*. She employed quicksilver light tilting and catching in mirrors or defined by a window frame, shivering on the rim of cups and bowls, lending a moon-grey tint to a square-shouldered, glass-stoppered bottle. In those canvases, which went beyond the frame, were suggestions of another world in which artefacts and flowers were their own wild coloured selves. Within the frame, the painting mediated with that world where flowers and things were indifferent to her, to those she loved and even those she did not quite love.

Her work became more about time and yet less about time. In this painting or that painting, it was early morning or late afternoon, but time had little to do with the length it took to complete the picture. Frequently when she returned to her easel the following day or perhaps the day after, the subject would have re-arranged itself. Re-capturing it became a retrospective act.

When she paused after a particularly rewarding and creative painting session she realised how drained and bone tired she was. She was glad to have Thomas drive her home. It was a chilly dusk by the time they turned in the gates. The leaves were dropping and the ground beginning to harden, steeling itself for the freeze to come.

'Come, Mama. You must look at what we've done.' Violet danced with impatience on the gravel as she pulled open the door of the carriage. Her self-confidence and assurance were manifesting themselves in a new imperiousness. Kate considered these necessary attributes for modern young girls, and while Jacques agreed, he pointed out the necessity of tempering such qualities with consideration for others.

The girls had been busy gathering up bits and pieces that lay around the garden, under the shrubs and hedges. They had taken more from the sheds—a selection of cracked flower pots, a slab of paving stone, a wooden handle and a ragged twig broom, which they had assembled into a loose pile and painted with a desert brown wash of muddied water. In between the twigs they had stuck the heads of pale mauve Michaelmas daisies, scarlet late flowering dahlias and bright yellow chrysanthemums.

Hands on both hips, Violet demanded, 'Well, Mama, what do you think?'

Isabel and Lily hung back. When Violet was in one of her dominant phases they became pale shadows of their bossy cousin, a situation Violet encouraged.

'Did the three of you do this?' Kate injected a tactful note of wonder into her voice.

'It was mostly me, Mama.'

'Well, sweetheart, it looks like the joint effort of at least three very artistic people working very hard. Don't tell me you were those people?'

She was rewarded with a small dimpling smile from Lily, a shy nod from Isabel and a shouted, 'We are but mostly it was me,' and waving arms from her daughter.

The piece showed innovation and creativity. Kate

walked around it, bending to examine a bent twig, to touch a blossom, to admire the slant of a stone. 'Have you a name? Masterpieces must have a name.'

'That's what Uncle Jacques said it was. A masterpiece.'

'He said it was a garden sculpture too, Violet,' added Isabel, savouring each syllable of 'garden sculpture'. She had obviously learned off the phrase.

'And so it is. Well done, the three of you. We'll make artists of you yet.'

'I'm going to be a real artist, just like Uncle Jacques,' Isabel announced.

'He's not your uncle,' said Violet. 'But we're going to have an exhibition and invite everyone who is important so that they'll buy our sculptures and we'll be rich, just like Uncle Jacques.'

Kate had reached the blessed comfort of the porch, resplendently lit by Jacques's latest buy of modern gaslights from Paris, when she was overcome by a fit of coughing. The foggy autumn had brought on her annual wet cough early, and that evening it was aggravated by the damp garden. She had never come to terms with the misery of the English winter, and she dreaded facing into the relentlessness of months of cold and damp. She should not have lingered outside but how could she have refused the girls?

Violet was proprietary of Kate and wielded her residency at number 17 with Damoclean intensity. While Polly was devastated at her daughters' wishes to live permanently with Kate and Jacques, her time was more than taken up with her long-awaited son. Arthur was a year old. He had been born a sickly baby and was growing up a sickly child, but at least he was alive. White-faced and with deep shadows under her eyes, Polly had whispered to Kate that since his son's birth, Gussie had become 'less demanding'.

Jacques, drawn by the sound of voices, opened the front door. He was accompanied by Cecil, all blond curls, white frock and smiles, who raised plump arms to be lifted up by Kate. Jacques slipped an arm around her waist and nuzzling her head spoke into her hair. 'I've arranged to have supper served in the drawing room tonight. Just the two of us, and Thomas is lighting the fire.'

'Have you considered exhibiting?' he asked after they had shared a bowl of oysters. They were lying back on a heap of cushions enjoying a sharp white wine and the heat from the logs. Kate rose up on one elbow and looked down at him.

He ran an index finger along her jaw line. As well as being an adoring lover, he was an enormously affectionate man and seldom allowed an opportunity to pass without stroking or touching her in a loving way. 'A joint exhibition at some stage would be something to think about. We could open in London and move to Paris.'

She reared back in horror. 'You mean you and me? Us? Jacques, have you any idea of what a laughing stock you would be? And me too although that wouldn't matter as much. Anyway I won't be ready for years and years. If ever.'

'That's not what your Mr Rumple says. Seriously, *ma belle*, he is enormously taken with your work.'

Kate laughed off the compliment An insidious tickle of thought at the back of her mind had her far from pleased by what she saw as Jacques's intrusion. Her painting time should be her own. Without her permission, Jacques should not interfere and Mr Rumple should not comment. She bit back the retort that bubbled on her lips. Jacques was her *raison d'être*; she would allow nothing to come between them. She sat back on her heels, 'Darlingest Jacques, you know how much I love painting.'

He nodded.

'But don't you know that I love you even more?'

He put on his mock amazed expression, eyebrows quizzically raised. 'No. I don't. Please show me.'

The volume of love that each had for the other was an ongoing joke between them. In demonstration she bent down to kiss his lips, and when he began to unhook her bodice her painting became unimportant. She shivered in delicious anticipation, as she did each time they made love.

Jacques was stretched out on the bed, his head resting on a pile of vividly braided silk bolsters. He had pulled back the bed curtains for an unrestricted view of Kate as she dressed her hair. No matter how often he observed the procedure, he found it a movingly sensual experience, bringing back boyhood memories of the hours his mother, aunts, sisters and cousins spent over elaborate hairdressing rituals.

Styling took place seated in front of a bank of looking glasses, some stationary, more handheld, others angled for best advantage, all full of drifting, mysterious shadows. The women twisted this way and turned that way, taking or leaving at whim the suggestions solicited for style and embellishment, deliberating before placing a clip here, a hairpiece there, curling a tendril around a finger, touching a brush to a fall of curls; perhaps using an ornamental velvet bow or a comb resplendent with feather decoration. When satisfied with their hair, they finished off their toilettes with puffs of perfume from one of the silken-tasselled crystal phials lining their dressing tables.

Kate, who had not an ounce of vanity, was impatient about the time involved in personal grooming, employed few artifices, and had reduced the act of dressing her hair to simplicity. After a vigorous brushing, she simply caught it in a bundle, hoisted it to her crown, wrapped it in a ribbon, shook her head, and where it fell into place she clipped it in at the nape of her neck. Invariably small tendrils escaped to frame her face, and the finished result was as though she had spent hours being coiffed. Preferring the body's natural scent, she did not favour perfume, an inclination Jacques wholeheartedly endorsed.

He rose, stood behind her and slid his hands into her loose hair. He loved its silken feel and length and the scent of flowers that clung to it. Taking the brush from her, he started brushing, long slow strokes starting at her crown, easing strands of rippling hair in and out of the bristles, tugging gently all the way down her back.

As their eyes met in the looking glass, he said, 'I have a surprise.' Jacques loved surprises: whether it was taking everyone cycling in Hyde Park, or arranging for Kate and him to join a party at one of the Monday popular concerts, known as 'the Pops', visiting the British Museum with four questioning children in tow, or buying a cricket set for Cecil, which with squeals of ownership the girls appropriated.

'Are you going to tell me or just sit there smiling like the cat that got the cream?'

While Jacques's command of English was grammatically perfect, he felt he lacked the idiomatic turn of phrase of a native English speaker, and he particularly loved the richness of Kate's Irish similes and metaphors, which she racked her brain to remember from both her mother's conversations and Aunt Muriel's letters.

'Well now. Let me see. Will I, won't I tell you?'

Their eyes, full of merriment, met in the looking glass.

She jumped up from the dressing table, scattering hairpins, combs, feathers and lengths of ribbon in all directions. 'I'll torture you until you tell.' And to show she meant business, she approached him with a long hatpin.

He hid behind the gold-leafed armoire. It had been his idea to decorate the room in shades of maroon verging on pink, and to use velvets, brocades and shot silks to create opulent warmth. Hatpin at the ready, Kate stalked him on tippy-toes. 'Help, help,' he cried as she appeared around the corner.

Neither heard the discreet knock on the door. Dolly, presuming the room to be empty, entered with an armful of bed linen. Realising her error, she withdrew quickly, smiling and shaking her head in disbelief. Never had she imagined being employed by a master and mistress who played hide 'n' seek with each other. Oh, the pleasure and joy of such happiness diffusing through the household.

'So, what's this great surprise of yours?' Kate finally asked Jacques, resting her hand across her chest to stop her fluttering heart.

'Well, I have two. First the Athenaeum is hanging *A Type of Beauty*.

'Congratulations.' Her tone was muted. At his suggestion for the sitting she had worn a scarlet gown, tempered with a black bonnet and black lace gloves. The completed picture not only confirmed that he was a maestro with the brush, it also proved conclusively that he knew precisely—and better than she did—the colours that most flattered her complexion. That he had such power left her feeling slightly claustrophobic.

If he was surprised by her lack of response he did not show it. He knew she would react differently to his second piece of news. 'And I've asked Thomas to get us a Christmas tree.'

Kate squealed her delight and clasped her hands in pleasure. 'Oh, darlingest. That's quite perfect. The Queen will have nothing on us.' Kate loved everything about the English Christmas—decking the hallway with greenery and berries from the grounds; the pervasive air of festivity and revelry; religious services and carol singing; homes redolent of the aromatic richness of roasting goose, baking mince pies, boiling puddings and spiced wines. 'Let's make it our best Christmas ever.'

Jacques smiled indulgently; Kate promised that before each Christmas, and, each New Year's Day, she solemnly pronounced that it had been 'the best ever'.

Chapter Twenty

For a man who throughout his twenties and thirties had no particular ambitions to be a father, daily Jacques was surprised at the joy he got from watching the world through the eyes of the children.

'Well, Dolly, how did they do today?' The girls were finishing their lessons as he joined them in the morning room, which had been turned into the schoolroom.

'Well, sir. Really well. They try hard.' She bobbed a small curtsy, and Violet, Isabel and Lily grinned with delight. Jacques had come up with the idea of Dolly teaching them for two hours each morning. She was a natural imparter of information, and they were thriving under her tutelage. He planned for Cecil to join them in the new year.

'In that case I have an important announcement to make.' He smiled down at the serious faces. Being a slender man, against the more robustly built Englishmen of the time, he cut an unprepossessing figure, but his charisma was enormous, and he had the aura of authority that comes with success. He was always immaculately turned out in black broadcloth and crisp white linens. 'Say thank you to Dolly and put away your slates and books.'

The girls' eyes widened as he took his watch from the

pocket of his waistcoat and tapped its glass with his forefinger. 'Anyone here like surprises?'

'Yes, me, me,' went three voices.

'In that case you must be ready to come into town at precisely eleven o'clock tomorrow morning.'

'What for?'

'If I told you, Violet, it would no longer be a surprise.'

'But I want to know. Now.' She tossed her head petulantly. 'Is Cecil coming too?'

'You will know all tomorrow,' said Jacques firmly. 'And yes, of course Cecil is coming. Now off you go and ask Charlotte politely to give you lunch in the kitchen.'

'I don't want to eat in the kitchen. I want to be with you and Mama.'

'You either eat in the kitchen or not at all.' It was a threat Jacques was capable of carrying out. On occasions he knew he was too soft with the children, but not on that day. He wanted to lunch alone with Kate prior to kidnapping her for a modelling session. He had a burning idea for a dry-point drawing. While inspiration was rolling fresh in his head, he wanted to carry out some preliminary sketches.

The girls, jigging with excitement, were present on time the following morning. Violet burst through the door, a whirl of embroidered royal blue velvet and golden ringlets. Isabel and Lily were in more subdued brown wool capes with fur collars and matching muffs.

'Where are we going, Uncle Jacques?'

For once, Violet allowed Lily's form of address to pass unchallenged and added her own. 'Please can you tell us now?' She was almost standing on top of him, her plump shoulders moving impatiently under her cloak.

'Well, let me see.' Jacques was in particularly good humour as they mounted the carriage. The preliminary sketches of the previous afternoon had worked out extremely well—much better than his usual preliminaries. Kate was an extraordinarily good model, sensitive to his every mood. She was also his muse and quite inspirational.

'We're on a very important mission.' The girls' lips pursed in anticipation. It was bitterly cold, with snow nudging its way into every crack and crevice, but they were well wrapped up and the carriage was warm from Thomas's heated clay bricks. Isabel was looking out of the window, Lily's muffed hands rested neatly in her lap, Violet fidgeted with the braid at the edge of her cloak: all three were swinging their legs. 'I have some important shopping to do and I need your help.'

Lily gave a little giggle. The importance of helping delighted her.

Violet was suspicious. 'Are we going to buy presents? It's nearly Christmas.'

'As you ask, yes. We're buying Christmas presents. In the new toy shop in Holborn.'

'Will we be getting presents for us?'

'We'll be buying for the important people in our lives—those we love.'

'Will *I* be getting something?'

Although Jacques was not judgemental, on occasions he found Violet's brash acquisitiveness annoying. 'Those who deserve gifts usually receive them.' He marvelled at the difference in the girls' personalities: Violet constantly demanding; Lily full of wide-eyed gratitude, and Isabel happy with the simplest of pleasures and beginning to show an interest in painting.

'I know what I want for Christmas.' Violet's legs swung violently. In her present mood she was irrepressible.

Isabel was still looking out of the window, and Lily was silent. Jacques had never heard her ask for anything. 'Is there something you'd like, Lily?' He was curious about her and he wondered what she thought about during her long silences.

'A new doll would be nice,' she said hesitantly. 'A small one.'

'I want a doll too. A big doll with a pretty face, yellow hair and a long gown with frills and lace,' Violet rattled off.

Jacques planned for them each to choose a toy. As usual Violet was dominating, but with her constant chattering and opinions there was never a dull moment. There was a swirling urgency in his veins that he couldn't identify, and, like Kate, he wished to ensure this was their best Christmas ever. 'Well, let's hope we fulfil your dreams.'

Despite it being several days to Christmas, the shop was brightly decorated, crowded with shoppers and resonating with the voices of cautioning parents, nannies and childish shrieks of delight. The shelves were packed with toys of every description, size, shape and colour; Jacques's eyes were drawn to a well-displayed red, blue and yellow wooden train set, which he planned to buy for his son, who had woken up with a head cold. Kate insisted on confining him indoors.

Squealing excitement, Violet ran towards a collection of dolls with elaborate gowns, pained expressions on their porcelain faces, and improbably cascading curls. Isabel and Lily followed more slowly. Jacques was taken by Lily's expression of wonder as she stood motionless, her hands clasped behind her back, her eyes darting from doll to doll, oblivious to the indulgent smiles of adults reliving their own childhoods.

'I like this and this and that too,' went Violet, hopping from one leg to another, pointing to three of the largest dolls.

'Which is your favourite?' Jacques hunkered down so that his eyes were level with Lily's.

'They're all beautiful,' she whispered. She shook her head. 'I don't know.'

'Well, you can't have them all, sure she can't, Uncle Jacques?'

'I don't want them all. I just like looking at them.'

'You may each choose one. It will be my Christmas gift to you.' Jacques was still down at the girls' level.

'Thank you.' Isabel did not go in for effusiveness.

Shyly Lily raised her face, smiled beatifically and planted a solid kiss on his cheek. 'Oh, thank you so much.'

Violet was too busy debating her choice to notice.

Jacques left the girls making the decision of their lives while he returned to examine the train. He wanted something special for Cecil. Sometimes as he watched Kate's absorption in their son, he was consumed with a feeling he had reluctantly come to recognise as jealousy.

The days preceding Christmas were magical. The tree arrived with the maximum of fanfare, on another morning when snowflakes, a shade lighter than the snow-coloured sky, fell in quantity, webbing the corners of the windows and frosting the buttresses of the house. The seven-foot pine sparked all the surprise Jacques hoped for.

'Oh, la, la!' Kate stood in the porch, with a fringed shawl thrown over her ruby red gown, determinedly trying to ignore the cold and her cough, clapping her hands like a child.

Thomas produced two large boxes of decorations. 'Regretfully, sir, they're from Germany. I couldn't find anything worthwhile made in England.' The boxes yielded up a treasure trove of clear glass icicles and hand-blown globes in greens, maroons and yellows, as well as embossed silver and gold papier-mâché ornaments in the shapes of moons, butterflies, fish, birds and flowers.

Kate called for a seasonal bowl of punch and some of Dolly's shortbread. Jacques pronounced the punch 'vile', and insisted on opening a bottle of champagne. The one bottle became two, and then four when he invited the servants to join them. As the adults stood around raising glasses to each other, the children enjoyed a celebratory sip. The library never looked lovelier with the winter light skating over the surfaces and the forest green of the walls acting as a perfect backdrop to the tree. When Charlotte took the children to the kitchen to be fed, Jacques slipped an arm round Kate.

'May I ask you something?'

'Of course you may.' She snuggled deep into his chest.

'Will you marry me?'

Jacques's proposals were part of the fabric of their lives.

She wriggled free, wrapped her arms round his neck and kissed him soundly. 'Thank you, darlingest, but no, I won't.'

'Why?'

Usually she sensed the question and was able to defuse it before he asked. But that afternoon she had relaxed into Christmas with the tree and champagne. 'I'm honoured, but in the eyes of our Church, you know we can't get married and we don't need to. And anyway as far as I know the decree absolute has never been applied for.'

'Perhaps I could look into it.'

'No. Let us just leave things as they are.'

'What about Isaac Newton?'

'I know nothing of him or his whereabouts.'

'Perhaps he's dead?'

Her voice softened. 'Perhaps he is. But we have no way of knowing. Why should we change what's perfect? Remember, I tried marriage once and I don't recommend it. I have decided...'

Jacques joined in her game, 'Decided what?'

Over the years she had perfected the art of the light-hearted, humorous reply when Jacques raised the subject of marriage. 'Our saints are rather too pious for the likes of us and disapproving of divorce, and even worse living in sin, but the gods and goddesses of India are deliciously naughty and get up to all sorts of shenanigans.'

As she knew he would, he asked, 'Shenanigans? What are they?'

'Come, let me show you.' She winked, took him by the hand and led him up the stairs and into the bedroom, where each night they slept entwined.

Jacques felt blessed with Kate; she was a passionate lover, wonderful company. She had an enquiring mind and was a constant source of good humour and good fun, but during the winter months, no matter how warm the fires, she was constantly chilled and coughing. 'Cold hands, warm heart,' she told him when he worried about her blue lips and icy hands and feet. On occasions, despite warming pans, hot water bottles and the thickest of comforters, it took all the heat from his body to take the chill from hers.

Each autumn he suggested spending the winter in the more clement climate of the Côte d'Azur, but when it came to the point to make bookings and organise accommodation they were reluctant to uproot from their home, and as Kate would indicate with one of her mischievous smiles, 'Winter passes and becomes spring and my cough goes.'

The hope of alleviating Kate's deep-seated chill brought Jacques to the International Fur Store in Regent Street. He sat on a gilt chair, was fussed over by the senior sales lady, and shown a selection of luxurious furs modelled by young, out-of-work actresses. When the red-haired mannequin with the boldest of eyes paraded in front of him wearing a long sealskin coat in glossy black, he did not hesitate. It was the perfect replacement for Kate's ancient fur. He added a matching hat. Kate suited fur or rather fur suited Kate.

As he watched the coat and hat being boxed, wrapped and ribboned, the title for the dry-point came to him. Kate and he had fun naming his works: sometimes they were in immediate agreement, other times they argued titles backwards and forwards. There had been no dispute with *Waiting for the Ferry*; they'd settled on *The Orphan* without too much difficulty, although Kate maintained the golden lights of the grasses made the painting too happy for the connotation of its name; they had rather liked the contradiction of *Holyday*. They were extraordinarily fond of *Summer* or *L'Été*, as Jacques preferred. He was particularly pleased at the way he'd managed to capture the summer sunshine streaming through the translucent paper of the Japanese parasol, and he planned to look further into the simplicity of Japanese art.

But the dry-point had them baffled, and it shouldn't have because, as though guided by his guardian angel of creativity, he was inspired from Kate's first sitting to the moment he signed off in pencil and added his red monogram stamp. It was a labour of love: delicacy combined with durability. It was the portrait that best captured Kate's spirit. Unlike the majority of his prints, he had worked it in pure dry-point, which allowed him to merge fine touches of line for the drawing of her face, with rich textures in the burr and wiped ink tone for the collar of her coat and hat. He would call it *La Frileuse*.

When Jacques returned home, he stood quietly and happily surveying his domain. The moment was broken when Cecil came running out and clung to his leg, followed by Kate, who reached up to hug him. 'You were gone for a long time. We're waiting to put up the Christmas angel. The girls are doing so much bickering that I told them you'd supervise a joint effort.'

Jacques and Cecil held the ladder while Violet and Lily ascended; Isabel remained on the floor looking on with Kate. Finally the Christmas angel with her soft feathery wings was placed on the top of the tree, Thomas positioned and lit the hand-dipped candles, and Isabel, her voice full of wonder, echoed Kate's sentiments: 'This is everything and more.'

'Are you free this morning, Mavourneen?'

Kate smiled at Jacques's pronunciation. Excellent as his English was, he had difficulty getting his tongue round Irish words. He was intrigued at her Irish heritage as he was at her Indian upbringing. *Ravissante Irlandaise* and Mavourneen were his special terms of endearment, and in moments of passion he claimed the scent of India clung to her.

'What are you planning?' She injected enthusiasm into her voice. Despite her dearest wish, it hadn't turned out to be their best Christmas. She was out of sorts: feeling not quite ill, but not wholly well either. Although she worked hard at making it a happy and peaceful family time, attending the few parties to which they had received invitations, and shining at their soirée on New Year's Eve, she was surprised at how pleased she was to return to the simplicity and predictability of their everyday domestic routine.

'How do you know I'm planning anything?'

'Because I know you so well.' She knew him better than she knew herself. He made no effort to hide his many moods from her; she loved his emotional openness and could read his every nuance of happiness, sadness, expectation, childishness and enjoyment. Much as she knew he loved Cecil, she also knew that he was rendered uneasy by the closeness that existed between her and their son, although he never seemed threatened by her loving relationship with Violet.

'I have a thought.' Presumably from his edgy behaviour, furrowed look of concentration and the way he was running his fingers through his hair, it was an artistic thought. Invariably, they emerged as fully fledged inspirations. Fearful they might disappear, Jacques liked to implement them immediately. 'I want to do a picture of you standing outside the National Gallery.' He had already painted the scene using a well-dressed couple and titled it *London Visitors*. The time on the clock on the steeple of the church of Saint-Martin's-in-the-Field, seen through the portico, read 10.35. The overall grey tone of the painting was intended as a wry observation on the British weather.

Posing outside, exposed to the elements, was the last way she would have chosen to spend that morning. Although she was enjoying the touch of brightness in the spring days and the sense of hope in the air, the weather was still sharp. She would much prefer to curl up with *David Copperfield* in front of the fire, but she would not, could not, disappoint Jacques. His enthusiasm for painting, particularly a new composition, made him difficult to refuse, and when artistically wound up he was impervious to anyone else's lack of enthusiasm. 'Why the Gallery?'

'For authenticity, *ma petite à moi*.'

'Authenticity? What are you up to?'

'Immortalising you as a student, so that for posterity you'll be known as an artist in your own right, not just remembered as the love of my life and the beautiful model who was the inspiration for my best works.'

He cupped her face in his hands and kissed her soundly on her nose. Instead of reciprocating with a hug, she shivered—the shiver, her mother would have said, was a goose stepping over her grave. She pushed aside the morbid thought. She had lost count of the number of occasions she had modelled for Jacques. They were special times of heightened physical, mental and emotional intimacy. 'Can I wear the fur?' His Christmas present was such a success that she hardly left it off, and she had passed on her old coat to Dolly.

His laugh was hearty. 'No. Of course you can't. Students are supposed to be penniless—even students who live with rich benefactors!'

Kate flicked a pellet of bread at him across the table.

267

That morning the smell of food had her feeling nauseous and she had eaten virtually nothing. Jacques had tucked into his favourite breakfast of orange segments and kedgeree and kidneys, followed by toast and coffee. He happily straddled the gastronomic divide between English and French, enjoying what he considered the best foods from both countries.

'It's still very cold,' she said, knowing as she spoke that the weather was unlikely to change his mind, although fairly she also knew if he suspected she was feeling poorly he would not ask her to model.

'Yes, we'll be frozen with the cold and that wind,' he said cheerfully. 'But it'll only take a few hours. You can wear anything except the fur, but make sure you're comfortable and warm.'

Jacques took pleasure in Kate looking her best. He bought her gifts of diamonds and pearls and encouraged her to buy new gowns. 'I'm a hopeless fashion case,' she would laugh at him, as she appeared in yet another loose wrap. She was interested in the latest fashions and loved the feeling of silks and fine cottons against her skin, but she disliked being tightly corseted, which was necessary for the nipped-in waists of the time but which reduced flexibility and ease of movement.

He gave an elaborate sigh. 'I don't suppose I'll ever understand women.'

'Probably not, Jacques darlingest.' As Kate rose from the table, she was overcome by a spell of dizziness. She bowed her head and stood quietly resting her hands on the damask, waiting for the buzzing in her head to pass, grateful Jacques had returned to reading his newspaper. She went slowly up the stairs to her room and sat by the fire. She could no longer ignore the fact that she was unwell, and she was not getting better. Her limbs ached, her body sweated, and as well as a persistent cough she was constantly tired.

She reached for the bell rope, and when Dolly entered she asked, 'Do you remember mentioning something about a cough mixture?'

'Yes, Miss Kate, shall I ask Thomas to fetch some?'

'No. You get it. Thomas might mention it to the master and I'd prefer him not to know. He'd worry.'

'He'd worry even more if he realised how poorly you are.'

'I'm not poorly.'

'Beg pardon, but you are, miss, and you have been for some time, and in this weather you'll catch your death going posing outside.' Dolly withdrew with a disapproving bob of her head. Not for the first time Kate wondered at how the servants, without ever being told, appeared to be aware of Jacques's and her every move.

Although she did nothing but stand in the place and position designated by Jacques, Kate found the morning's posing strenuous, as she fought off waves of weakness. Perhaps when the weather turned warmer she should take the waters at Bath.

Halfway through the sitting, which turned out to be a standing, Thomas produced a hip flask of sherry and some triangles of shortbread, as well as a woollen rug, all of which Kate gratefully recognised as Dolly's doing. When Jacques agreed to a break, during which he tidied up his preliminary sketches, she wrapped up and lay back against the wall, sipping and nibbling: by then she was ravenously hungry.

That evening, while Jacques was adding touches to the

picture, Dolly handed Kate a small dark brown bottle labelled 'Freeman's Chlorodyne'. Its label declared it to be the greatest medical discovery of the century.

'I feel better just looking at this,' Kate told Dolly.

'It's supposed to cure every ailment under the sun. Diarrhoea, croup, epilepsy and the ague.'

'Well in that case it will have this bothersome cough of mine gone in no length of time.'

From her first spoonful of the disgusting-tasting, viscous mixture Kate felt better. Over the following weeks, as spring gave way to summer and blooming saturated the air, she recovered much of her spirits.

She began rising early to catch the birth of day, slipping out the back door to visit the section of the grounds where Thomas kept a cluster of beehives. While the lingering threads of early morning mist dissolved, she watched as the hives brightened, their wooden slats becoming smooth and pale as candle wax, and when the sun grew warm, the bees emerged—their eternal quest for honey satisfied in the profusion of arching and winding yellow, red and pink roses.

Arms entwined, she and Jacques whiled away the long lilac evenings wandering the pathways—hearing and seeing the fluttering flocks of wheeling starlings falling like smuts of coal dust into the clusters of midges; breathing in the scents of lavender, sweet pea and the roses that blossomed in profusion; or, when it showered, inspecting the crescents of silver light trapped inside the drops of summer rain.

'You and your rain,' he murmured into her hair, after splattering showers had ruined his plans for a day of outdoor painting. He embraced each artistic innovation with enthusiasm and was particularly delighted that the introduction of metal tubes of paint did away with the necessity of blending powered pigments outside.

'England's rain is soft, so unlike the rain in India.' As a child Kate had so often seen the dark clouds of the monsoon paint their sombre mood on the sky, watched as they gathered from horizon to horizon, seeming to press down on the tops of the tallest of trees. The air after the long dry months was so lavishly perfumed with rain that everyone was drunk with excitement. '*Pauos alla*,' the servants called. 'The rain is coming.' In a few seconds the first drops were a heavy fall. In minutes they were a cascade, and within an hour the monsoon was a ceaseless torrent, so thick that it was difficult to breathe. The downpour was followed by a lull, during which the sun shone intermittently and rainwater steamed from the warming earth. That was the way of the first days of the monsoon, but when the great rain came it could pour without pause for seven days and nights.

'I've been looking into visiting India,' Jacques said. He knew how much Kate wanted to return. He also knew that winter cough of hers was stubbornly refusing to clear, and he worried about exposing her to disease, but perhaps the sea voyage would be beneficial. 'I believe the weather is at its best in the Northern Provinces in January. Perhaps we'll go then.'

Nuzzling her face into his shoulder, Kate threw her arms around him. 'Oh, Jacques, happy as I am here, there's nothing I'd like better.' She stood back from him and in the dusky garden held her face to the sky and breathed deeply. All around her were the scents of patchouli and sandalwood, and hot sun, cool rain and dry dust caressed her skin.

Chapter Twenty-one

Kate's father looked remarkably well for his sixty-three years. But then it was a well documented fact that older men who took on younger wives invariably received a new lease of life. Meetings between father and daughter were infrequent since Kate had moved in with Jacques. A frisson of hostility, although well contained within the boundary of politeness, still existed.

'Well, well.' The major, as he still insisted was his title, exuded his characteristic collective affability towards all present. 'Well, well,' he repeated, stooping down to shake Cecil's hand, 'aren't we quite the little man, eh?'

Cecil was looking particularly adorable. He was wearing his first pair of pantaloons and a matching blue jacket, a mini-version of Jacques's shirts and white stockings with patent shoes. Only a few weeks previously, when Jacques had suggested taking him out of dresses and cutting his hair, Kate had been so upset that her eyes had filled. It was bad enough that his golden blond curls were darkening at the roots. 'Oh, please, no. Let him enjoy being a baby. I don't want him forced into boyhood ahead of his time.'

'Rearing a boy along the same lines as a girl is detrimental to manly development.' Jacques spoke with authority. He prided himself on being a forward thinker on a variety of subjects, particularly the raising of children. Eventually, after cogent negotiations, it was agreed that Cecil's boyish progress would be better served without wearing dresses, although for the foreseeable future his hair would remain uncut.

The major patted Violet's head. As of old, he was seeking to enclose everyone in a claustrophobic shelter of false bonhomie. 'I suppose you can recite the ten times tables?'

'I can,' she said, swinging on her heels. 'Dolly taught me and Mama hears me. Dolly teaches me lots.'

'I have no doubt she does. And do you like learning?'

'I don't know, sir.' Violet liked discovering and knowing and being the best but she was not so sure about the process and disciplines required for learning.

Kate stepped in. 'Violet is a very special student. We're reading the works of Mr Dickens together.'

Violet glowed with her mother's praise.

The major turned his attention to Kate. He spoke quietly. 'Happy at last?' As she inclined her head, he said, 'Well, you should be—finally getting your own way.' He was right. Her sole wish for her children was that they would be as fortunate with their lives. Her father wasn't finished. 'Now that your husband is dead, perhaps you will persuade Monsieur Tissot to make an honest woman of you.' Under his breath and watching for her reaction, he added, 'And save the family from further disgrace.'

Kate's head spun. She felt as if she had been felled by a swift blow. How typical of her father to hurtle such a momentous piece of news at her in such a casual, thoughtless way. She turned away her head, blinking tears of hurt. 'I didn't know.' She had no curiosity as to how Isaac had died.

But the major had turned to Cecil, lavishing attention, sitting him on his knee, asking questions, his stern features softening at the childish answers. 'I presume, he'll go into the army, as I did,' he said with the aplomb of a warrior who had single-handedly quelled the Sepoy Uprising. He rumpled the child's hair. 'Girl's curls. These should be got rid of.'

Upset as Kate was, she would not allow her father to exercise his dominance in her home. She leapt to Cecil's defence. 'His hair will be cut when Jacques and I decide.'

'But if he's going into the army...'

'Well, he's hardly likely to be enrolling at the age of five. He may wish to follow in his father's footsteps and become an artist. You'd like that, wouldn't you, sweetheart?' she addressed the child who was looking in smiling bewilderment from one adult to the other, his brown eyes softening, as Jacques's did when he was puzzled. Cecil was not a talker, he lived much of the time in his head.

After Dolly had taken the children from the drawing room, no longer able to contain his curiosity, Kelly rose, ostensibly to stretch his legs by wandering round the room, but in reality to carry out his own assessment. Kate, as always on edge in her father's company, and more than ever that afternoon, followed his movements with her eyes, as well as with the tilt of her head and shoulders. She wanted him gone so that she could tell Jacques that Isaac was dead.

The major had seen opulence in his day, but from what he had observed this house combined opulence with taste. Gilt tables with a variety of *objects d'art*, and a series of slender, erotic sculptures occupied the corners. Bowls of summer roses wafted scent, and the walls were lined with contemporary paintings and English hunting prints, as well as a selection of Jacques's portraits of Kathleen. Even he, neither a believer nor a respecter of art, recognised love in every line of the paintings of his daughter.

'We're thinking of moving to Jersey,' he announced, half-turning from perusing *La Frileuse*.

'Indeed, sir. I'd have thought if you were considering moving, it would be back to London.'

'The less expensive cost of living is our main attraction.'

Kate was puzzled; she understood her stepmother to be independently wealthy—it was rumoured she had inherited a sizeable sum. Even her father with his spendthrift ways should be more than comfortably off for the remainder of his life.

'The weather is more clement in the Channel Isles and, of course, there's the new baby to consider.'

'New baby?' Was there no end to her father's shocks? Kate had never considered the possibility of him starting another family.

'Yes, God willing, in about three months' time.'

'Congratulations are, indeed, in order.' Jacques stepped in as Kate appeared to be at a loss for words.

'That's good news for you, Papa.' Kate injected as much warmth into her tone as she could manage. 'I hope your wife keeps well.' She had not met her stepmother. Polly and Gussie had spent a weekend with them in Yorkshire, after which Polly declared the new wife '*formidable*', giving the word its French intonation.

Her father looked at Jacques while answering. 'Regretfully my wife is rather poorly. And may I enquire how sales of your paintings are?'

Jacques was taken aback as much by the abrupt change of topic as by the commercial question, which should not be asked in polite society. In the circumstances he felt compelled to answer, 'Well, thank you, sir. They sell faster than I can paint.'

The major offered a slim tooled leather box to Jacques, who fingered out a cigar. As they clipped the ends of their cigars, lit up and sat back, relaxing into their first puffs, Kate found herself wondering if Jacques missed the men-only evenings of good food, fine wines and artistic conversation in the Athenaeum Club, which in her opinion he too seldom attended.

'Perhaps I might talk to you alone?' Charles Kelly asked Jacques.

Kate was brought back to the present. 'No, Papa. I would prefer to remain.'

'It is all right, *ma petite à moi*. Please leave us.' There was a glint of firmness in Jacques's embrace of her eyes.

Kate knew her father too well to want to leave him alone with Jacques. With time, and with her happiness and Jacques's more philosophical outlook on life, she had reached the stage, reluctantly, of giving him the benefit of the doubt, trying to believe that in the cases of Isaac and Captain Palliser he had acted in her interest to the best of his ability.

But now?

What could he want alone with Jacques other than to try to pressurise him into marrying her? Her father may have been vocal on the importance of his Catholicism but that wouldn't stop him pushing his daughter into a marriage, unrecognised by the Church, but more socially acceptable than having her live with Jacques. She loved

Jacques deeply but had no wish to marry him. To avoid him losing face, she had no choice but to leave the room.

Her father made a hurried departure less than a half an hour later, and as Kate and Jacques stood in the porch with Violet and Cecil, the four of them waving goodbye, Jacques slipped an arm round her shoulders. 'Come, *ma chérie*, I need to talk to you.'

For once she was unable to read his expression or know what he was thinking, and that was because he was uncharacteristically sombre.

They were hardly seated in front of the small summer fire when Jacques came straight to the point. 'Your father asked me for a loan of money.'

'Did he say anything else?'

'No. Should he have?' Jacques's gaze was steady; he was incapable of pretence.

Kate's anger and hurt quivered her arms and legs and wrenched her face into shapes of disappointment. She was surprised her father hadn't mentioned Isaac's demise, and she was outraged that he would presume on Jacques's hospitality to make a request for money. But where he was concerned money held precedence over honour and integrity. It was terrible to feel so ashamed of him. 'What did you answer?'

'I didn't. I said I'd need to talk the matter over with you.'

'You actually told him that?'

'Yes. Of course. What do you think we should do?'

Jacques was an amazing man. Not even husbands consulted their wives about money matters, but he constantly sought her opinion on every aspect of their life together. With him it was a constant 'we', never 'I'. She left her chair and came to sit on the floor, with her head resting against his knees. Time enough to tell him about Isaac. But before she could answer, she was overcome by an overwhelming urge to cough.

She tried to stifle it, but, as though it had been gathering strength and momentum over the weeks when it had lain relatively dormant, in the space of a gasp for breath it began its eruption. As she rose to leave the room, spluttering an excuse, it exploded out of her. She was incapable of moving. The hand she raised to cover her mouth came away smeared with bright red blood. She tucked it into the pocket of her skirt; no matter what, Jacques must not see it.

He jumped to his feet alarmed by her deathly paleness and the way she was clutching at the doorknob. 'What is it, *ma belle*?' His eyes widened in fear. If he feared anything in life, it was that something might happen to Kate. 'You are unwell.' He grasped her wrist. 'We'll have to get Dr Mackintosh to visit.'

'No. It's nothing.'

'It is. You've had that cough for a long time. Much too long.' He sighed. He had been remiss. Instead of waiting around for the Royal Academy to make contact, he should have insisted they spend winter in a warmer climate, and he most certainly should have called the doctor. But as usual he had been relieved to believe her assurance that all was well. She was obviously unwell.

Kate licked at her lips, which felt dry and cracked, but she had regained most of her composure and Jacques had not seen the blood, which felt hot and sticky on her palm.

Perhaps Dolly could get a stronger medicine.

In his concern for Kate, Jacques had forgotten her

father's request, but she had not. She wanted the matter sorted as much as she wanted to take Jacques's mind off her health. She sat back into her chair and spoke slowly. 'My father has an embarrassing habit of borrowing money which he doesn't re-pay. You're not the first and you probably won't be the last, though I would have thought with a wealthy wife borrowing wouldn't be necessary.'

'I am not sure she's that wealthy.'

'Did he say so? '

'No. But there was talk in the Athenaeum. Something about diamonds and bonds and stocks tied up in a trust.'

'And you didn't think to tell me?'

'At the time, it didn't seem important. But with a baby coming, should I make him the loan or just settle a sum on him?'

Kate's eyes widened. Despite Jacques's reputation for parsimony, she had seen the opposite in his generous donations to charity and to people who were less fortunate—but this...? 'Absolutely not. You will do neither.'

'But he is your father.'

'Yes. But that does not mean you have to support him, his wife and child. He's hardly destitute or likely to be.'

Jacques chuckled. Kate looked at him as though he had taken leave of his senses. 'What's so funny?'

'This is the first time you've told me what to do. You're usually so circumspect.'

'Well...as you said, we *are* taking about my father.'

Kate felt another bout of coughing coming on. She took several deep breaths and swallows, kept eye contact with Jacques and tried to smile.

'Tomorrow you must see the doctor.'

She stood tall to her full height, proud and fearless with

her head back. Jacques was reminded of the happiest day of his life, when she had stood by his fire in her muddy boots and told him she loved him. 'Look at how well I am. Can't you see there is little wrong with me? Why should we waste his time?'

'Because you're the most important thing in the world to me. If anything happened to you, my life would be over.'

That was not a conversation she had ever envisaged, it wasn't one she wanted to pursue. 'Nothing's going to happen to me, but if it did your life would go on. You'd continue painting.' Her tone of voice was forceful. 'You'd have to.'

'Mavourneen, come here.'

Their love-making that night reached ardent heights never before achieved, but their mutual passion did not calm Jacques's anxiety, and next morning, before Kate was awake, he sent Thomas with a message for the doctor.

Instead of remaining in bed, as Jacques and, indeed, Dolly considered more appropriate for a visit from the doctor, Kate got up, bathed and dressed. She took an unprecedented length of time over her toilette, choosing the red silk gown she had worn while sitting for *A Type of Beauty*, plaiting her hair in the latest Parisian style, and even going as far as carmining her lips and rubbing a little of the red into her cheeks.

As she came down the stairs, Jacques and Dolly were in the hallway. He came forward, arms outstretched, smiling in delight. '*Te voilà, ma belle*, you look very beautiful. And very well too.' Had he been worrying unduly? Where Kate was concerned his anxiety had a habit of veering out of control. Looking at her, smiling, wearing his favourite gown, she did not look as though she needed the services of a doctor.

Dolly remained silent; she knew all about the benefits of female artifice.

As Kate heard the carriage crunch up the driveway, she pinched her cheeks to make them even rosier. When Dolly showed in the doctor to the small morning room that she had made her own, she was the picture of relaxation, sitting in a plump armchair by a crackling fire. Slipping a bookmark into *Pride and Prejudice*, she directed him to take the chair opposite.

Dr Mackintosh was big and hearty and soothing. He was a doctor who lived for his patients, a passionate advocate of Hippocrates and the Hippocratic oath, as well as being a firm and vocal believer in the power of God and of His will being done. On his rounds he was attended by a Negro footman, a huge placid fellow, who took up a watchful position by the door and averted his eyes.

The doctor had heard of the luxury of the French artist's house, and of his infatuation with his mistress, who had been variously described to him as beautiful, plain, a fortune-hunting adulteress and a wealthy Irish Catholic divorcee. But nothing had prepared him for either the natural loveliness of Mrs Newton, which was compounded by her air of dignity, gentle voice and quiet graciousness, or the tasteful lavishness of number 17.

She displayed no false modesty as he carried out his examination. His expression remained locked into a pleasant mask of inscrutability as he noted the dryness of her skin, took her pulse with soft but deft fingers, and finished by listening to her lungs for rather longer than was necessary. Biding further time, he made a show of calling for his footman and consulting his reference book, but he had seen enough not to doubt his initial diagnosis. This was an illness wrought with social sensitivity. He wondered what precisely he should say to Mrs Newton; how far should he go in his explanation.

Hands loosely clasped in her lap and face upturned enquiringly, she appeared untouchable, serene, in control and unafraid. He stroked his chin. Thinking. She had no need to know that she had the symptoms of an illness that currently accounted for one in four deaths. Since its contagion had been established, it was a notifiable disease, with campaigns to stop spitting in public places, and pressure to enter sanatoria.

The sanatoria for the poor resembled prisons, although those for the middle and upper classes offered excellent care and medical attention, but still some fifty per cent of patients were dead within five years.

No, he would not recommend a sanatorium, and, in this case, he would think further about the implications of 'notifiable'. Exposure to the mountain air could be beneficial—he had heard rather than seen proof of the advantages of the Swiss sanatoria, with their modern medical care and lines of beds on verandas opening to the clean, invigorating air. Perhaps he might discuss the possibility with Monsieur Tissot. His face ruddy with earnestness, he beamed encouragingly and rubbed his palms together. 'I prescribe plenty of rest and good food. For the present, I suggest abstinence from wine and red meat.'

Kate's question was tentative, 'May I expect to be better soon?'

'Yes, I'm sure you will, and the warmer weather should

help.' His answer was bouncingly optimistic, and as he intended, she felt the better for it.

As Dr Mackintosh and his footman were being shown out, Jacques intercepted them at the front porch. Throughout the doctor's consultation, he had fretted, cursed his feelings of inadequacy and despised himself for his relieved acceptance of Kate's assurance that his attendance was not necessary. He should have been by her side—if the situation were reversed she would have been with him, but fear for her and his all-consuming horror of illness had made a coward of him. He had watched with futile horror as his once dynamic *grandmère* choked to death from an enlarged goitre, and he had listened to the doctors conferring and admitting there was nothing to be done. He kept his voice light. 'Mrs Newton is all right? Nothing serious, I presume?'

'As I'm sure you understand without her permission, I cannot discuss her health.' If such a dual display of simultaneous emotions were possible, Jacques managed to widen his eyes anxiously and to purse his lips in relief. The doctor's further words puzzled rather than pacified him. 'Mrs Newton is considering taking the waters at Bath? Perhaps that might be better postponed.'

Jacques took a step backwards and shook his head. It was the first he had heard of it. 'I believe Bath is a place favoured by those with consumption. I do not consider it a good idea to have Mrs Newton exposed to such an illness.'

'As you say.' Dr Mackintosh's expression was without emotion. There was no point in mentioning Switzerland.

'When can we expect her to be better?'

The doctor's eyes raked Jacques. In his experience, the

most intelligent people could be the most medically obtuse. 'It's difficult to say but time is a great healer.'

Like a talisman Jacques held on to the fact that it would take time for Kate's health to be fully restored.

Dolly was not as easily pacified. She strode around from the side of the house, waving an arm, as the doctor was mounting his carriage. 'A moment of your time, please, sir!'

'Really! What do you want?' Dr Mackintosh was not used to dealing with servants.

Dolly stood firm, her earnest, troubled face looking upwards. 'I want to know how best to care for my mistress.'

Having met Mrs Newton, the doctor understood both the whispered rumours and malicious gossip that circulated about her in society. He recognised her as the type of woman who heightened the passions of others—be those passions good or bad. From the maidservant's inquisitive, knowing look, he would not be surprised if she was aware of both diagnosis and prognosis. 'Fresh air, rest and what she'll eat of good wholesome food should help.'

Dolly bobbed a curtsy. 'Thank you, sir. It is the consumption, isn't it?'

Dr Mackintosh did not answer and he did not know what impulse made him call out the window of his carriage, 'If you have any worries, you may contact me.' Even more unusually, he handed Dolly one of his cards.

Chapter Twenty-two

Jacques was an avowed monarchist and he followed Queen Victoria's activities with great interest, daily reading aloud the court diary and commenting to anyone within earshot on her various engagements. 'Here's an occasion we cannot miss.' He put down his newspaper and looked expectantly around.

Kate, a shawl thrown around her shoulders, was seated by the window reading *Sense and Sensibility*; Cecil leaned against her knees spinning his top on a tin tray; Violet, Lily and Isabel lay on their stomachs in the middle of the room, bickering over scrapbooks, cards and pieces of ribbon. It was what Kate termed one of her 'better days', which were increasingly precious. Outside, the afternoon was heavy and greasy with rain, which engorged into slow drops and zigzagged down the windows.

She slipped her finger into the book as she closed over its cover. 'So, Jacques, what can't we miss? Listen, children. I do believe there's another treat in store for us.'

At the hint of any sort of expedition, Violet became a tornado of animation. She jumped to her feet, scattering paper scraps and dried flowers, and oblivious to Isabel's squeals. 'Where are we going? What are we going to do? When?'

Jacques threw his arms wide and asked, 'Would anyone like to attend the Queen's birthday celebrations?'

Lily stopped tidying up and sat back on her heels. Her eyes widened and her mouth opened in an ooh of delight. She was an ardent collector of anything to do with the Queen. 'Are we really, really and truly going to her party?'

'Well, not quite her party. How about her special fireworks display?'

The idea of fireworks aroused Cecil from his spinning. He was so obsessively interested in anything to do with fire that Jacques had gone around the house ensuring the safety matches were locked away.

The children converged on Jacques, throwing themselves at him, asking, 'When can we go?' 'Are we going to the palace?' 'Can we talk to the Queen?' Watching and listening, Kate's heart was filled with conflicting emotions: of joy and sorrow. These days tears were never far from the surface.

She was not herself, as Mama would have said if she were still alive. Of recent weeks Kate found herself hungering for her mother, remembering the touch of her fingers through her hair, her gentle voice and the soft swish of her muslin gowns. Her hungering wasn't for want of care. Dolly's devotion to her was humbling: flannels, dipped in bowls of cool water, wrung out, folded and lain gently across her forehead, and menthol vapour rubs that warmed her chest. Most horrendous of all, and according to Dolly, backed up by Dr Mackintosh, the most efficacious was the mug of thick, globular buttermilk at eleven o'clock each morning.

The May evening was balmy and the roads leading to Hyde Park black with carriages filled with revellers dressed in their Sunday best. Jacques, his hands resting on a silver-headed cane, looked with pride on his entourage—which included Dolly, who with a stubborn dignity that boded no argument had become her mistress's shadow. The city was a fairyland, wearing festive garb of coloured paper streamers and Chinese lanterns strung between buildings. A band of men playing fiddles and a piano accordion had attracted a crowd, clapping and laughing. Children weaved between adults, waving Union Jacks and blowing whistles; men and women mingled round great metal drums, roasting chestnuts and drinking ale from mugs.

With Thomas and the children carrying rugs, fold-up hunting seats, cushions, champagne and the picnic paraphernalia packed into a wicker basket, they hurried across the grass until Jacques found their designated space. They settled in the soft dusk to wait for darkness—the children scrapping and chattering like magpies, Dolly doling out treats, Jacques sitting close to Kate, joining her as she sipped champagne and nibbled on chocolate and strawberries.

'Mama, look, look!' Violet pulled at Kate's arm. In the navy twilight, a thunderous explosion sent a deep shudder through the earth and split the black sky into a million fragments of tiny glittering fires.

By the light from the giant shimmering firework chrysanthemums raining down from heaven, Kate saw Jacques, his head close to Cecil's, presumably deep in some flame-related explanation. Bursts of gold and silver, overlaid with blue and red and green, spun through the air—whirling, floating before dropping gracefully into oblivion—to be replaced by fresh shooting stars joining the non-stop galaxy. The incandescent sky lit the upturned faces of children and adults alike as they stared and counted aloud the starbursts from each rocket: 'One, two, three, four,' and finally a thrilled 'five!'

The glory of heaven and the joy of living.

Next morning it was a different story. Kate woke pale and exhausted. 'I'm not surprised,' said Jacques, who constantly sought for explanations for Kate's debilitation. 'What with the fireworks and the children it was quite an outing.' He didn't seem to remember the days when Kate was indefatigable, busy from dawn to dusk.

After he had disappeared to his studio and Dolly was occupied with the children's lessons, Kate discovered spottings of blood and what looked like pus on her kerchief. She tossed the kerchief into the small fire and sat, arms wrapped around her body, rocking from side to side.

This was going to be another bad day, one of the days that she struggled to ignore, but had to give in and rest quietly on the chaise longue, pulled close to the window so that she could look out at the grounds. While she would have the inevitable book by her side, frequently she was too exhausted even to pick it up, much less read. But she was never too exhausted to greet Jacques or the children with a warm smile, a thoughtful remark and an interested enquiry.

It was different in the dark of those nights when she woke feverish and frightened, bathed in sweat, the unthinkable throbbing certainty behind her eyes, consuming her brain, demanding escape from the bed and Jacques's arms. Her disentanglement was purposely rough, as she wanted him to wake up, to be the one to sponge her body and to speak words of love and consolation. But he never woke. Indeed, his soft snoring never faltered.

But miracle-like, as soon as her feet touched the floor, the door would open a crack and Dolly would be standing in the dim gas light holding a fresh nightgown. Sometimes that was enough: Kate would change, return to bed, Jacques's arms and blessed sleep. Other times, when the dark night of her soul would not be pacified, Dolly would drape a shawl round her shoulders and lead her by the arm through the shadowed corridors, down the stairs to the morning room, where she tucked her into her favourite armchair, bellowed the fire to flames and stood companionably on guard until her mistress felt able to return to bed.

Dr Mackintosh called frequently. He handled Kate with gentle sensitivity. In her eyes and demeanour he read questions she wasn't ready to ask. He knew enough about human nature to know she was thinking, always thinking, trying both to deny and come to terms with the implications of her symptoms.

He managed Jacques with bluff heartiness, cloaked in elaborate comments about the weather and cricket—being wrongly informed that Monsieur Tissot was passionate about the game. He nodded at the various remedies put forward by Dolly, rubbing his hands and pronouncing each one, 'Good, good.'

No more was said about taking the waters at Bath. Sometimes Dr Mackintosh wondered should he have been more open with his diagnosis, should he have presented Mrs Newton and Monsieur Tissot with the grim facts, and given them choice? But he believed patients were best served in their own homes, surrounded by family. Despite the continuous research and analysis of lung lesions, reading of worthy papers in medical institutions and various theories put forward, there appeared to be no cure for the cursed disease that progressed from a spitting of blood to a spitting of pus.

He recognised the pain of pretence in number 17, its destruction, the way it was tearing apart loving relationships and reducing a warm and vibrant home to a house of sham. The charade that had taken over the lives of the house's occupants was permeating every room, corner and mood.

When Polly visited, complete with baskets of homemade biscuits and preserves, she stayed her distance from Kate, although she was uncharacteristically jolly, chatting about Arthur and his exploits. On the rare occasions when Gussie joined her, he did little more than echo her sentiments about their son's brilliance.

As Kate's health deteriorated, her weight loss became obvious. She kept her dressmaker busy taking in her gowns, even ordered some new ones, and took endless trouble over her toilette, despite being hardly able to raise her slender arms to dress her hair. As her energy levels dipped, she encouraged Violet and Cecil to stay overnight at Hill Road with increasing frequency.

When summer began to turn to autumn, gradually and painfully Kate began to accept the possibility—a slim possibility was all she would concede—that she might not get well, although there remained a small but stubborn corner of her heart that sturdily refused to believe she wouldn't.

Jacques had drifted back into pre-Kate perfectionism, which took the form of pestering the servants, checking on the gardens, nosing round the kitchens, suggesting health-inducing menus to Charlotte, and riling Jane by running the tips of his fingers along surfaces in search of dust. In the confines of his studio, in a feverishly compulsive manner, he painted a series of rather depressing domestic scenes in predominantly brown overtones.

Alone he quivered with fear, his expression wrenched into shapes of hopelessness. The more he tried to be brave and accepting, the harder and deeper his fear of Kate's illness ran.

On occasions, he was able to re-capture the words of *plámás*, as Kate called the extravagant flattery he used with such Gallic sincerity. '*Ma toute belle,*' he would peer at her anxiously before swinging her round and round, until she laughingly pushed him away. Laughing was the last thing she felt like doing. Pretence was a lonely place.

'Jacques, why don't you dine at the Athenaeum?' she asked one afternoon as they circled the garden. The gillyflowers were in full bloom, filling the air with their sweet and heady scent, their outermost petals bright with sun.

He squeezed her hand resting on his arm. 'Don't you know I prefer to remain here with you?'

'Well, yes. And that that's all very flattering but if you went out at least we'd hear the latest gossip,' she tried but did not succeed in tempting him. He was quieter than she'd ever known him, plodding through the days without optimism. He no longer spoke of their future.

Much to Violet's annoyance, Isabel was in the first stages of realising her dream of becoming an artist. She had joined Jacques as his helper, tidying his studio, fetching and carrying his paints and canvases to the designated setting in the grounds. As she eased into the creative world he occupied, she became knowledgeable in the language of the artist, asking about colours and brushstrokes. Absorbed by her interest, the sad lines of his features would relax a little as he became lost in expounding on the art he loved.

Standing back from a long session at his easel, over a period of days that mimicked the past, and which Kate and he had embraced in joyous pretence, he tucked his brush behind his ear and clasped his hands in a prayer-like pose. 'I am particularly pleased with this. Come, *ma chérie*, look.' The painting focussed on four figures and the garden bench set against the pergola of tangling orange nasturtiums and red geraniums. Kate, wearing a face-framing bonnet, was looking at Cecil, whose tam-o'-shanter struck a note of frivolity. Violet nestled against her mother while Lily, still somewhat the outsider, hung over the back of the bench. 'What do you think, what shall we title it?'

For a moment Kate forgot. She was back in the peace and tranquillity of previous years, posing, Jacques painting and the children being children, all of them happily living out their hours among green lawns, scented shrubs and coppery sunlight filtering through the treetops.

'What do you think, Isabel?' Kate had grown exceedingly fond of her eldest niece.

'Are you asking me?' The child beamed.

'Yes,' said Jacques and Kate simultaneously. As their eyes met across the young girl's head they were startled by the power of their emotion. It was a somnolent afternoon of indolently voiced birds and nodding pink and purple asters. For the first time in weeks there was urgency in Kate's limbs and a new vitality in Jacques's physique.

'It's lovely.' The awe in Isabel's voice reminded Jacques of that day in another time, another world, when he had brought the three girls shopping for Christmas presents. 'Everyone on the garden bench.'

'*Voilà.* That's it. *The Garden Bench.* Thank you.'

As Isabel packed away his equipment, Jacques scooped Kate into his arms and carried her indoors. For a short time the world became theirs again.

Chapter Twenty-three

Two weeks later Kate summonsed Dolly to the morning room. 'Close the door and sit down.' She pointed to the chair opposite. 'I want you to listen carefully.'

Kate, with her arms folded and her pale hands arranged across her lap, looked exquisitely calm, but impressively sad. As she spoke she watched Dolly closely. 'I know I have pulmonary consumption.' The last rays of the sun drifted across her face. Dolly's lips pursed, neither confirming nor refuting the words.

Kate's last vestige of hope slid to sorrow before arriving at the beginning of angry acceptance.

Without wanting to know why or how, she knew Dolly was well informed about her illness. She had clung to the hope that she would come up with a cure for her symptoms. But no longer. 'I need to be able to talk to you, Dolly, make plans…'

'But the master?'

'The master is not ready, so for the present all of this must remain our secret. You understand?'

Dolly nodded and hoped her trembling lip would not give her away. She was frightened at what lay ahead and in awe of her mistress's courage.

'I want you to help me to live as best I can for as long as I can.'

'Bed rest is important. The doctor says so.'

'As long as I can move about, I don't want to spend my days in bed.'

'You're wrong, miss.'

'If I am wrong, it's my decision. Will you help?'

Dolly made no effort to stop her tears.

Some days later, she appeared with a bottle of medicine. It was a cloudy brown colour. 'There's this Russian man called Dost...something—perhaps you know of him, he writes books? He has a disease of the lungs and he takes this medicine every day, as well as the waters at some spa place in Germany. He has been ill for five or six years but he is still well enough to do his work.'

'Thank you. You have brought me hope and the best news possible,' Kate's smile was radiant. She would grasp at the most slender straw of hope. 'Dostoevsky is a well known writer and if he can live with this illness, I can too.'

Dolly was under no illusion about the effects of consumption, but she had thought it only stalked the poor. Throughout her childhood she had seen the ragged misery of its progress in the back streets of Dublin. She had watched it claim her mother, aunts, uncles and cousins. The symptoms and the outcome were the same. But she said nothing. How could she take away hope from her mistress?

The medicine gave Kate a temporary boost of energy. But the morning came when she did not come down for breakfast. Jacques returned upstairs. He drew back the silken curtains from around their bed. His cheeks were damp with knowing as he looked down. 'Mavourneen, you are ill?'

She rose as far as she could manage on one elbow. 'Yes, darlingest, I am.'

'Really ill?'

'Yes.'

His howl of grief was raw and of such devastation that Kate knew why up to then they had avoided discussion of her health.

She lay back on the pillows and reached towards him.

He grasped her hand like a lifeline.

'My greatest joy in life is the time we've had together. We've been lucky. Few people have what we have.'

A sob rose in his throat, he looked at her with wild eyes, pulled back his hand and stumbled from the room. He retreated to his studio for three days, and when he staggered out unshaven and reeking of wine, he was a shadow of his former self, gaunt and red-eyed.

'I want you to fetch the priest.' Kate had ignored Dolly's bowl of potato soup with its scattering of parsley and was slowly eating a small square of chocolate, savouring the melting of each tiny portion on her tongue.

'Oh, miss, whatever about being able to get medicines, don't you know a priest is out of the question?'

'Nothing is out of the question.' Kate opened the bedside locker and reached in. 'Please go to the oratory in Kensington and give Father Mathew this note.'

'And if he's not there?'

'God is not that cruel.'

The priest returned with Dolly in his carriage. He remembered young Kathleen Kelly well. He never forgot the penitents who were overly scrupulous. They would walk a hard road throughout their lives.

After spending more than an hour with Kate, Father Mathew asked to see Jacques. Whatever was said in the sickroom remained between the three of them. But like a miracle answer to Kate's prayers, Jacques was touched by a new resolution. He began sitting with Kate, chatting, reading to her when she was awake, sketching her while she lay sleeping. While he had always been slim, over the following weeks, he grew skeletal.

'Please say you'll marry me?' he asked at twilight on a November afternoon. He had a great urge to be married to Kate, as he saw it, to fulfil the ultimate of his grandmother's prophecy of this great love.

Kate locked fingers with him—hers were pale joints and marbled knuckles, and his weathered and long and strong. She drew him towards her, resting the side of his head against her lips while murmuring, 'I am the words and you are the melody.' The meaning of the Hindu wedding ceremony held a special significance for Kate. She had whispered it to herself when they had first made love and now she was sharing it with him. 'Darlingest, we could not be more married than we have been for the past six years.'

She hated denying him but no matter how he pleaded, she wouldn't relent about marrying. She would not leave him with an indelible mortal sin on his soul. The thought of the everlasting flames of hell burned bright in her imagination. Long after she was gone, she prayed that Jacques would draw comfort from his religion as well as his painting. Closing her eyes, she drew his head deep to her breast, spoke the words again, and running her fingers through his thick curling hair she comforted him.

'I cannot watch the master destroy himself and his talent,' she confided to Dolly later that evening.

'He's desperate.'

'I know. He will not be able to live his life properly until I am dead.'

Dolly was horrified. 'Don't say that, miss.'

'You are no good to Mrs Newton if you don't look after your health,' said Dr Mackintosh sternly during his next visit.

'What do you recommend?' Jacques was hard pushed to keep the sarcasm from his voice.

'Mrs Newton is travelling a hard road and it will be made easier if she knows those she is leaving behind will be able to cope.'

On his way out, the doctor handed Dolly a small brown glass bottle. Its cork was protected by a scrap of cotton held in place with a curl of string.

'Do you know what this is?'

Dolly nodded. She knew more than she wanted to or needed to know about laudanum. She had long thrown away the bottle she had removed from Miss Carmody's bedroom. But she still felt enveloped in the pall of suspicion at running away. Miss Kate had insisted she tell her story to the master, and she had been somewhat reassured by his advice to say or do nothing.

'It's only to be used, and sparingly, in an emergency. No more than a few drops in a little water.'

Violet and Cecil climbed into bed alongside Kate, one either side snuggling against her shoulders. Cecil's curls were boyishly clipped and little tufts of hair stood up around his crown. His face had thinned. He was beginning to have the look of the man he would become, and that was his father.

Over the round collar of her dark green frock Violet was wearing the butterfly pendant that her father had left on the mantel of Mrs O'Connor's parlour all those years ago. During the past months, she had lost much of her natural ebullience. She leaned over Kate and with fingers as soft as velvet stroked her forehead. 'Please, Mama, may I stay and help Dolly to nurse you better?'

Violet's short life had been filled with too many 'please Mamas'. More than any child should have to endure. 'No, sweetheart, you go to Aunt Polly. She's looking forward to having you.'

'I'd prefer to stay with you.' With her blonde prettiness and definite views, Violet was a feminine version of her father.

'Me too. I'll stay too. I can mind you but only if I don't have to do those horrid lessons.' To Jacques's dismay, his quiet son had become vociferously vocal in his dislike of learning. His small scrubbed face scrunched in misery as he peered around Kate as though expecting his father to materialise in order to enforce sums, reading and writing, which were the bane of his young life. 'Where's Papa?'

'He's attending a meeting at the Academy of Arts in Piccadilly.'

'If he's gone out, it must be important.' Like everyone, Violet knew Jacques seldom left Kate's side, much less the house and grounds.

'It is. Don't ever forget he is one of the Academy's most important exhibitors.' Kate touched their cheeks with the palm of her hand. 'Don't you ever forget either that nobody could love you more than me. And now it's equally important that you don't disappoint Aunt Polly by being late.'

'It's good to be loved, isn't it?'

'Yes, Violet, it is. It's the best feeling in the world.'

'Are you better enough for me to have a love hug?' Violet was kneeling up on the bed anxiously peering down at her mother.

'Not today, sweetheart.'

'I'll give you a hug. The hugest love hug in the world. I don't mind getting your cold.' Cecil leaned in towards Kate. She averted her head on the stacked pillows.

'Soon, we'll be able to kiss Mama properly,' soothed Violet, getting down off the bed and smoothing the skirt of her frock. 'Come on, Cecil.'

Kate watched hungrily as her children crossed the room. She held her smile in place while they turned at the door and blew kisses in her direction. She raised herself up on her pillows as far as she could manage, and blew kisses back, holding her lips to the heel of her palm until the door closed. She heard them skipping along the corridor and down the stairs, with Violet calling for Thomas to hurry up so they wouldn't be late for Aunt Polly.

When the last sounds of their leaving died away, she picked up her rosary from the bedside table and began reciting the Sorrowful Mysteries. As her fingers caressed the beads, she drew comfort from the repetitiousness of the prayers and her head began to fill with swirling shadow memories: the plum-coloured twilight and Mama rocking on the veranda, looking out beyond the banyan trees; Isaac, pale hands fluttering and timid eyes flickering; Miss Carmody, shoulders back, head tossed, a parody of indignity and outrage; Poonam on the bank of a river, holding the tail of a cow; and Polly's cherub babies sitting in a row on the edge of her consciousness.

She shook her head—she was only twenty-eight years of age —and dislodged the images. She finished the decade, made the sign of the cross, kissed the crucifix and draped the circlet of beads round her neck.

Thomas and the children would be well on their way to Hill Road by now. No doubt Jacques was still being lunched by the Academy dignitaries. She held their faces in her consciousness. They knew they were loved and dear to her but she was glad she had told them again and again.

She rang for Dolly. Faithful Dolly, who drew her happiness from her mistress's well-being. That shouldn't be the way of life but it was. Perhaps in future decades it would change.

A knock and Dolly entered. There was sadness in the set of her features and the slump of her shoulders. Kate gestured for her to draw near. 'Dolly, I can't thank you enough for all your care and attention...and the buttermilk.' Instead of her voice lightening, as she intended, it cracked on the word buttermilk.

'Oh, miss, that's all right. Just try and get well.' The words were spoken sadly and automatically.

'I won't, Dolly. We both know that. But I am grateful for all you've done for me. Now I want you to please bring me the bottle of laudanum.'

Dolly moved from foot to foot, made a loose sign of the cross. 'Tonight, please God, you will have another good sleep.'

'No. Now. I want you to fetch it now.'

It was a long time since Dolly had been ordered in such a peremptory manner, and never by Miss Kate—but once a servant, always a servant. She dropped her gaze and left the room. When she returned carrying the bottle, reluctance was stamped on her features and controlled her every movement.

'Thank you. Leave it on the locker.'

'I don't think…'

'You don't have to think. I said leave it.' Kate had to fight to keep her voice imperious. Otherwise, she feared her resolve would weaken.

Lower lip quivering, Dolly put down the bottle on the edge of the locker farthest from the bed, and stood, with head down and hands wringing, in the very way that Miss Carmody had spent months training out of her.

'Now go, Dolly. And thank you.' Kate's voice gentled.

When Dolly hesitated, hovering on the brink of speaking, Kate spoke more firmly. 'You're to go. Now.'

Dolly backed across the room, opened the door, eased out and carefully shut it behind her.

By turning sideways and stretching her arm, Kate was just able to reach the bottle. She grasped it around its middle and brought it into bed. With its base resting on her belly, she loosened the cord holding the cloth around the stopper, slid out the cork and took a long slow mouthful, then another and another.

Looking out the window at the denuded trees caught against the cold skyline, she saw Poonam, with her ringed toes and red sari and her hair as black as a raven's wing. The bottle slipped from the grasp of Kate's fingers and she lay back against the pillows. There was Mama again. Smiling, drawing her into her warmth, urging her towards her.

With a soft sigh and a last breath, Kate slipped from the bed, through the waiting shadows to join Poonam. They would hold the tail of the cow, and together cross the rippling waters to the far side.

Epilogue

Jacques Tissot was grey-haired now and proud of the curving luxuriance of his silver moustache. He was still slender but instead of black and white he had taken to wearing the colours of nature—boots the tan of autumn leaves, a muddy brown jacket, a wide-brimmed hat in the beige of undergrowth, and soft creamy shirts. Kate would be proud of the comfort of his informality.

As his carriage turned into the driveway, crunching up the gravel of number 17, he could imagine the rise of her eyebrow and her smile of satisfaction. He hadn't been back to Grove End Road since the day of her funeral. What an awful day that had been. He had stumbled into the waiting carriage en route to the railway station and Paris, trying to hold himself together by giving a last heartbreaking order to Thomas: 'Make sure you burn Mrs Newton's mattress.' The words still echoed in his head.

The day of Kate's burial was even worse than the previous four days, when he had sat by her open coffin. Although she had made her confession, and when she died had her rosary beads around her neck, she was refused burial in consecrated ground in Kensal Green Cemetery.

303

Suicide. They said. As well as being in an immoral relationship. And having two bastard children.

He had walked away from the house, his home that was too full of the whispering ghost of Kate to remain. He had left behind his paints and unfinished canvases. Without properly realising the implications, he had also abandoned Violet and Cecil—and truth to be known at the time he had not cared or thought of their future. With the death of Kate, the compassionate and loving core had vanished from his relationship with them.

He did not know what happened to Dolly. He had heard she was arrested a few days after the burial, but whatever came to pass it hadn't resulted in Kate being moved to consecrated ground.

He was pleased when his friend Lawrence Alma Tadema and his second wife Laura bought the house. If rumours were to be believed, he was as interested in its refurbishment as he was in his painting, and Jacques looked forward to viewing his innovations.

In Paris he had found bitter solace in séances, where he communicated at length with Kate while committing to canvas the series of paintings he entitled *Women of Paris*. When exhibited they were another commercial success, but more importantly for him they somewhat curbed his sexual torment. His Catholic religion too began to resume a new importance as he stormed God as to why He had taken Kate. Despite his terrible grief—or perhaps because of it—he became absorbed in illustrating the life of Christ and the Old Testament.

When Paris became too lonely, too full of the memories of those halcyon June days when he and Kate had wandered the city, he journeyed to Palestine, where he completed out hundreds of drawings illustrating incidents in the life of Christ. Again, they were successfully exhibited in Paris. Now they were to be shown in London, and there was talk of publication by the firm of Lemercier in Paris for a fee of 1,100,000 francs.

Author's Note

An exhibition of Jacques Tissot's paintings was held at Leicester Galleries, London in June 1933 (Ernest, Brown and Phillips Ltd, catalogue number 556). His son, Cecil George Newton unexpectedly turned up. It is popularly believed that after leaving the exhibition he was never seen again but records at National Archives, Kew show he died in 1941 at Lancing under the name of Cecil Ashburnham. He was in the army but gazetted out in 1916. His rank is uncertain.

A marriage was arranged between Kathleen Kelly (Kate) (1854–1882) and Isaac Newton, a surgeon attached to the Indian Civil Service by her father 'Major' Charles Frederick Ashburnham Kelly (reputedly his grandfather was a doctor who emigrated from Ireland). Charles Kelly posed as a military man but was an administrator with the East India Company, based first in Lahore, then Agra, retired to London; her mother Flora Boyd from Belfast died during their posting in India.

Kate travelled from England to be married in Agra. En route she captured the fancy of Captain Palliser (using name and dates, the best fit is Captain C H Palliser of the Bengal Cavalry; but he also could be a ship's captain, Lloyds shipping records don't begin until 1881). Records show

Kate was married on 3rd January 1871. (I visited Agra as part of research.) When Newton learned of Palliser's dalliance, he returned his bride to England without consummating the marriage.

Palliser's daughter Muriel Violet M Newton was born in Conisbrough, Yorkshire on 20th December 1871, on the same day as her decree nisi was granted. Major Kelly remarried. Kate and daughter went to live with her sister Mary P A Hervey (Polly) at 6 Hill Road, St John's Wood.

Kate's son, Cecil C (*sic*) Newton was born in March 1876. Legend has it that Kate and Jacques met while posting letters—there is a post box equidistant from their houses. The following year, she moved into 17 Grove End Road, St John's Wood with artist Jacques Tissot (1836–1902), although she is not named as resident in the 1881 England census, which lists her and her two children as living with Mary P A Hervey. There is no documentation but Tissot is believed to be Cecil's father—timing is right, likenesses show physical similarity.

With the exception of his relationship with Mrs Newton, Tissot lived a detached existence. (Most comprehensive information from Michael Wentworth's *James Tissot*, OUP 1984.) He was born in Nantes to a middle-class merchant family, educated with the Jesuits, attended École des Beaux-Arts in Paris where he was a contemporary of Monet, Manet, Degas and Whistler. He made his name, reputation and money by painting contemporary social scenes.

During the unrest following the 1871 Franco-Prussian war and establishment of the Third Republic, suspected of involvement in the Paris Commune, he moved back to

London where he had held his first exhibition in 1864 at the Royal Academy. *The Farewell* (1871), one of the first paintings he produced after relocating to London, was much admired when exhibited at the Royal Academy and is believed to have launched him in England.

Realising London's potential as a source of wealthy patrons, he changed his name to James and bought a thirty-year-old mansion in St John's Wood. (Now a Grade II listed building, renumbered 44, which I have seen over.) Tissot's paintings of contemporary social events and conversation pieces were as commercially successful in England as they had been in France. A particularly fine example is his lush expansive view of *The Ball on Shipboard* (1874), depicting a gala that was part of the annual sailing regatta off the Isle of Wight. It was panned by critics when exhibited at the Royal Academy, but was snapped up by Agnew's, the foremost dealer in British art. The painting is now in the collection of London's Tate Gallery.

His work was also critically annihilated, with Oscar Wilde referring to his paintings as those of 'over-dressed, common-looking people', and John Ruskin using the term 'mere painted photographs of vulgar society'. Henry James wasn't impressed either.

Kathleen Newton was his model, mistress, muse and the great and only love of his life. She lived with him for six years and was the model for some of his most inspired and sensitive works. They lived a relatively private life and as part of this withdrawal from the outside world, Tissot focused on portraying her in their elegant home and carefully laid out garden. In Victorian times, gardens were repositories of social and aesthetic meaning. With its pond and iron colonnade, the garden at number 17 served as the backdrop for paintings such as *Holyday* (c1877), *The Hammock* (c1879), and *The Garden Bench* (1882).

When she died—she had tuberculosis and committed suicide—he was overcome with grief, and prayed beside her coffin for four days. After her burial, which because of her suicide was in unconsecrated ground in Kensal Green Cemetery, he abandoned his house, the children, his painting equipment and several unfinished canvases and returned to Paris.

A year later the house was bought by artist Sir Lawrence Alma-Tadema. About 1912 it was converted into apartments and gradually declined until 2003 and its renovation and modernisation by Bleier Estates (UK). It is now owned by a Syrian businessman. Number 44 has featured in the BBC's 2004 television adaptation of *Sherlock Holmes and the Case of the Silk Stocking* and Hammer House of Horror's 1963 classic, *The Children of the Damned*.

Looking to reclaim his place in the French art world, Tissot reintroduced himself with an ambitious series of fifteen pictures titled *La Femme à Paris* and succeeded in presenting himself as a Parisian insider after years abroad. He became interested in spiritualism and took part in séances, during which he believed he communicated with his late mistress.

By the late 1880s he had re-embraced the traditional forms of religion and devoted his energies to projects illustrating the Bible. In pursuit of archaeological and topographical authenticity, he visited the Holy Land. In 1895 he exhibited in Paris a set of 365 New Testament subjects, followed in 1906 by 95 based on Old Testament themes. (As he died in 1902, these were finished by his assistants to his designs.)

Characters

All main characters in *A Type of Beauty* are as historically accurate as possible with information sourced primarily from National Archives, Kew, London.

Fictional characters include: Miss Carmody, Dolly, Aunt Muriel, the Montgomerys and their servants, Poonam, Mrs O'Connor, Louisa and the honourable Mrs Caulfield as well as Thomas and Mr Rumple.

Works

- ◆ Tissot's paintings are exhibited worldwide, including part of a Russian exhibition held 2007–08 in London's Royal Academy.
- ◆ The ark of the tabernacle in Hollywood movie *Raiders of the Lost Ark* was modelled on Tissot's reconstruction.
- ◆ Tissot canvases, prints and drypoints fetch millions of dollars/pounds at auction.
- ◆ A lucrative online industry exists in Tissot copies.

Bibliography

Inside the Victorian Home (a Portrait of domestic life in Victorian England), Judith Flanders (Penguin, London, 2004).

One Last Look, Susanna Moore (Penguin, London, 2005).

Emma Brown, Clare Boylan (Abacus, London, 2003).

A Passage to India, E M Forster (Penguin, London, 2005).

Katey, Lucinda Hawksley (Doubleday, London, 2006).

The Mutiny, Julian Rathbone (Little, Brown, London, 2007).

The Holy Cow, Tarun Chopra (Prakash Book Depot, New Delhi, 2000).

The Irish Raj, Narinder Kapur (Greystones Press, Northern Ireland, 1997).

A Princess Remembers, Maharani of Jaipur (Rupa & Co, New Delhi, 1995).

Anila's Journey, Mary Finn (Walker Books, London, 2008).

The City of the Djinns, William Dalyrmple, (Flamingo, London, 1994).

Mrs Duberly's War, ed Christine Kelly (Oxford University Press, 2007).

Parrot Pie for Breakfast, Jane Robinson (Oxford University Press, 1999).

Victoria's Wars, I F W Beckett (Shire Publications, 1998).

The Victorian Workhouse, Trevor May (Shire Publications, 2005).

The Victorian Hospital, Lavinia Mitton (Shire Publications, 2004).

The Victorian Domestic Servant, Trevor May (Shire Publications, 2003).

The Victorian Schoolroom, Trevor May (Shire Publications, 2006).

The Workings of the Household, Lydia Morris (Polity Press, USA, 1990).

The Victorian Web: <www.victorian.web.org>.